PRAISE FOR M. L. BUCHMAN

Tom Clancy fans open to a strong female lead will clamor for more.

— *DRONE*, PUBLISHERS WEEKLY

Superb! Miranda is utterly compelling!

— *BOOKLIST*, STARRED REVIEW

Miranda Chase continues to astound and charm.

— BARB M.

Escape Rating: A. Five Stars! OMG just start with *Drone* and be prepared for a fantastic binge-read!

— READING REALITY

The best military thriller I've read in a very long time. Love the female characters.

— *DRONE*, SHELDON MCARTHUR, FOUNDER OF THE MYSTERY BOOKSTORE, LA

A fabulous soaring thriller.

— *TAKE OVER AT MIDNIGHT*, MIDWEST BOOK REVIEW

Meticulously researched, hard-hitting, and suspenseful.

— *PURE HEAT,* PUBLISHERS WEEKLY, STARRED REVIEW

Expert technical details abound, as do realistic military missions with superb imagery that will have readers feeling as if they are right there in the midst and on the edges of their seats.

— *LIGHT UP THE NIGHT,* RT REVIEWS, 4 1/2 STARS

Buchman has catapulted his way to the top tier of my favorite authors.

— FRESH FICTION

Nonstop action that will keep readers on the edge of their seats.

— *TAKE OVER AT MIDNIGHT,* LIBRARY JOURNAL

M L. Buchman's ability to keep the reader right in the middle of the action is amazing.

— LONG AND SHORT REVIEWS

The only thing you'll ask yourself is, "When does the next one come out?"

— *WAIT UNTIL MIDNIGHT,* RT REVIEWS, 4 STARS

The first...of (a) stellar, long-running (military) romantic suspense series.

— *THE NIGHT IS MINE,* BOOKLIST, "THE 20 BEST ROMANTIC SUSPENSE NOVELS: MODERN MASTERPIECES"

I knew the books would be good, but I didn't realize how good.

— NIGHT STALKERS SERIES, KIRKUS REVIEWS

Buchman mixes adrenalin-spiking battles and brusque military jargon with a sensitive approach.

— PUBLISHERS WEEKLY

13 times "Top Pick of the Month"

— NIGHT OWL REVIEWS

HOLD THE WEST LINE

A MILITARY ROMANTIC SUSPENSE

M. L. BUCHMAN

Copyright 2026 Matthew L. Buchman

All rights reserved.

This book, or parts thereof, may not be reproduced in any form without permission from the author.

Receive a free book and discover more by this author at: www.mlbuchman.com

Cover images:

Airport in winter © Jun Seita

Focused Army male soldier © serhil.bobyk.gm

Beautiful brunette © Shell114

Christmas snowy banner © Maxborovkov

SIGN UP FOR M. L. BUCHMAN'S NEWSLETTER TODAY

and receive:
Release News
Free Short Stories
a Free Book

Get your free book today. Do it now.
free-book.mlbuchman.com

Other works by M. L. Buchman: (* - also in audio)

Action-Adventure Thrillers

Kate Stark
Final Taste
Ice Burn
Knife's Edge

Miranda Chase
*Drone**
*Thunderbolt**
*Condor**
*Ghostrider**
*Raider**
*Chinook**
*Havoc**
*White Top**
*Start the Chase**
*Lightning**
*Skibird**
*Nightwatch**
*Osprey**
*Gryphon**
*Wedgetail**
*Air Force One**

Science Fiction / Fantasy

Deities Anonymous
Cookbook from Hell: Reheated
Saviors 101

Contemporary Romance

Eagle Cove
Return to Eagle Cove
Recipe for Eagle Cove
Longing for Eagle Cove
Keepsake for Eagle Cove

Love Abroad
Heart of the Cotswolds: England
Path of Love: Cinque Terre, Italy

Where Dreams
Where Dreams are Born
Where Dreams Reside
*Where Dreams Are of Christmas**
Where Dreams Unfold
Where Dreams Are Written
Where Dreams Continue

Non-Fiction

Strategies for Success
Managing Your Inner Artist/Writer
*Estate Planning for Authors**
Character Voice
*Narrate and Record Your Own Audiobook**
Beyond Prince Charming: One Guy's Guide to Writing Men in Romance

Short Story Series by M. L. Buchman:

Action-Adventure Thrillers

Kate Stark Stories
Miranda Chase Stories

Romantic Suspense

Antarctic Ice Fliers
US Coast Guard

Contemporary Romance

Eagle Cove

Other

Deities Anonymous (fantasy)
Single Titles

The Emily Beale Universe
(military romantic suspense)

THE NIGHT STALKERS
MAIN FLIGHT
*The Night Is Mine**
*I Own the Dawn**
*Wait Until Dark**
*Take Over at Midnight**
Light Up the Night
Bring On the Dusk
By Break of Day
Target of the Heart
Target Lock on Love
Target of Mine
Target of One's Own
NIGHT STALKERS HOLIDAYS
*Daniel's Christmas**
*Frank's Independence Day**
*Peter's Christmas**
Christmas at Steel Beach
*Zachary's Christmas**
*Roy's Independence Day**
*Damien's Christmas**
Christmas at Peleliu Cove
HENDERSON'S RANCH
*Nathan's Big Sky**
*Big Sky, Loyal Heart**
*Big Sky Dog Whisperer**
*Tales of Henderson's Ranch**

SHADOW FORCE: PSI
*At the Slightest Sound**
*At the Quietest Word**
*At the Merest Glance**
*At the Clearest Sensation**
WHITE HOUSE PROTECTION FORCE
*Off the Leash**
*On Your Mark**
*In the Weeds**
FIREHAWKS
Pure Heat
Full Blaze
*Hot Point**
*Flash of Fire**
Wild Fire
FIREHAWKS SMOKEJUMPERS
*Wildfire at Dawn**
*Wildfire at Larch Creek**
*Wildfire on the Skagit**
DELTA FORCE
Target Engaged
Heart Strike
*Wild Justice**
*Midnight Trust**
NIGHT STALKERS RELOAD
*Guard the East Flank**
*Hold the West Line**

Emily Beale Universe Short Story Series

THE NIGHT STALKERS
The Night Stalkers Stories
The Night Stalkers CSAR
The Night Stalkers Wedding Stories
The Future Night Stalkers Reloaded
DELTA FORCE
Th Delta Force Shooters
The Delta Force Warriors

FIREHAWKS
The Firehawks Lookouts
The Firehawks Hotshots
The Firebirds
WHITE HOUSE PROTECTION FORCE
Stories
FUTURE NIGHT STALKERS
The Lift (Science Fiction)

ABOUT THIS BOOK

CAPTAIN ABIGAIL ROSE, A LEGACY "MAINIAC" PILOT FROM THE fine state of Maine, hides her heart behind professional armor and the roar of her mighty Chinook helicopter. She is used to outperforming every man in the sky—and scaring them off in the process.

But Delta Force operator Derek Kylie refuses to be intimidated. When a training-op first meeting morphs into a lethal rescue mission, their one-night stand becomes a high-stakes complication.

Facing rogue agents across the Atlantic, Abby and Derek must navigate a labyrinth of betrayal and desire, proving that the most dangerous part of the mission is the connection neither expected.

---

*And return afterward for a free bonus story
and a recipe from the book.*

1

YOU HAVE A VISITOR.

Colonel Emily Beale tried to make sense of the message on her secure phone, but she'd been awake for thirty-six hours and couldn't decipher its hidden meaning. A slow scan of the airfield at Fort Campbell, Kentucky, showed that she stood alone on the unlit tarmac. The last bird of the two companies of MH-47G Chinook Spec Ops helicopters, which had been her sole focus for the entire time, had departed less than a minute ago.

No "visitor" here. Just herself and the lingering exhaust fumes dissipating into the night. The lights of the tail helo ducked beyond the silhouette of trees against the stars, leaving only the heavy beat of the big helos' twin rotors to fade into the waning night traffic from Route 41 along the eastern edge of the base.

A crescent moon was trying to punch through the high horsetail clouds that presaged an incoming weather system. Predicted as the first big storm of November, she'd believe it only after it showed up.

A reminder beep. Oh, right. Phone message. She definitely needed sleep soon.

In the last day and a half, she'd formulated an emergency, set up the scenario, and given the crews a scant hour's notice to create an action plan and implement it. Both heavy assault companies of the Night Stalkers 2nd Battalion had just winged aloft headed for a simulated combat search-and-rescue *crisis* staged eight hundred kilometers away at Fort Bragg's gunnery range. She added to the challenge by pre-staging their action assets down in Fort Rucker, so they'd have to go to Alabama first—though they didn't know that's why they were going there yet.

She'd handed off the task of setting surprise traps along their possible routes to her assistant, Lieutenant Colonel Trisha O'Malley. Not only did her red-headed sidekick possess an evil bent when it came to training, but it would also be good practice for training the commander in her—Emily had taken away half of Trisha's counterattack forces *after* her plans were set. Interestingly, it hadn't thrown her into one of her normal verbal fits of incomprehensible Boston-accented protests against God, The Army, and whatever else she worshipped. Instead, she watched Emily steadily for about five seconds, grinned evilly, then headed off while issuing a maelstrom of commands. Emily would have liked to hear what she had in mind; but Trisha moved at a warp speed beyond her own capacity at the best of times.

Now, with the twenty twin-rotor Chinooks departed, half of the entire regiment's heavy-assault team—the rest were based in Georgia, Washington State, or currently deployed—the night's silence unfolded enough to hear the honking of late geese headed south in the overhead darkness.

She didn't want a visitor.

What Emily wanted to do was go home. But the Montana ranch and her family seemed impossibly far away.

Montana ranch.
Phone message.
Visitor.

She pulled out her phone, though she didn't remember tucking it away, and checked the message again. The visitor wasn't here; she'd already figured out that much. Nor at her Fort Campbell office. Oddly, not out on the ranch either, at least not exactly.

Oh right, someone else was telling her she had a visitor somewhere. Not some*one* telling her—some*thing!* The message had been a carefully nondescript alarm from her top-level security alert system.

The message was from inside the secure Tac Room she'd built at Henderson's Ranch. Someone had entered who wasn't supposed to be inside there. Only three people other than herself had access to that space—none of whom would be labeled a visitor.

It was the sole office of what they figured was the smallest and least known intelligence agency in the nation—they themselves didn't know of any smaller ones. Of course, *no one* knew about them. Perhaps twenty knew of the room's existence, but most of them were the family's ranch hands who didn't care. A bare handful knew the room's purpose, and she kept it that way. The only likely *visitor* was former President Peter Matthews, who had set up their agency while he still had the power to do so. However, Emily knew that her childhood friend was currently in Africa in his "retired" role as Secretary of State, and even he couldn't open the door.

Deciding that a deserted airfield in the middle of a secure Army base was a safe enough place from which to find out who the hell had showed up in Montana, she first checked the GPS readings of the Tac Room's three operators. Two were in the ranch house lounge off the big kitchen; typical for an after-dinner evening. Lauren was in Hawaii on vacation with her husband.

She called the Tac Room, wondering who had broken in and if they'd answer the phone. Yet there was no break-in alert; rather, someone had attempted to login on the computer system there—and failed. Who had *slipped* in? The US government had spent a lot of money to make sure that was impossible. Neither Claudia nor Michael could have missed that, unless...

Over a thousand miles west, the evening sun would still be up, shining golden off the first real snow of the season. The cold-sharpened air would smell of horses and larch pine. November was incredibly late for the first snowfall, but she loved seeing the seasons brush across the ranch the way they never brushed the DC of her youth or the Kentucky of her present. Hopefully, she would see it soon.

Someone did answer and spoke with no introduction. There was no need for one; she knew the voice instantly.

"Hi, Emily. We need to talk. In person. It's *majorly* important."

The phone fell from Emily's nerveless fingers. She heard a small tink as the screen cracked on the tarmac.

2

"Is this über-weird or is this über-weird?"

"Not giving me a lot of choices there, Captain Ethan Merced." They'd started using each other's full title and name two months ago when they made captain together, and the charm of it hadn't worn off. His wife and four-year-old had picked up on it as well and called him nothing else. Which, as Ethan appeared less charmed about, Abby encouraged at every opportunity.

"Kinda obvious anyway, Captain Abigail Rose."

Abby kicked the tail of her big helo sideways to pass between the tops of two particularly tall oaks fast approaching on her helmet's visor display. Night vision and radar pointed them out—not a challenge at all. Then the next tree, just beyond the first pair, had her slewing hard the other way. Hard enough to turn her last name into a grunt from Ethan: *Ro-hose*.

She sighed; the mission *was* weird. Who sent two full companies, totaling twenty Chinooks, along the same Black Route all at once? And on one hour's notice? That was unusual even for the US Army's 160th Regiment. This Black Route was a five-hour, thirteen-hundred-kilometer training run from Fort

Campbell, Kentucky, down to Fort Rucker, Alabama, out to Fort Bragg, North Carolina, and home—all in the moonless darkness. They were nicknamed the Night Stalkers for a reason.

Colonel Emily Beale, that's who. Their commander would, of course, have a hidden lesson buried inside the op that would later be revealed as deeply meta-on-meta—obvious in retrospect but that no one except the colonel could have thought up. The woman was seriously deep, which would have brought up any number of jokes by Abby's cousin, who'd opted to continue in the family's Maine lobstering tradition. *Ocean t'ain't deep, it only comes up t' here on the ducks,* then he'd hold a hand palm-down at his hip. Ricky loved that one; he wasn't exactly a deep one himself.

For now, *Charlene One*—technically *Charlie One* but neither Abby nor her twelve-ton baby girl were down with that—was the lead bird of the twenty. The Fort Campbell flight controllers had learned that one quickly enough. Mainiacs—as natives of Maine, the nation's greatest state in the Union—didn't get angry. They didn't get even. Instead, they strived to make you look utterly ridiculous for their own amusement. After the third flight controller in a row discovered that his Army boots had been permanently converted into high heels when he wasn't watching—and been forced to show up to a surprise inspection either wearing those or barefoot—*Charlene One's* name and reputation were firmly secured.

Not that she could see a hint of the others on tonight's flight. She inspected the inside of her visor, flipping quickly through several of the screens using the thumb control on the cyclic between her knees. Nothing. She returned to her primary piloting screen. Ethan would be monitoring systems' health, threat analysis, and a couple of other displays. As pilot-in-control, her duties were to watch the overlapping images of light-amplified night vision, infrared imaging, and wire frame of the landscape including buildings, power lines, and other known features—and not hit anything.

The Night Stalkers had made most of the innovations for night vision, starting back in the 1980s. She couldn't imagine those early pioneers who had died while tackling the first-ever Black Routes with nothing more advanced than a high-quality map and balls of steel. Those deaths had driven the early days of simple light amplification to the limits. Now she flew with near-daylight vision and overlaid wire-frame mapping to let her anticipate the terrain well beyond what lay within line of sight. She had no nostalgia for the old days.

For tonight's op, she and her teammates were given a ceiling of a hundred feet—to the tops of their rotors, which placed the belly of her massive twin-rotor assault bird down at a tree-scraping eighty. Their mission? Hug the terrain in the dark for five solid hours in an NOE—nap-of-Earth flight, the most exhausting other than in a fully engaged battle—and arrive within plus-or-minus thirty seconds of preset times at the three successive destinations, each over four hundred kilometers apart. At each location, they were to land for precisely thirty seconds before racing to the next.

If only it were that simple.

Though never in so large a flight group, it was the type of route she'd flown throughout testing and qualifications. Then Colonel Beale had taken over the regiment, and anything predictable had gone out the window.

This time, their twenty birds were all spaced one minute, five kilometers apart. That meant that if you were outside your time window, you were in the next bird's slot. Worse, other birds in tonight's training flight had been blocked from her situational awareness satellite feeds, and they were all too low to be seen on radar. Which was kind of the point. They'd been warned that, if they delayed one another or bunched up, the entire mission would be declared a failure. To avoid any chance of coordination, each bird had been given a separate radio frequency and a slightly different route as well. Only their destinations were in common.

With the cancellation of the rather brilliant Raider and Defiant helicopter designs, the Chinook remained the fastest helo in the fleet, capable of scooting along at three hundred and twenty kmph, nearly two hundred miles an hour. The Osprey and new Valor could go faster, but the ungainly tilt-rotors certainly didn't fit within the Night Stalkers' need for managing stealth and tight spaces. So, rather than shifting to new cutting-edge brilliance as planned, the 160th Special Operations Aviation Regiment—SOAR—would be sticking with their own customizations of the three platforms they'd adopted at their founding forty-four years earlier.

Which was fine with her. They were Night Stalkers; the pilots were what mattered most. Like Cousin Ricky on the lobster boats, she was a legacy in the heavy metal of the Chinooks. Granddad had flown them in Vietnam, Dad in Desert Storm, and she'd survived two tours in Afghanistan before that mess finally shut down.

Canceling the new birds, which their most elite Spec Ops fliers needed, wanted, and had helped design, ranked several steps below incomprehensible. It was as if the top levels of the Department of Defense had shipped their brains to Fiji or—

"Oh!"

"What?"

"Colonel Emily Beale..." The full name thing was habit forming. It was time Abby declared that it had run its course. "The colonel is up to something."

"Duh!"

"No, I mean something other, Ethan. Something hidden." A section of the Cumberland River ran in the right direction, so she dropped down to ten meters from belly to water, now watching out for bridges she'd have to pop over rather than power lines to duck under.

"Such as?"

"They took away Raider and Defiant." And she left it there to see if he reached the same conclusion.

It didn't take him long. "They wouldn't!"

"They might."

"Come on, the DoD ain't that stupid."

Abby wished. In her experience, the Dummies of Defense —as the Department of Defense command in the Pentagon were often called—were *absolutely* that stupid. "Colonel Beale isn't breaking the training regimens for the fun of it…"

Ethan sighed. "She's trying to find a way to keep the Night Stalkers relevant."

Because the DoD was maneuvering, with their typical complete lack of foresight, to make them *irrelevant*. "Sure, let's cut the budget by axing the one regiment that Spec Ops depends on for transport into and back out of The Ugly. Why? 'Because we're idiots and it saves us money even as it guts a key element of the nation's security.'" She did the last in a fake hick accent that totally stereotyped about a third of the country.

Ethan merely groaned.

But if the colonel was fighting back, it meant tonight's mission was only the beginning.

At the Tennessee-Alabama border, *Charlene's* threat sensors picked up a pair of incoming MH-6M Little Bird helicopters.

"Shit! We aren't equipped to fend off those!" Chinooks boasted four whole guns. They could do immediate-area ground defense, but up against missile-equipped birds? Two steerable M134 Miniguns and a pair of lousy little M240D medium machine guns, all facing to the sides, weren't going to cut it. They usually flew with their own attack Little Birds and Black Hawks to protect them when the airspace turned nasty.

She checked the rapidly resolving image as they

approached close enough to reveal details. They weren't MH-6 transports with a bench seat on either side for delivering Delta Force or Rangers into battle. These had a stubby wing on either side from which missiles and Miniguns could be mounted. These were AH-6—as in attack-helicopter—*Killer Egg* Little Birds. The things were lethal out to five kilometers; her Miniguns were effective to only one.

"Encrypted text message," Ethan reported. Rather than a traceable transmission on the encrypted radio, someone had sent a short blast up to the satellite, which came back to them in an untraceable signal, which was then decrypted.

"Surrender or die?"

"My guess too," Ethan agreed. "But no. They're our escort for the rest of the exercise."

"Well, that's handy." She tested a sigh of relief—but didn't feel it. Needing their protection meant that there would be more twists and turns inbound during this exercise.

The Little Birds fell in to either side of her Chinook…then began falling behind.

Abby eased back on the thrust control. The Chinook could outstrip the Little Birds by forty klicks an hour. That meant that she had lost most of her flexibility for achieving their assigned landing times. "How bad?"

She didn't have to be clearer for Ethan to know what she meant. "Uh, at their max cruise, we can still make our assigned time with, wow, a whole two minutes of flex in the next hour. That's assuming nothing—"

Just as they hit a stretch of clear water over the Lake Martin Reservoir on the Tallapoosa River, a Black Hawk came racing toward them from the west.

It didn't report in as being friendly.

3

They arrived at Fort Rucker shy one Little Bird from *mechanical issues*—it had recorded a simulated hit to its main rotor from the unfriendly Black Hawk. Per new training orders, they had autorotated all the way down, just as if they'd actually been hit. You did that to one of those new Valors that the DoD-heads had selected and the crew would be dead.

Instead, her Little Bird crew was down safe, except they'd mired in the mud alongside the Tallapoosa River. Now they sat there, waiting for the beaten Army National Guard Black Hawk to circle back and lower a cable to extract them from the swamp. The Night Stalkers had beaten the ARNG's Black Hawk bad. The single Little Bird strike they'd managed before being declared damaged definitely belonged in the lucky-shot category. Her guardian Little Bird would remain parked in the stinking swamp for a long time before the Black Hawk could be bothered to extract them.

Abby hit Fort Rucker, Alabama, seven seconds ahead of her mark. Parked it clean.

A pair of nine-man DAGORs—Deployable Advanced

Ground Off-Road, Spec Ops light-tactical vehicles—raced toward them. Big tires, a suspension designed for crossing absurdly rough terrain, seats, engine, and roll cage. They were bare-bones, insanely durable, and could travel five hundred miles on a single tank of a variety of fuels, so long as the passengers were absolute masochists. They were not comfortable rides.

"Ramp! Ramp! Ramp!" The air marshaler who'd guided the last few feet of their landing was shouting.

Only thirty seconds allowed down didn't leave much time for doubts and guesses.

Charlene was parked on a supposedly friendly base, so Abby called the order back to Sam, her senior crew chief. Five seconds later, she felt the cool November air roll in off the Alabama lowlands as the wide tail ramp hit the ground. It brought back memories both good and bad. Too many trips down here to face the brutal instructors at ACE, Aviation Center of Excellence, and that was the good bit.

The sharp pine resin and noisome swampy scents that the two DAGORs pushed in as they rolled aboard made Abby's stomach churn.

It hurt despite her best intentions to never again think of or repeat her mistake when she'd been a gullible second lieutenant here, one dazzled by a major's attentions. By the time she'd found out he was married, she'd been sufficiently compromised to ruin her career if she didn't acquiesce to his wishes. Then she'd figured out he was just as vulnerable, more so for taking advantage of a lesser officer. But a woman never won tit-for-tat battles in this *man's* military. At least not until she'd thought to send a letter to the major's wife. He'd become far too busy to bother her after that.

"Nineteen...twenty..." Ethan was counting seconds since they'd gone wheels down. Their brief had said *precisely* thirty seconds on the ground.

"Twenty-one…"

Abby resisted the urge to turn around and watch. A pair of DAGORs was a tight fit for a Chinook with little more than inches to spare. The crew chiefs, who must be doing their jobs while clinging to the hull's structure like chimpanzees, would tell her when they were ready.

"Twenty-five…twenty-six…"

"Brakes set! No chains!" someone shouted over the intercom. His voice was so distorted that she couldn't even tell which of her crew it was.

"Raise ramp twenty percent up." Abby kept her voice calm, because that's what pilots did in times of crisis. That should keep anything from rolling out the back of the cargo bay. But they couldn't close it until the DAGOR's engines were shut down and no more exhaust was pumping into the cabin.

"Twenty-nine…"

Abby eased up on the thrust control. *Charlene One* was now near her max load as they'd just acquired nine thousand pounds of vehicle and another forty-five hundred of men and their gear. She'd be over her limit if she hadn't just burned off three hundred kilometers of fuel. Someone on the ground knew that.

"Thirty!"

She was airborne. Abby held the hover at one foot. Orders were to land for precisely thirty seconds, not a word about staying in the neighborhood up to her time limit. Thank God she'd hit seven seconds early. With her plus-minus window, that gave her team thirty-seven seconds before they *had* to clear out. Until then, if the load shifted unexpectedly, she'd only crash down one foot.

"Chains on." The call that the vehicles were now anchored to the decking and couldn't shift during maneuvering came at nine seconds remaining.

Charlene still felt tail-heavy. It was minor, but she could feel it. "Shift two guys as far forward as you can." She could trim it out, but that might limit handling in an extreme flight envelope.

Abby eased up to twenty feet as the balance shifted to neutral and then she set off northeast toward Fort Bragg. Her companion Little Bird had taken on a quick sixty gallons of fuel that should see them to the next stop—if they weren't shot down on this next leg.

"This far enough forward?" a voice asked from close behind her, deep enough for the sound to carry through her helmet. It wasn't one of her crew chiefs, which was what she'd meant. Actually, it was better that they stayed by their guns.

"Ethan," she spoke to her copilot over the intercom. The balance was good; it was time to hand off the second leg to him.

"I have control."

Once she felt his sure motion through the joined controls, she eased her hands away and flexed them. They ached from fighting the desire to hold on tight over the last two minutes, but a tight hand on the controls had no finesse.

She flipped up her visor and had to twist around to face the voice—almost clipping him with her helmet.

A wiry soldier sat in her jump seat, blocking any view she might have backward down the bird. No, not a soldier. By the MICH helmet, he was a Delta Force operator. The warriors from The Unit, as they styled themselves, weren't inclined to be big, and he wasn't. By his outline against the red running light in the cargo bay behind him, that was all she could tell. Unit operators were selected for endurance, speed, incredible marksmanship, and utter fearlessness—and a whole lot of other criteria they weren't mentioning in public.

Not wishing to blind night-vision-equipped pilots, Fort Rucker, which was fast falling behind anyway, had very little light facing upward. Inside the cockpit might as well be the dark side of the moon except for the dim glow of the night-vision-compatible instrument panels.

Whoever he was, his shadow *was* close.

4

"A-yuh, that's far enough forward." She had a Yankee sarcastic twang and sat short in her seat. Derek hadn't realized she was female until she spoke—a low, throaty voice but very female. He'd been meaning to just mess with a guy, not practically stick his nose in a woman's face.

With her visor up, his night-vision goggles let him see her face just fine. She'd have no visibility inside the cockpit, but he could see that her smile quirked to one side when she was being funny. He saw the arched eyebrow telling him he was in dangerous territory. No way to differentiate color through the NVGs, but he'd bet those eyes were light above the wide cheekbones. Nice face. And he liked that the humor reached her voice even while it threatened to prick him with sharp objects.

He found a headset hanging on the back of the pilot's seat and pulled it on. "Derek Kylie. Thanks for the ride."

"Abby Rose. Welcome aboard." She slid down her visor, turning into one of the Night Stalker cyborgs, looking far more machine than woman, and faced forward. "Any idea what's coming next?"

"Typical," Derek laughed.

"Typical?" Her tone went arch at his perceived insult to her gender's abilities. And it tried to go mean, but she didn't pull it off with that amusing so-very-Yankee accent.

"Typical for a *training op.*" His big sister had whupped no-underestimating-women into him fair and square. She was the one with Papa's big build and had followed into his rodeo career just fine. "I didn't even know we were headed northeast until I saw your departure path. For actual missions, they're far more inclined to tell us where to go and what to do."

She sighed. "They are. Or it could be that Okie accent of yours convincing them they didn't want to tell you."

"Good ear."

"Two of them."

"Yep, I'm just an Okie from Muskogee. Maybe that *is* why command never tells me shit."

He could see her fine fingers moving on the cyclic, but it was the copilot who was currently the pilot-in-control. Nothing changed on the displays he could see, so she must be toggling views inside her helmet while they talked. Couldn't be a Night Stalker pilot without an exceptional ability to multitask. He'd heard plenty of idiots call their pilots, especially those riding the comfortable seats in the big Chinooks designed for long-haul flights, *armchair warriors.* They'd hauled his ass out of too many hairy places for him to have anything but the utmost respect for them. Only the second time he'd run into a female pilot though, which meant this woman was seriously special.

Derek liked special.

5

"What the hell?" Abby's gut clenched as several warnings flashed simultaneously inside her visor. Several categories of threat sensors had just freaked out.

A fast-mover jet slicing in from the south, barely above their own flight level.

She called her lone Little Bird escort. "Inbound on our six. Target and prepare to fire."

"On it." They were already spun around and flying fast for a head-on with the jet, not that they stood a chance. She could definitely get to like that Little Bird pilot.

A message flashed down from above—but not on the satellite radio. It was local with no apparent point of origin.

"Flight *Charlene One,* this is Overwatch. The in-bound is a CCA. Do not fire."

She could feel Ethan freeze on the controls. She wiggled the cyclic slightly, and he flinched. Not enough to affect the flight, but enough that she could feel it through the controls. Then she felt him resume controlled flight. The whole interchange had lasted no more than a second or two, but when flying NOE

—nap of Earth—at nearly three hundred klicks, errors were typically measured in tenths of a second.

Abby gave him the moment to say he was sorry, which he did by not saying anything. And she replied the same. They'd flown together long enough that much of what needed saying didn't need to be said.

"Who the hell is flying that thing?" Abby felt the itch between her shoulder blades like a hard-driven knife blade, which must have been what snapped Ethan's attention out of piloting mode—he got a little intense and hyper-focused, even by her standards. "I thought the Collaborative Combat Aircraft were still in basic flight testing. Someone please tell me that isn't an armed autonomous AI drone flying beside me."

It must be the Anduril YFQ-44 by its standard inverted-T tail and thin wings. They weren't even through the first flight test as far as she knew, yet the long thin fuselage of the aircraft flying beside them matched the specs she'd been studying for the fun of it.

"I could tell you, but that might spoil the fun." Mr. D-boy. Mr. I'm-too-cool Delta operator. They were cool…and scary as could be.

"Go ahead, spoil the fun."

"There's a 24th STS dude embedded with our Delta team. Never told us why he was here. Guessing that's why."

They were the Air Force's contribution to the Tier One teams of Joint Special Operations Command. The Army contributed Delta and the Navy stood up DEVGRU, which everyone except the Department of Dense knew as SEAL Team 6. The 24th Special Tactics Squadron were definitely good guys to have around. Whether you needed a precision air strike or someone to run a couple hundred supply flights per hour into a recently captured airport using nothing more than a handheld radio and an apple crate to sit on, they were the guys.

"Turns out he's not the one actually flying it."

Abby could hear the tease and refused to rise to the bait as she watched the CCA slide into formation to the side where she'd lost the Little Bird…and a little ahead.

Derek waited.

She didn't have time for a guessing game in a combat situation, not even during a simulated one. Unless it wasn't a guessing game. The STS dude wasn't here to fly it, which meant he was only here as a safety pilot to *monitor* it in case the stupid thing's brain went kerflooey. It wasn't a nicely useful drone—the damn jet *was* flying itself. Using its own unknown set of programming and misconceptions.

"Well, isn't that just Jimmies on an Italian?"

"Who on a what?" Ethan had given up asking long ago, but Derek fell for the trap.

"Jimmies, you know, those sprinkles on ice cream. Chocolate ones are the only real ones by the way, just in case you ever buy me an ice cream."

"O-kay." Not being stupid—Delta meant he was very, very smart—his tone said he knew he had one foot in the trap. "What's with sprinkles on a person?"

Her trap snapped closed in her thoughts with a bright *snick!* "An Italian, or an Italian Ice to the uninitiated, is called a snow cone in the more heathen parts of this fine nation."

"Heathen. Like any state that isn't Vermont?"

"*Downeast.*" She slashed at him. "The great state of Maine. Never insult me like that again." Then she heard his chuckle over the intercom. Yep, he'd already paid her back for her trap.

"Yes ma'am," he sassed her. In her peripheral vision, where it wasn't blocked by her helmet, she saw his hand sweep up into a sharp salute. "So, having an experimental Air Force CCA horn in on a Night Stalkers' training mission is about as logical as chocolate sprinkles on a snow cone. Got it! But if that's the case, how do you explain my team being here?"

"What do you call a moose with no friends?" She let him

stew on that while she looked again for whatever was flying overwatch from somewhere above them. Until the CCA showed up, this had been a strictly Army operation. No longer. Which meant that in addition to one of their own Gray Eagle drones, it could be any of the standard sentry birds—a Navy E-2 Hawkeye, P-8 Poseidon, or the like. Except those would show up clearly. Yet another drone? If so, it was a stealth bird without even a hint on her extremely sensitive threat radar.

"No matter what I say, I'll be wrong," Derek finally conceded.

"It be alone-some." She gave it her best Downeast dry tone. Mainiacs were prone-*some* to tacking *some* onto words in the strangest ways. At least according to anyone from *away*—those who didn't have the God-given gift of being born in the greatest state. To her ear, it was a quantifier of more, or less, but a little more than less.

"So, my team and I are here because...what, we don't have any friends?"

"Oh, the man is sharp."

Ethan laughed, and Derek joined in with that good chuckle of his.

"We still have our uses."

Abby glanced over in time to see Derek make a gesture to the men behind him. Seconds later, a request came up on her visor to permit a data link.

"That you?" Certain things you didn't mess with, and letting strangers into her helo's systems was one of them.

"STS," Derek confirmed.

She authorized the connection, but read-only. No data would travel back to the US Air Farce Circus's man, whether or not he was a clown. And she slotted it as an isolated view on its own screen, not the full-display request.

The new option popped up on her menu: *CCA*. She selected it with the thumb controller.

Night Stalkers trained hard to absorb and process huge amounts of visual and auditory data rapidly. When threat sensors lit up over navigational views requiring targeting and firing solutions, only to be interrupted by damage reports, a girl had to stay on top of it all.

The CCA selection gave her a flash of nausea. The unexpected shift as her viewpoint jerked a hundred meters to starboard and thirty meters up. As if someone had tried to yank the rug of the landscape out from beneath her feet and only succeeded in shifting it. Now it was her own bird showing up to port and below, from the CCA's view. Even as she watched, it picked up flights climbing out of Charlotte Douglas International Airport. Each shifted from yellow, when spotted, to green as it tagged the aircraft with its flight number. Green must be *known aircraft*. Not the way her Army-built helo's display reported, but she got the idea fast enough.

Which all meant she wasn't doing her job as a copilot. She flipped back to the tactical screens for her own bird, pausing to check the aircraft's health status. All nominal.

"What the hell game are we playing?"

Derek laughed. "When you find out, be sure to tell me."

"Maybe yes. Maybe no." There sure wasn't anyone she could ask. She was the lead bird on this twenty-long daisy chain flight of Chinooks. Except it didn't mean anything as they weren't connected. So, she was the lead on a flight of one Chinook, one Little Bird that she trusted after its amazing flight during the earlier face-off with the Black Hawk, and a CCA she wouldn't be trusting this side of the North Maine Woods. "Guess we're just waitin' a bit on that overwatch bird to tell us what's going on," she nodded upward.

"It had better be soon," Ethan spoke up. "Our assigned time at Fort Bragg is in four minutes."

Crap! Abby checked the route map and the timing. During her inattention, Ethan had kept them within their assigned plus-or-minus thirty-second window—barely. His sole job during NOE ops was to fly; her job included everything else. Hard against thirty seconds over their time meant zero leeway for surprises as she'd used at Fort Rucker. They'd get thirty seconds on the ground and then have to scoot—ready or not. "Try nudging up three knots."

Ethan did. But the Little Bird, up at its limits, began falling behind.

"Ease back." It was up to her to handle threats *and* navigation. "My bad."

"We got this," Ethan floated up to clear a set of power lines. The CCA was above the power lines already; the Little Bird slid under and then dodged through the trees on the far side. Ethan eased back down before twisting sideways around a barn. Most of the Black Route avoided towns and homes, but in a few places there simply wasn't a choice.

"Two minutes." Abby announced to the crew chiefs. "Sam, we don't know what's coming or going, so I want the ramp on the ground within one second of our wheels."

"Roger that."

"You sticking or going, Derek?"

"My guess—"

Overwatch cut him off. "Emergency re-route to 35.131 by -79.06. Half squad. Debus."

Abby punched the new latitude and longitude into the NavComp as Overwatch read them out. *Debus* meant a hot insertion—rapid deployment. But it was only going to be half their load, which meant they had to stay on the ground while the remaining load was shifted and re-chained to the deck.

"Huh," was all Derek said before Abby heard the click of him dropping off the intercom. A half turn of her head showed that the jump seat behind her had been folded away and no one blocked her view of the packed cargo bay. She missed having him there. Who knew when she'd see him again. The

Spec Ops world was small, but not *that* small. With the approximately three hundred Delta Force operators and the Night Stalkers' two hundred aircraft, their meeting again soon didn't seem likely.

Facing her readouts once more, she saw something good had come of the change. "Those coordinates are fifty-four seconds closer than Pope Airfield on the other side of the base. So, we'll be early instead of late."

"Good-some news."

Ethan earned her laugh. She waited a beat for Derek to inject a comment, but he wasn't there.

6

Derek didn't like dividing the team. Especially sending half of them into an unknown situation of a hot LZ. Even a *simulated* hot landing zone had to be approached with serious caution. He also didn't like that someone up there was messing with them.

And not just Colonel Beale. She might be a legend, but she didn't command the kind of power that could launch half of Delta Force from Bragg to Rucker on a C-5 Galaxy super transporter, merely so that they could be dragged back by helo. Although he'd only met her twice, Beale struck him as a woman well able to get her way.

And what the hell was that Air Force drone jet doing here? After its first flight, there should be another year of flight testing and refinement before an overtly stupid AI was flying lethal hardware on a training mission.

Don't think, boy. This the Army is. Just do.

Yes sir, Drill Sergeant Yoda, sir!

As the helo slammed to a halt, he had someone stationed at every chain. From a dead stop, the bird settled a foot...and touched down. Damn, but these pilots were good. At his signal, they dumped the chains on all four tires of both vehicles. He saluted his number two as they accelerated backward off the ramp. The forward non-exiting DAGOR backed as if their bumpers had been stuck together until it reached the middle of the cargo bay and slammed on its brakes.

The crew chief had them adjust six inches forward as they juggled the chains. They had the rear ramp lifting with five seconds to spare. The crew of Abby's bird were as good as its pilots.

Derek surveyed his team as they double-checked their personal gear, even after such a short move. That's the way he liked it—nice and tight.

The half team that was gone? He had to dismiss them from his thoughts. He'd find out more in the after-action report, but until then they were out of his hands. So, what were he and his squad in for?

He didn't even have to catch himself as they pulled back aloft at thirty seconds, because they were that smooth. Telling himself to stay out of their way didn't slow him down much; he headed up front toward the lady pilot. Derek eased into the cockpit, a little disappointed to see that Abby Rose was once again the pilot-in-command. No one in his right mind would distract a pilot flying NOE where death by crashing lay well inside a single second's inattention.

"I can feel you shifting my weight." Her tone was now deadpan and professional. Abby hadn't turned at all in his direction.

Even with one team and DAGOR gone, it was still twenty tons of helo. He didn't know whether to retreat back to the cargo bay or—

"Sit your butt down already." The Maine accent was also lighter. *Your* only had a hint of being *yo-ah*.

He swung out the jump seat, sat, and pulled on the headset again, but left the mike swung up in the off position. It was a very different experience with her piloting. No words. No excess movement. No jokes that he could imagine included a raised eyebrow or that sideways quirk of a smile he'd glimpsed. Instead? He felt like he was back in Space Mountain, hanging with his two young nephews screaming with delight as they roller-coastered through the dark. As Sis was a single mom—she'd consistently outridden her rodeo husband, which he hadn't taken well—Derek was always her *date* for the boys' annual Disneyland treat. Honestly? He'd miss it if they ever outgrew the place.

By the time his NVGs resolved the obstacles ahead of the helo; they were already slashing by. His night vision was for slipping into a building unnoticed and taking down individual targets, not for cruising along at a couple hundred kmph. He knew the Night Stalkers had special displays to do that. They'd practically pioneered night vision after losing one of their founders in a nighttime run that, he recalled with a shiver, was pioneering the Black Route runs like this one. But those views were projected inside their helmets, and he didn't dare interrupt her to ask about them.

"You can talk," Abby's voice still lacked the earlier teasing tones. "Just don't, you know..."

"Be my distracting self?"

"Ayuh."

"How far ahead can you see?"

Ethan was the one who answered, though he didn't turn from his tasks. "Three layers. Wire-frame of everything accurate to a couple meters, programmed from detailed satellite surveys. Radar to pick out any changes. All overlaid by ten-eighty night vision, made up of mixed IR and enhanced visual. Near range is practically daylight visibility. For distance, we can see the shape of what's behind the next hill."

"Which," Abby was indeed carving around a knob or hill or whatever they called them now that they'd crossed back into

Kentucky, "is useful except when it distracts you from the object right in front of you."

Even with the description, he struggled to imagine such a thing—and couldn't. And the ten-eighty thing was straight out of Delta. A thousand and eighty degrees. Three times three-sixty. Not only aware of everything around you as in a three-hundred-and-sixty-degree circle, but two more circles—above and below. But Delta mostly lived in the horizontal world. Not the Night Stalkers; nastiness could come at them from any direction. They traded Delta's Situational Awareness for all-around Airspace Awareness.

Derek's gut tried to slide out his ass, saying Abby had entered a hard climb. He didn't see anything to avoid, but she topped out and cliffed off the other side like the peak of a rollercoaster ride. "What was that?"

"Power lines. We worked hard on night vision, but it wasn't enough. So thin that the radar barely showed it, but it's dead clear on the wire frame."

"That's gotta be a head splitter."

He saw Ethan's nod against the starlight outside his windshield. "A top reason for pilot failure. Imagine that three-layer view. Now overlay tactical displays and aircraft status. You add in that CCA," a head tip to the side where Derek assumed it still flew, "and you've got a whole other headache."

Derek had been delivered to plenty of battles and exfiltrated back out without ever thinking much about what it took to do that. Delta Force were simply the best. The British SAS came close, and the Russian Spetsnaz had too—until decimated by their position as the first troops into the Ukraine War. But he was starting to think that The Unit wasn't the *only* best out there.

He knew he was biased partly by gender. Women were under twenty percent in any branch of the service and way under one percent in Spec Ops. But he figured his chances of meeting—connecting with—another woman like Captain Abby Rose were damned low. Of course a woman in the Spec Ops world had her pick. Unless she already had. For all he knew, she was doing it with her copilot. Against all the rules, but there were certain rules that folks flat out ignored. Mostly it was only the bad breakups that hit the courts-martial.

Too bad he hadn't buddied up with any Night Stalkers who he could ask about Abby—major oversight in hindsight. He couldn't ask Ethan. But...there were the four crew chiefs hanging out in the back with his team.

"I'm gonna go check on my guys. Thanks for the tour." He waited for a reply, but he didn't get one.

7

She sighed. At least she was consistent. Abby could always grab a guy's attention, but she'd never had any luck holding onto it. In bars back home, she had to hide her skills and her brains. Not like she was a conversation killer on purpose, but she had a real knack for it. *I fly helicopters for the US Army;* guys didn't like being outperformed. *I've flown in twenty countries on five continents;* most guys in Maine bars had never traveled farther than the tax-free liquor stores just over the New Hampshire border, *I—*

What was the point? She scared off guys in Fort Campbell bars just as effectively. Though spooking away a Delta operator might be a new low for her; an honor she could have done without.

Something flickered at the edge of her awareness. "Ethan, check the CCA position. See what that damn thing is up to."

"Nothing much. Holding position. It's enough higher that they won't be running ten million bucks of experimental aircraft into a hillside anytime soon."

Higher. That meant—

"Send it wide!" Abby punched the left pedal, doing one of

her favorite Chinook tricks—making twenty tons of helo spin about its vertical axis without banking. Because she had twin rotors, she could fly the nose and tail in different directions. Which meant she could send the nose left and the tail right until she was on a new course, twisting around the fuselage center point of the cargo hook. And, this close to the ground, she could do it while diving for the dirt without having to worry about catching her long thirty-foot blades while in a steep bank.

She twisted so sharply that she passed behind the Little Bird off her port side. Behind *and* below. If she'd been low before, now she was hugging the terrain. *Sorry, buddy.* The Little Bird was there to protect her, and she had a bad feeling about what lay close ahead.

Or... She'd just messed up royally by departing her designated route in a direction that was backward-some. It was definitely abrading the time window second by second, but that was the least of her worries at the moment.

"Check the CCA view," she ordered Ethan. She couldn't afford to look away from the obstacles flashing by.

"Identified twelve hostiles."

"*Twelve?*" Was every Night Stalker in the entire regiment aloft tonight?

"They're—shit. They're small."

Drones! If she ingested even one of those into an engine, they'd be down in the dirt. Except Chinook helos had one major drawback. If the drive train broke, they couldn't autorotate down to a tricky landing. Instead, Chinooks tended to shred at altitude and rain down on the ground in several thousand tiny pieces.

She checked her display again—nothing. The drones weren't stealth or the CCA wouldn't have seen them.

Diving low and outside had saved her...but from what?

Drones were such a threat that she couldn't believe Colonel

Beale would put them in her path. Not even Trisha O'Malley would do that.

She keyed the radio. "Little Bird. Turn to heading two-six-zero. Climb to thirty meters. What are you seeing due north?"

Abby only had to wait seconds for the report. "The CCA. Otherwise, clear skies."

The Air Force collaborative combat aircraft wasn't collaborating; the Air Force had programmed it to give a *false* report of a drone swarm.

She slammed the controls over to swing back to course and climbed back to the hundred-foot cap.

Then she had an idea and hit the radio again. "Put a simulated round through that damn CCA's little brain."

Ethan reported six seconds later. "CCA has suffered a hundred percent simulated destruction."

8

"She's a wild one." Derek joked to Sam, the master sergeant crew chief.

Abby's first sudden maneuver had caught them all by surprise. With no banking, they hadn't been driven deeper into their seats. Instead, the bird had twisted sideways, tossing the unwary against hard surfaces. He and Sam had been standing near the center of the aircraft, so they were only dropped to the deck when their feet had gone sideways without them—instead of slamming up against hard objects.

The only real injury was that Hot Rod, who'd been lounging in his normal driver's seat in the DAGOR, lost a hold of his muscle-car magazine. Between the abrupt twists, turns, and air currents—with its pages flapping like a bird's—the magazine disappeared out the open Minigun window. It was wide and tall enough for a crew chief to swing the big gun where it was needed, but it had slipped by.

Everyone adapted fast; the second hard swing elicited no more than grimaces excepting a steady stream of curses from Hot Rod.

"Major Roberts says she's the Number One Chinook pilot, after him, of course."

"Tall Texan, white cowboy hat?"

Sam nodded.

"Shit. Next time you see him, tell him that Derek still says *thanks*. Hauled my team's ass out of Ecuador when no one should have been able to. So, what's Abby's story?"

Sam's smile said that it wasn't his smoothest play, but he did swing up his helmet's microphone to switch it off. "Nobody climbs that hill."

"What? Why not?"

Sam shook his head. "Scares 'em off. Seen plenty try. Too smart for 'em. They bounce off like a hard wall."

"Plays for the other team?"

Again the head shake.

"Any reason not to try?"

"How do you feel about pain?"

"Hey, I'm Delta."

Sam laughed and thumped him on the shoulder. "Good luck, bro. You're gonna need it." Then he swung down his mike and headed along the cargo bay toward the other crew chiefs.

Derek watched to see if he was filling them in then voting whether to toss him out at altitude; no one glanced his way.

He squeezed along the side of the DAGOR and sat in the passenger seat. Hot Rod sat in the driver's seat, still griping about his lost magazine. No help there. After the two hard maneuvers, with no sign of a third, most of the others were doing what Spec Ops warriors did best while waiting for the action to start—sleeping.

Derek was bolt-wide awake. By brute force, he shifted his thinking. Based on what he'd already seen tonight, what battle scenario had command cooked up for him? Would they be dumped into the back forty at Fort Campbell the way the other half of his team had been dumped at Bragg's Range 37? At the other extreme, were they going to meet planes that would ship them all overseas tonight? That was unlikely as most of the big lifters—C-17s and C-5s capable of carting around multiple helos—were back at Fort Bragg.

That meant a ground action at Fort Campbell. What was Abby Rose like in real life, away from her helo?

Shit! Back exactly where he'd started.

9

All the way back to Fort Campbell, Abby felt even more edge-of-seat than usual from an NOE flight, which she hadn't thought was possible. Waiting for the hammer to drop, on top of the strains of such advanced flying, had left her wiped out—but the hammer never fell. Not a peep from her radar and not a single word from Overwatch.

No new attack. No last second reroute. No surprise aircraft.

The second after it declared itself dead, the CCA had disappeared to parts unknown. Not that she was paranoid about what the Air Farce was up to, but she made sure to maintain an aerial dance with her sole remaining Little Bird—despite the added layer of complexity—in case the damn thing returned. It didn't.

For a lack of any other instructions, she cleared her flight with the tower and landed once more at Fort Campbell, wheels down to the second in her slot. By the time she and Ethan had run the Shutdown checklist and she'd pulled her helmet and scrubbed a bit of life back into her scalp, Trisha O'Malley was standing front and center outside her windscreen.

Colonel Beale's second-in-command was grinning like the

evil red-headed demon she was. Pleasant, jovial, pretty, and utterly ruthless. Her breath blowing dragon's steam in the predawn chill only added to the image.

"Looks like the debriefing is starting early," Ethan kept his tone steady. Steadier than she felt anyway.

When someone pulled open her right-hand door, she almost tumbled out on top of him. MICH helmet with NVGs tipped back, sidearm in the middle of his vest for a quick draw, rifle over his shoulder—Derek Kylie. Now in the low glow of the field lights, she could see that unlike many D-boys who wore their beards past scraggly and into horrific, his was neatly trimmed. His lean face matched the rest of him, and she'd take his smile to mean that she hadn't scared him off completely.

Too exhausted to notice more, she climbed down from her high seat and circled to face Trisha. They traded salutes. Then she looked over her shoulder. Not at Derek, but up at the sky. She'd been on the ground for over ninety seconds. The next Chinook in the flight should be landing by now but she spotted no running lights. No noise except the fuel truck approaching to top up her tanks and the light rumble of the DAGOR unloading down *Charlene One's* rear ramp.

Trisha answered the question that Abby's thoughts weren't yet organized enough to ask. "Half didn't meet the time limits, especially on the unplanned load up and load outs."

Abby would have to remember to tell her crew chiefs they'd done good.

"The rest fell for the trap."

Abby turned back to Trisha. Her brain was slow shifting out of her own tactical situation into the whole flight's. "They decided that the drones projected by the CCA were real and got out of the air?"

Trisha nodded, her smile huge. "We have Chinook and Delta teams scattered all over farm fields from here to Bragg.

The CCA worked the line from the rear the moment that you folks dropped off half of the D-boy and Ranger teams."

"How many?" How many would be counted among the dead or captured.

"One successfully deployed to Fort Campbell."

Abby looked around the tarmac, but hers was the only helo here. "Who else?"

Trisha pointed at her. "You spoiled my fun. Of those not disqualified for being too late, everyone else failed the CCA test. They either let the CCA integrate with their systems, so that the false drone readings appeared on their own equipment as well, or they trusted the CCA's equipment over their own and dove for a safe landing. Only one person shot the Air Force bird." Again the finger pointed at her chest.

Someone held up a hand for a high-five and she slapped it. Then she turned to see Derek grinning down at her. A single horse-hand taller than her own five-five, he looked as pleased as if he'd been the one flying.

"So, was it me or the CCA that you trusted less?" he asked.

"Both."

He tried to look hurt and ended up looking cute—at least for a scary-as-shit D-boy.

"Wait! You're the one who prompted me to connect to the CCA. Would you allow an unknown drone to integrate with your comms network during a mission? I didn't know it was a trap until later, but it was all a little too convenient in retrospect."

"Sam said you were smart." So, he'd been checking up on her. She needed to have a chat with her crew chief about doing that—like *never* again.

Then she spotted Trisha's expression. "You had a plant on each flight to suggest that connection to the CCA's data feed."

"That wasn't a question." Trisha laughed. "Can't wait to

tease Emily about slipping that past her, but I can't find her. Bitch is probably asleep."

"No, I guess it wasn't a question." Abby knew that, in addition to being top-flight SOAR officers, Emily and Trisha were close friends, but it was still kinda shocking. She couldn't imagine anyone calling the austere Colonel Beale by her first name, never mind by a curse. That woman was more daunting than a whole squad of D-boys.

"Emily dumped the debrief on me, but that won't be for a couple hours. At the moment, I've got Chinooks spread across six states. Time to go sweep them up. Captain Kylie, we do have a planned exercise for your teams here at Fort Campbell tomorrow night. And yes, you'll get a pre-mission briefing and time to plan for a change, but that's tomorrow. We want the Night Stalkers to fully experience what you guys can deliver." Then that evil grin flashed again. "And vice versa. Until then the corporal can set you up in Transient Quarters." Trisha waved at the person who'd been lurking in the background.

Abby made a point of thanking Ethan and each of her crew chiefs before releasing them. Derek did the same, sending his team and the DAGOR off with the corporal. Soon it was just the two of them standing in the dark together. Trisha had mounted her broom and flown away when Abby wasn't watching.

"Food?" Her constitution was feeling the one-hour planning and five-hour op badly.

"Derek." He tapped his chest and grinned at her. Then hooked a thumb in the direction of the departed DAGOR. "However if you want to share room service—"

She sent him a look.

He grimaced. "Yeah, bad line. You're throwing me off my game, Abby. Food sounds great."

"I've got no use for someone playing games."

"One strike I'm out?" He actually looked worried that might be the case.

"Usually yes, but we'll call that one as just a stinky-foul hit."

Derek nodded his thanks and waved for her to lead the way. She didn't hold out much hope. Unit operators were known for being the unruly renegades of the US military. Perhaps not as bad as SEAL Team 6, but close.

But she was tired, hungry, and it had been a long time since she'd found a decent man outside of her chain-of-command to even consider.

Counting herself as weak, she even slowed down her usual fast stride to let him keep up with her.

10

EMILY MADE IT BACK TO THE RANCH EVEN MORE SLOWLY THAN usual—sixteen hours to cross half the country. With no military flights headed in the right direction, she'd fought through inconvenient airport locations, a broken plane, and a drunk who should have been ejected at altitude instead of merely cornered—the not-so-gentle application of her hand-to-hand combat training had definitely garnered his attention and cooperation—and ended with him zip-tied to an attendant's seat in the aft galley. The flight attendants had appreciated the help, but it had led to interviews and paperwork once they'd landed which made her miss the connector flight of an already bad layover—winter-time flights to western Montana simply weren't very common.

The flights themselves were consumed by paperwork she'd fallen behind on and planning she hadn't had time to do in Fort Campbell. Trisha's after-action report had made her laugh. She'd never considered planting a key friendly aboard each helo to unwittingly sabotage their systems. How Trisha managed to get a CCA from the Air Force testing and qualification teams was an addition to her never-ending mystical collection of skills.

The results had her frowning until she read the detailed accounts by the various pilots. Trisha had slammed them up against a helo pilot's greatest fears.

During her own time in Afghanistan, their greatest fears were RPGs and surface-to-air missiles. Drones back then had been strictly US hardware, large birds flying high on surveillance or kill missions. Now they constituted a whole new level of ugly. Small, incredibly maneuverable, and—with the innovations of the Ukraine War—lethal. No one had missed the recent downing of a twenty-million-dollar Colombian military Black Hawk by a three-thousand-dollar Russian drone used by the extremist guerilla drug- and kidnap-runners still operating in the deep jungle.

Only one Chinook had made it through last night's test, captained by Abigail Rose and Ethan Merced. Digging deeper into the debrief, Emily spotted Trisha's note.

Capt. Abby Rose and D-boy Capt. Derek Kylie showed strong connection and cooperation.

Leave it to Trisha to bury it in an after-action report. She *knew* they represented the sort of people Emily was looking for. Her husband Mark and Colonel Michael Gibson, then Trisha and her husband Billy, Emily knew the power of that deep integration offered by the inclusion of a permanently embedded Delta Force liaison within a Night Stalker operation. Surely, Trisha hoped that Emily would miss it so that she could lay a massive tease trap for later.

Emily sent a simple text: *Push them hard in tonight's exercise.* Trisha would definitely know who she meant, and her own nonreaction would be a tease back.

The jolt of the landing in Great Falls, Montana, came as a complete shock. She'd been so deep in the report, she'd completely missed the passenger jet's descent and final approach. She rubbed her eyes. Were her piloting instincts failing her?

The more likely answer, of severe sleep deprivation, came home to roost the instant after climbing into the ranch's helicopter that Mark had flown down. She didn't even stay conscious long enough to kiss him before sleeping through the twenty-minute flight out to Henderson's Ranch.

He had half lifted her out of the helo before the slap of cold air woke her. "No, wait. Put me down before you hurt yourself."

Mark laughed and held her closer. If anything, ranch work had made him even more powerful than the first time he'd held her thirteen years ago. Retired and mid-forties, he'd mellowed from that long-ago company commander…but not changed all that much. Nothing she'd like to do more than curl up in his arms and be carried to their bed—as long as he let her sleep.

"The girls?"

"It's a school day." One p.m. her time had become noon local. Which meant—

"Dilya."

"What about her?"

"Where is she?"

Mark looked down at her. "Dilya?"

Emily sighed. The girl could be bloody invisible when she wanted to.

"Hi, Emily."

Mark banged his nose on the back of Emily's head as they both twisted to look down at her. Except Dilya wasn't *down* anymore. She'd been a little slip of a girl when their unit had rescued the war orphan from the middle of a battle in northern Afghanistan. She'd been starved for too many years to ever be more than slender. Her dark brown hair still ruffled long down her back, and her green eyes still seemed too large for her narrow features, especially highlighted by her mid-tone skin.

Mark set Emily down rather abruptly as he grabbed for his

nose. Thankfully he first let go of her feet rather than her head. Still, a hand on Mark's shoulder was all that kept her from dropping to the snow-dusted dirt.

"You're in Montana." Emily didn't know quite what comfort she'd found in stating the obvious.

"So are you." Dilya smiled at her, and her dog, a too-smart Sheltie named Zackie, wagged her tail in agreement. "We need to talk."

"So you said."

Mark looked from one to the other of them as he held his nose before cursing, "Dabbit!" And he stalked off without even giving her a kiss. Mark knew about the Tac Room, probably knew its purpose, but he wasn't one of the four authorized to enter there. Usually he liked it that way. Not at the moment.

Of course Dilya wasn't authorized either, but that hadn't stopped her. She'd had years of practice, first at the secret forward military base they'd rescued her to, then later as the First Child's nanny and the First Lady's dog handler in the White House. Emily still hadn't heard the story of how Dilya ended up owning the First Lady's dog when she left the White House.

"Sorry," Dilya looked more sad than sorry.

"Your timing has been better." Then she recognized the new pained look on Dilya's face as clearly as Mark had recognized that nothing important would happen as long as he remained within earshot. "New Hampshire?" Last she'd heard, Dilya had been living with a boy near Mount Washington, the tallest point north of Tennessee and east of the Black Hills.

"All he cared about was his trains."

"Trains?"

"He works on the tourist cog-rail line that goes up to the top of Mount Washington. I thought he'd be…"

"…interested in the same things you were?"

Dilya sighed so heavily that even the irrepressible Zackie

looked sad. "He was, still is, into tactical online war games. But that's as far as he wants to take it. Ultimately, we just annoyed the crap out of each other." She stroked Zackie's head. "Our Shelties grew as grouchy with each other as we did."

"I'm sorry." Emily was never brilliant at moments like this. She knew what to do when she was someone's commander and superior officer. But Dilya was the adopted daughter of the man she'd met at West Point, then flown with for years, and the woman who'd been Emily's top gunner back in the day. Emily and Dilya were more friends than anything else. Out of other ideas, Emily rested a hand on Dilya's arm in sympathy.

Dilya nodded hard, brushed once at her eyes, and retreated without moving a muscle. "We need to talk."

Emily dropped her hand. "Is it okay if I get some sleep first?"

Dilya's look said no.

Now it was Emily's turn to sigh sadly. Well, she wasn't going to leave the high-pressure world of Fort Campbell only to crawl into the high-pressure world of the Tac Room, no matter how anxious Dilya was.

Emily looked about the Montana ranch compound; she might be barely conscious but at least she was home and that was a blessing in any form.

But the two-story log-built lodge would be busy with ranch operations; there might also be a chef's masterclass based on the number of vehicles parked in front of the lodge. Their master chef often ran those over the winter—for income off the tourist season. The big horse barn rarely had a quiet corner. Mark had gone to the multi-bay garage; he and Doug, the ranch manager, maintained most of the tractors and such themselves. Zackie's attention was riveted in the opposite direction where Stan and Jodi would be running a new class of war dogs through training. The soft, chilly breeze from that direction must be suggesting a whole pack of potential playmates.

She looked up at the achingly blue sky that stretched on forever. After growing up in DC and spending the bulk of her adult life in helicopters and military bases, she'd fallen in love with the ranch's Big Sky. The snow shone beneath the midday sun, but it wasn't much more than a filling around the winter grasses. The air was crisper than a fresh-picked apple and alive like nowhere else she'd ever been.

"Do you ride?"

Dilya's eye roll said she was being dense.

"Give me a break, kid. I've been awake for three days." And she wasn't as young as she used to be. Twenty years back when she'd been a freshly minted SOAR pilot, her current state of sleep deprivation was nothing out of the norm. Now in her mid-forties? Not so much.

"I spent *how* many years working for First Lady Melanie Anne Darlington Thomas?" Dilya didn't make it a passive-aggressive sneer. It was more of a jog-your-elbow reminder. Dilya had never developed any nasty streak past the eye roll she'd had down cold long before she spoke English.

The First Lady, Zackie's putative owner, was a masterful horsewoman from a grand Tennessee farm. Emily had seen the wall of awards to prove it. She'd even managed to convert her husband to the sport, though President Zachary Thomas never excelled any better than Mark, or herself. "Oh, right."

What had Dilya been up to that had made Emily drop everything when Dilya insisted they talk? She was only... "How old are you now, anyway?"

"Twenty-five." Again, no *duh!* Just a fact.

At that age she'd become Captain Emily Beale and been commanding combat flights for the 101st Screaming Eagles. Dilya's specialty wasn't flying helos. But it was—

Emily felt her first true chill since arriving in Montana's

winter. Dilya had been trained by having parents who were the top military sniper and a military strategy consultant to multiple Presidents, and had lived a dozen years within the White House. There she'd been gathered under the wing of one of the nation's top spies. Who knew *what* the hell the girl delved into now, with that as a background. But it explained why she'd dropped everything and come on the run when Dilya called.

She hadn't even thought of telling Dilya to come to her in Kentucky until she was halfway home. It was a good decision on two counts. First, Emily didn't want to risk mixing whatever worried Dilya with her own day job as commander of the 160th SOAR. Second, hadn't she been wishing to get home just minutes before Dilya's call?

"Let's go steal a couple horses."

Dilya brightened. "Yes, let's."

11

The instant Dilya found out that Wind Runner was Mark's mount of choice, she insisted on riding him. He was the feistiest mount on the ranch, teaching Mark many hard lessons. Of course, as a retired 160th company commander, Mark was used to learning that way.

Dilya proved her horse handling abilities by showing Wind Runner exactly who was in charge before the saddle was even cinched. He and Zackie had a brief sniffing negotiation, which appeared to reach a satisfactory conclusion as there were no complaints about the Sheltie's presence in the horse's stall. At ten years old, no Sheltie slowed down measurably at play. But long runs over rough ground—with the snow dog-knee deep—were best done tucked deep inside a comfortable leather perch. Dilya loaded Zackie into a large saddle bag and, after an additional eye-to-eye negotiation, that too was settled.

Dilya insisted they ride out through the barn door facing the compound rather than the one that led toward the trails. She led them in a wide circle of the ranch's compound, that—Emily fought to hold in the laugh—just happened to pass the open equipment garage bay where Mark and Doug were rebuilding the hay mower for next season.

When they trotted past the garage, Mark just shook his head and shot a smile at Emily that said everything was okay between them. He too had plenty of experience over the years of Dilya as a force of nature.

Love you, she mouthed to him.

I know, he offered his standard reply before turning back to his repairs.

She and Dilya rode up past the cabins where Julie's truck showed she was inside doing winter maintenance after the heavy tourist season. Over the ridge, the swimming hole had ice around the edges though the middle remained open.

They rode into the first roll of the foothills. To the east of the ranch lay the vast flats of the Great Plains. The ranch itself nestled in a narrow band of the Front Range breaks. The Montana Front Range was so dramatic that she could never tire of it. Bounding the far side of ten thousand acres of ranch, the Sawtooth and Lewis Mountain Ranges punched aloft like snow-covered claws scraping at the blue sky.

Mark often called them a frozen tidal wave. When iced up as they were now, they appeared on the verge of crashing down upon the ranch. Emily, on the other hand, had always thought of them as a great bastion, holding the world at bay whenever it tried to overwhelm her. Though in her current state, they appeared to waver and shift. If only she could tell whether they were following Mark's expectations of imminent tsunami inundation or fighting a titanic battle as they rose to her defense.

Dilya still hadn't spoken and Emily was too exhausted to go first. The only sounds were the creaking of the saddle leather and the call of a rock pigeon. Zackie watched everything with a Sheltie's excitement but no horse-annoying squirms. She followed the dog's gaze upward to spot a pair of bald eagles soaring high aloft, their white heads and tails shining in the sun.

"You two have something real."

Emily laughed. "You can't give up yet, Dilya. I was thirty before Mark and I got together. Your second mom might have been twenty-five, but Archie was thirty-one when they got together and adopted you."

"I know. I know all that. I just...thought I'd already found it."

Again Emily had no real reference. Her heart had gone from the mad crush on her childhood neighbor, the six-years-too-old man destined to become President, to Mark with very few noteworthy wanderings in between.

Dilya had never been one to speak quickly. In the beginning, she didn't have the English and probably suffered from shock after witnessing her parents' murders and then wandering lost and starving in the Hindu Kush Mountains. Living as a nanny in the White House, she'd certainly overheard a lot—had made a hobby of it—but her natural discretion meant that she rarely and discreetly revealed what she had learned. And then she'd come to the attention of the ex-CIA master spy, Miss Watson.

"Did Miss Watson send you?" Emily gave in to the silence. Please let it not be that.

"Kinda sorta." When Dilya descended into any form of slang, Emily knew she was dissembling.

"Not being helpful, Dilya."

"Not wanting to get us all killed, Emily."

12

When Dilya noticed that Emily had reined Chesapeake to a halt, she was forced to circle around and come back. She stopped when they were knee-to-knee. Emily faced the ice-crusted peaks, while Dilya and Wind Runner faced the vast flat of the Great Plains. Her attempts to *not* come up with any metaphor of the vast wasteland she was feeling inside didn't make it one bit less obvious.

Her parents murdered. While she loved her adoptive parents, she'd lived with them for only a few years. She'd mostly grown up as that oddest of fixtures, the only person to live in the White House other the first couples and their kids. Because she served two separate two-term President's families, she'd broken FDR's record for the longest occupancy in the nation's first home by three months—a fact she'd kept to herself after she figured it out.

She'd always been *other*. If not for her friends from the high school Chef's Club—which had far more to do with studying geopolitics than cooking—she probably wouldn't have any friends at all.

And she'd just lost Jimmy Martin, which left a hole in her

chest bigger than anything except her parents' deaths. She'd been twelve when they were murdered, which lay half a lifetime in the past. This pain was fresh, raw, and still bleeding. She and Jimmy hadn't parted all that badly, but they'd done it very definitively. So definitively that Dilya wondered if she'd lose the friendship of the other Chef's Club members while she was at it.

If Zackie missed Merle, she wasn't showing it. Of course Zackie had always enjoyed new adventures. Also, she was ten years old to Merle's one and he appeared to relish annoying the crap out of her elder statesman years. Even now she was sitting in her saddle bag trading polite nose sniffs with Emily's Chesapeake before the horse turned her attention to the dry grasses sticking up through the snow. Sedate. Much more Zackie's style.

But Dilya was missing Jimmy more than she'd thought possible. She didn't think there was any going back. Jimmy was happy with his trains. Driving and servicing the equipment for the Cog Railway that carried a thousand tourists up Mount Washington each day satisfied him. He fit in so well that they'd offered him a precious over-winter contract. One night, he'd confessed his big dream in a bare whisper—that someday he might be the Cog Railway's train boss.

Sure, a good step up for the kid of a single-mom DC cop. But where did that leave her?

Dilya had walked through the heart of wars and listened to whispers in the halls of power. Gods, she sounded like a purple-prose journalist in her own head. But knowing those experiences, she couldn't sit still while the world careened down so many fractured paths.

"I left the mountain. I was less useful there than a turnip at a state banquet. And that was before the snow and ice closed the top of the mountain."

"And you left Jimmy," Emily's voice was filled with kindness. "It's okay to grieve."

"I don't...know how to."

Emily reached out and brushed a gloved hand over Dilya's hair until it landed on her shoulder. "You'll know how when the time comes."

Dilya shook her head, and Emily dropped her hand back to her pommel with a sigh. She hadn't meant to push her away—missed Emily's comforting touch the moment it was gone. Dilya had been too busy starving and running for her life to ever properly grieve her parents. Kee and Archie had shifted out of her life as they'd continued to serve, and Dilya had moved to the White House. Their mutual emotions didn't fade, only their relevancy in each other's lives. All without her noticing it happen. "I seem to always be too busy looking forward to remember to look back."

"At least that hasn't changed."

"I...don't know what to do with that comment either." The way other people saw her was always surprising and had so little to do with how she saw herself. Yet most of their statements were true once she considered them.

She'd met too many real geniuses during her dozen years at the White House to think of herself as more than the low side of smart—yet she still jumped ahead of most people's thoughts so effortlessly. *Beautiful* was just...weird. *Driven!* Jimmy had thrown that at her as if it was a bad thing. She'd seen pieces of the worst the world could hand out and knew she must fight to create something better.

Emily never judged her. Surprised her sometimes but never made her feel bad for who she was.

Neither did Miss Watson.

"I went looking for Miss Watson after I came off the mountain."

"She didn't end up here. She retired to a cottage in Choteau."

Dilya wished she could see the small town from here, but thirty kilometers was too far even on a clear day like this. Other than the church and the big grain silos, it was a one- to two-story town, which left it below the horizon. "She's not there. I went over every inch of her place. Again, no messages."

Just last year she'd disappeared from her office in the White House basement as a killer was hunting her. Dilya had immediately left her life as a nanny and dog-sitter in the White House and set out on the quest to save Miss Watson. The quest had almost cost her own life, but it also brought her back together with the Chef's Club. And Jimmy—her gut clenched at the freshening of the memory.

"What trouble is she in this time?" Emily didn't sigh or groan. The tactician was ingrained so deeply in her bones that she went straight to the next step without question. *That* was something that Dilya wished she could do, but she had a strategic bent of mind—always worrying about the implications of the bigger picture. She automatically saw a hundred possibilities all snarled up in a jumble of a thousand possible whys. Emily wanted to know what to do next—and had become expert in doing it.

Swallowing hard, it still took Dilya a moment to continue. "There were signs of a hard struggle, including at least one corpse. Not her, based on the blood splatter patterns."

Emily paled. It was one of the first times Dilya had witnessed such a thing from her. Nothing bothered Emily Beale. Dilya had witnessed her return from missions with a helicopter so riddled it should never have flown. With crew in the same condition, ones who'd only survived by the miracles of modern surgery. A few who hadn't. Emily was always the practical stalwart.

It took a bit of thinking to figure out why this time was

different. Emily was picturing a home invasion and murder happening in nearby Choteau. Dilya had never had the structure to separate individual acts of violence from war violence.

Her youth in Uzbekistan had been under a police state run by the world's *worst* dictator. She'd been six when five hundred protestors were herded into a dead-end street and the police snipers killed four hundred of them under presidential orders. That didn't rate as his worst atrocity either. Her family's eventual escape into the mountains of Afghanistan had seemed safe by comparison—until it wasn't. America was her first experience that types of violence became separable.

She tried to think if there was anyone else she should have taken this problem to, but she couldn't. So, she'd forge ahead as if this would impossibly end up okay.

"Firing from her bed, she left brain splatter of one attacker on a wall and a spray pattern and bullet embedded in the other wall commensurate with a through-and-through arm shot. No other marks to indicate that she herself was injured. She was taken. I came here to try to find out by who and to where."

Emily took three slow breaths, releasing gentle clouds into the frigid Montana air, before speaking. "To use our Tac Room."

Dilya shrugged. "It was nearby and it's the most highly connected asset I can access." The little room in the Henderson's Ranch horse barn boasted many uses, including direct-class access to most of the world's databases. "I got into the room, but I couldn't get past the system security. You locked it down too hard. I guess that's when it sent you an alert."

This time Emily did sigh. "Did you even think of asking for help? Lauren? Claudia? Michael even?"

Dilya could only shake her head. She could hear Miss Watson's voice to not make her mistake of being too much alone. In a crisis, who could she trust other than Emily? She'd chosen to shut out even Michael Gibson without questioning why.

"I didn't need them to—"

"Goddamn it, Dilya!"

She gasped. Emily never swore.

"Don't be so stupid! It doesn't suit you. No matter how skilled you think you are, you alone are far less effective than if you use a team. I gave up—" She waved a hand back toward the ranch.

Emily on the verge of tears? Dilya was even less prepared for that than her swearing.

"—so much. My daughters are growing up without me so that I can improve the *teamwork* of the Night Stalkers. So that our Spec Ops warriors can travel to the worst situations with some hope of coming back. That takes a team. Not a couple of pilots and a helo. It takes coordinated efforts of hundreds of people. You've got to think bigger than yourself. If you want to be a one-woman army, go ahead, but do me a favor. Dig your own goddamn grave before you go! And keep it far away from my family."

She wheeled her horse away and turned for the ranch.

Dilya tried to follow, she honestly did. Even Wind Runner looked at her to see why they were still standing lost on the frozen foothills.

"That's why I was asking you for help." It came out as a whisper. Until this moment, she hadn't thought about why she'd called Emily. Emily Beale had always been the best. And she built teams without even thinking. It was a skill that she had and Dilya definitely didn't. Without Emily, she didn't even know where to start.

13

Mark gathered her in his arms, again, when Emily tumbled off her horse.

Doug took Chesapeake by the reins and led her away as Mark carried her inside.

"Don't let the girls see me like this."

He didn't hesitate as he carried her upstairs, undressed her, and tucked her into bed wearing her favorite nightgown—the thick flannel one covered with red cardinals and chickadees perched on pine boughs. When he went to leave, she kept a hold of his hand.

Mark kissed her, then settled one hip on the bed. "That bad?"

She nodded. "I yelled at Dilya. Swore at her."

"Hey, you don't even do that for me." Her beautiful man managed to sound jealous, which almost made her smile—almost. Too bad she felt so awful.

"I left her on the high plain. Make sure she doesn't leave. She needs help."

"Any chance of me finding out what's happening this time?"

Emily was exhausted enough to tell him despite him not

being cleared for it. She could see by his eyes that he knew most of it, except the hard specifics and the most recent events. Their tiny team had been assembled to protect the institution of the government itself—identifying and blocking direct attacks against the highest levels of the executive branch. Their primary tasking was providing imminent-threat analyses to the Secret Service protection details embedded in and near the White House, without ever identifying themselves.

Mark nodded when she was done. "Hadn't connected a couple of those to you, but I should have. I thought Dilya was at the center of what you people do in that room."

"She's a part of it. Yet she isn't. Miss Watson was until last year. But she isn't. I don't know anymore. I'd long since handed off my part before I got the bump to command the Night Stalkers. The other three handle it." Again, no need to explain which three. "Dilya said Miss Watson was *taken*. She's probably one of the greatest security assets the country has. Her knowledge about everything from the CIA to the White House to—" the words threatened to choke her "—to our ranch. If she spills one wrong word… You… The girls…"

Mark silenced her with a finger on her lips, then gathered her into a hug to silence her fears.

It did.

Or else the three days without sleep caught up with her.

Whichever it was, Mark's hug was the last thing she remembered.

14

Dilya turned for the ranch. She'd wanted to wait until the middle of the night. Then she could return the horse and slip away. It was a chickenshit move, but it was far and away her first choice.

Except Zackie was shivering despite her thick coat. Wind Runner had begun pawing the ground with his impatience. When the sun sank below the peaks of the Sawtooth Mountains far earlier than official sunset time, the three of them were cast into bitter shadows. Unsure if she could find her way back in the dark, she followed the three sets of tracks in the snow. Two outbound, one inbound.

Riding alone.

Emily was right. None of her instincts led her to expect help from a team of anyone other than herself and her dog. Reaching out to Emily hadn't been enough. Or was it too much?

She didn't know, but she'd found a way to make one of the worst weeks of her life even more horrible. She'd lost Jimmy, driven half across the country to discover that Miss Watson had been taken by force. And now, perhaps worst of all, she'd unleashed Emily's fury.

Neither Kee nor Archie had ever unloaded on her; though she'd probably deserved it any number of times—not the least when she'd stowed away on their helicopter during a long-ago Spec Ops mission. They'd thought her a naïve little girl at the time. Instead? She'd been terrified of losing them and even more afraid that they wouldn't follow through and kill the men who had murdered her parents. She'd stowed away to make sure they kept their word, which they had. That they had done it to stop a war was a detail she hadn't understood until years later.

The heads of the former President and First Lady's protection details—practically her third set of parents—would do no more than look at her sadly when the occasional fit of being a teen in the White House had swept through her.

Emily's ire probably wouldn't hurt so much if it hadn't been so pointed...and accurate. She needed to go somewhere and think about this. But doing it while freezing to death at the foot of the Sawtooths was too reminiscent of when she'd nearly frozen *and* starved to death in the Hindu Kush—only to be rescued by Emily's team. Well, Emily certainly wouldn't be rescuing her this time.

Dilya crested the ridge overlooking the ranch's main compound. She was halfway down the hill before she spotted the three figures. They stood in the failing light halfway between the big lodge and the horse barn—all three facing in her direction when she hove into view. The big man who hadn't bothered to zip up his parka. The smaller man, his body so quiet that it would be easy to miss his presence at all. And the woman at his side. Emily's husband Mark, Michael, the greatest Delta Force warrior in The Unit's history, and Claudia, the Night Stalker pilot whom he'd married.

Oh God. She was in so much trouble.

15

Derek stayed stuck in his chair at the end of the briefing for tonight's mission and wondered what prairie dog hole he'd just stumbled into. Delta prided itself on being different. And while he'd flown on literally hundreds of missions with the Night Stalkers, they'd always just been an asset to an existing mission objective. Slot helicopter A into hazardous-as-hell-landing-zone B, deliver Rangers C and Delta D, to kick serious terrorist ass T. It wasn't that complex a formula—until now.

Here in Fort Campbell, it was *all* about the helos. How to reshape the plan to leverage their strengths in new ways while protecting those precious aerial assets. Until now, he'd merely laid out a place and a time, leaving the rest up to them.

Not last night. The challenges they'd faced to hit those time marks despite picking up slower helos in their aerial convoy, then being betrayed by Air Force's autonomous drone—he still felt sick that he'd unwittingly been a part of that. Major Trisha O'Malley had been the one to tell him to offer that connection to Abby last night and probably, no, *definitely* gloated about it afterward. But he'd been the one to actually deliver that betrayal aboard Abby's bird. Only her being way smarter than the average soldier had kept their lone flight clean.

He couldn't call it a date, though by the time they'd finished dinner and headed for last night's long-delayed debrief, he wished he could.

What makes a D-boy so arrogant? had been her first question as they sat down over Hot Brown sandwiches. It was an artery clogging experience of the first order: layers of turkey and broiled tomatoes buried in cheese sauce and topped with bacon, all served on thick-slice buttered-and-grilled bread called Texas toast. He'd almost ordered it again for breakfast, instead opting for the marginally healthier biscuits and gravy with a side mushroom omelet.

Name another outfit as good as we are.

She didn't even try. No need, as D-boys were the best counter-terrorism squad out there. Everyone, except the British themselves, agreed that they'd even bypassed the SAS they were modeled after. *That wasn't the question.*

So, how would you answer that question about the Night Stalkers? he'd countered.

Arrogance isn't one of my failings. And it wasn't. Abby hadn't bragged a single word about the skills she'd shown during the night. She simply did it and done.

He'd had to chew on that one awhile. *Male bonding?* was the best he could come up with.

I'd have said testosterone poisoning. Same thing I suppose. Damn but she was funny, especially when she was being half serious.

Derek had never been the sort of guy to think things through. It was a God-given truth that no plan survives the first contact with the enemy—thank you General Helmuth von Moltke the Elder for that truism. Delta's solution? Don't think too far ahead. Go in with a goal and years of training in flexibility—act in the moment to compensate as each situation went dynamic in a new and unforeseeably ugly manner. Delta thinking was very present tense.

He'd spent much of the dinner kicking himself for hitting on Captain Abby Rose with the bar-babe line. He didn't usually aim any higher than that. At least in that world, everyone knew what was what—high recreation, zero commitment.

She might be what his redneck father would have termed a *God-forsaken Yankee*, but he found her kind of charming. Kinda? He'd spent the entire meal focused on getting her to like him... and still couldn't tell if he'd succeeded. She'd tolerated him, but dinner had shifted rapidly from the personal to the professional. She was from Maine. There'd been something about a relation with nothing but lobsters on the brain. He couldn't tell if that was a saying, a secret Downeast code, or a harsh reality.

Then she mentioned that she flew the same hardware that two generations of relatives before her had. After that, the conversation never veered back to her or her past. Army aviation all the way up.

Once the debrief ended, Trisha having burned everyone's butt except theirs, they'd walked through the chill of the predawn darkness until she pointed out a building. "That's you." Then she turned on her heel and headed off toward a different section of base housing.

If she'd done that after the flight, he'd have been pissed. But he had learned a few things about her over dinner. If he was right...

"Hey—" He almost called out *Hook Girl*. *Hook* was a common nickname for a Chinook helo; partly the shortening of the name and partly the immense loads it could lift with its cargo hook. For once, he heard how bad that would sound *before* he said it aloud. "Goodnight, Wokka Girl!" He'd done plenty of cross-training with the SAS; the Brits loved the *wokka* sound of their CH-47s.

Abby froze in her tracks, covered her face with her hands and emitted a small groan of purest frustration before turning to face him. "Oh God. I'm so sorry." She was almost in tears.

He'd been right; no social skills at all. Over dinner, everything would be running aces as they discussed a technique or mission, then, within a heartbeat, Captain Abigail Rose went away and Abby would stumble onto the scene and become thoroughly awkward, even suffering serious foot-in-mouth disease—repeatedly.

Derek stepped up until they were as close as the moment she'd turned aside. He wondered what she'd do if he pushed forward into her personal space: scamper or try to scupper his ass. While it would be tempting to find out, neither would suit him much. Instead, he waited with his hands jammed in his jacket pockets. It kept him from reaching for her.

When she still didn't speak, he prompted her with, "Sorry for what?"

She flapped a hand helplessly about her indicating nothing that he could identify. "For not even saying goodnight? For being a hopeless conversationalist? For being an utter train wreck of a woman? Take your pick."

"Apology accepted."

She just gawked at him.

He put on his best Okie accent. "Though to be truth tellin', next time I'll be pissed as a hog without a waller if'n you don' say g'nite like a proper lady."

"That's it? What about the...other stuff?"

"Well, from my view, you're apologizing for the wrong things, so I don't see any particular reason for me wasting time accepting such nonsense."

"Nonsense?"

"I enjoyed talking to you more than I've done any woman in a long time." He gazed up at the last of the stars and thought about it before looking to her again. "Any *person* in a long time. You've got a very interesting and sharp mind, Wokka Girl."

"Well, I guess that's a sight better than *Hook* Girl."

"I could get to seriously like that you don't miss a thing. You're interesting as all hell, WG."

"Except for being a train wreck of a woman." She sighed and looked down at her boots.

"You seriously need to be a-gettin' you'self a mere."

"A *mere*?"

"A mirror, Abby."

"A mirror?"

So, the amazing Captain Abigail Rose, who could make flying a twenty-ton helo look as easy as a kid flying a paper airplane, didn't see the amazing woman he'd just spent a three-hour dinner with. Three hours in a DFAC. Army dining facilities weren't exactly mood-making sorta places, but neither of them had cared. At least he sure as shit hadn't.

"Abby…" How was he supposed to explain how wrong she was? The woman shone so bright he was afraid to touch her.

"What?" She looked up at him. She did like her questions.

Well, Delta had taught him how to walk through fear—by asking *why*. Why was he afraid to touch her? That was easy once he thought about it. The chance that she'd choose scamper over scuttling his ass if he got any closer. He'd bet one-to-three odds on those options. As he'd taken plenty of hard hits over the years, he decided it was his kind of a good bet.

He took a step in, rested a hand on her shoulder, and kissed her.

He kept it light, and she let him draw it out. She wasn't wholly on board but the vote on his bet was still out. When she shifted back, not stepping away, just a shift, he let her.

"Looking to get laid?"

"Not tonight." Definitely not his usual response, but it was a guaranteed way to lose his bet.

"And the part about the mirror I seem to be looking at wrong?"

"That's the reason I kissed the lady without asking permission first."

"Do you usually ask permission?"

He had to think about that one too. "Must say no." She shifted farther back. "Because usually the answer is pretty damn obvious."

"But I'm not?"

He laughed. "You got armor thicker than your Hook's." He made a point of looking around at the deep-blue sky. "The only thing obvious about you is that you are seriously wrongheaded about yourself." He went Okie again. "I gon' out and buy this here fine lady a mere right soon."

He'd been right about her eyes; that curly walnut-brown hair and strong eyebrows that emphasized their light honey-amber color. All through dinner he hadn't been able to look away any more than he could now. She stared at him until he wondered if maybe he needed a *mere* to check himself in.

"Goodnight, Captain Kylie." Then she kissed him as lightly as he'd kissed her and turned on her heel. This time she didn't look back.

16

Abby had been exhausted after the long training flight and her constant conversational screwups over dinner. Which should have meant only one thing, she wasn't going to sleep a wink. Past history taught her that she'd replay every step of the former and every misstep of the latter throughout the day when she was supposed to be sleeping.

What in her past had ever taught her to deal with an attractive man? Mum had died when she was a toddler and Gran'mum soon after. The two funerals were her first two identifiable memories. She'd been raised in a house of men: brothers, cousins, even neighbors. She was the only female of her generation for a fair way round the family tree. Which taught her all the rough-and-tumble lessons as a child and prepared for nothing that happened when she hit her teens.

Deal with them in banter, barter, or a brawl? No problem. Ones she was attracted to... Yeah, still no ideas.

How many times had she proven that with Captain Kylie last night? Out of his fearsome D-boy mode, he was funny, polite, and interesting. His brown hair tended to curl, which made him look more disheveled than scary, even though he kept it short. *It goes nuts if I let it grow another inch. I swear, it's trying to stage a rebellion. That, or Mama and Papa were lying and I'm part sheep.* He laughed easily...and he listened. Yet she kept tumbling out of the conversation with all the grace of a busted helo.

And after that kiss and promise to buy her a *mere*, she should have had ten times the trouble sleeping. Instead? She'd crashed into her bed for the best eight hours she'd had in a long while.

For her late-afternoon breakfast, she'd hit the mini fridge for fruit, yogurt, and granola, with a splash of honey. She stuck with hot cocoa because coffee shifted her up, then down, and she didn't like the variability when flying.

Not that she was avoiding Captain Derek Kylie, who would have eaten in the DFAC. And she hadn't sat between Ethan and Sam in the front row of this morning's debriefing or this evening's briefing to shut Derek out; it's where she always sat.

Trisha had other ideas.

"Due to last night's success by your team," as if she and Derek were linked by their survival, "you're taking the lead on tonight's training op."

And it was a doozy.

17

"Your mission, Derek Kylie, is to run the lead of a roll-up, but do it Night Stalkers' style," Trisha announced.

It was one of the techniques developed by Delta during the Afghanistan War. Oh, there was the full military acronym, but not even briefing officers used it. A roll-up op started with an initial piece of intel. That was used to stage a raid—typically of Unit operators delivered by the Night Stalkers. Immediately, new information was gathered from aggressive prisoner interviews, laptops, diagrams, caches of documents under floorboards, and anything else that came to hand. Sent back to operational HQ, a new target was identified, and an insta-warrant was issued by US-friendly twenty-four-hour-a-day courts that they'd built in every relevant jurisdiction.

With a fresh warrant, the raiding team would transit directly to the next site—gathering up any more terrorists and intel that came to hand there—then punch on to the next site after that. It was a race against word-of-mouth networks that would scatter the possible downstream targets. They'd built that method to three or four raids in a single night, vastly increasing their effectiveness. They often cut off whole branches of the tree rather than a single Taliban or ISIL cell.

For the teams, it was a brutal mission that stretched abilities and stamina to the limits. On bad nights the word-of-mouth network outstripped even their best efforts. Then they might drop into a heavily armed death trap. The roll-up's toll on manpower and equipment could be brutal, but the payoffs often ranked as exceptional.

Tonight, they'd be staging the same thing out in the Fort Campbell training range, but each was required to use a different helo technique. In typical usage, the quick Little Birds would deliver four operators per bird. Then the Black Hawks would come in to deliver the support layer, typically 75th Rangers. Depending on if there was room or not, if the battle zone wasn't some too-tightly-packed urban environment, the big Chinooks would come in to clear up the mess. Chinooks—with a rotor sweep of sixty by a hundred feet—didn't thrive in the typical Afghan or Third World street designed for a couple donkey carts.

But the big cities had the space.

The next war was far more likely to be in an urban center like Kyiv or Taipei, perhaps even Moscow, Beijing, or Warsaw. Oddly, wider streets opened up more opportunities for the Night Stalkers' MH-47G Chinook helos and their serious carrying capacity. In a pinch a Black Hawk could carry eleven troops and their gear; a Chinook could handle fifty with room left over.

Trisha had left the briefing room, leaving a full portfolio of their first target on the briefing room table for the team to plan with. Derek let out a harsh laugh.

"What?"

He suddenly had the attention of the five top helo pilots from last night's exercise, though the only one he cared about was Abby. "Last night, Lt. Colonel O'Malley promised we'd have time for planning after the briefing. Which is true—and almost completely meaningless."

The others squinted at him...except Abby, who laughed along. Oddly, he hadn't heard that laugh once over dinner. The wry tone, the skewed observation, and that crooked smile that always started on the left side, but no outright laughter. This time he'd finally tickled her funny bone but good, earning him what he could only term as a guffaw. He'd never appreciated what that meant until she let one loose. It was as unique as she was.

Bottom line, they could plan all they wanted for the first target, but Trisha had kept all the cards after that in her hands alone. Each of the night's successive targets would only be revealed in turn by what they found at the preceding site.

"Is she always that sneaky?"

"Yes!" Even the pilots who hadn't realized that the joke was on them agreed.

Delta trained for flexibility; Trisha's exercise plan didn't allow for anything else. He could get to like her.

Then a big guy walked into the room. Big guy with a silver oak leaf to match Trisha's. Derek saluted. "Bill? Where the hell did you come from?"

"Chicago." Typical Bill Bruce one-word answer. As far as Derek knew, Bill avoided the city of his youth like a plague. They'd gone through Unit Selection and training together, then Bill had dropped off the edge of the Earth. The few times his name came up, half the people thought he'd tapped out, but then there'd be word of a mission he'd been seen on. A *helicopter* mission.

"What? Are you like on a permanent embed with the Night Stalkers?"

He nodded, then tipped his head toward the table without looking at it. "Put that shit away. I'm your referee."

Derek looked down at the light table with the training

range map and *certified-actionable intel* projected there. He tapped the dimmer control to blank it.

"If you're referee, then we're screwed." Bill Bruce hadn't come in with mere Ranger or Green Beret skills like most of The Unit candidates. He'd come in from the SEAL teams with years of deep-field combat experience. Bill was a decade older, and it had taken everything Derek could give to keep up with him—while he made it look easy.

Bill just waited.

"Wait. If you're referee for tonight..." He glanced at Abby. "Damn her!"

Bill's smile matched the season, wintry.

Abby nodded. "As you said last night, *typical*. Typical Trisha O'Malley, that is."

What had been sold to them as a training exercise, which would include trainers as observers to give advanced notes during the debrief—wasn't. A referee meant full-on war games with—he checked his watch—eighteen minutes notice. She'd planned that too. "Who's the OPFOR?"

Bill's stoney face gave the answer; Derek didn't know why he'd bothered asking. The Opposing Forces would be as lethal as possible to make it realistic. Probably the next five Chinook and Delta teams from last night's exercise. And Bill, as referee, would sit as the impartial judge. He'd judge who was a casualty or not. Or had broken the rules of engagement. Or, in the unlikely event of actual success, if they'd achieved their mission goals within an unknowable time constraint.

And having Lt. Colonel Bill Bruce in that role meant it was going to be hard-ass by even Delta standards. Delta standards? Derek hadn't heard of a permanently embedded Delta liaison to the Night Stalkers since the legendary Colonel Michael Gibson. Now there was a man he'd like to meet just to see how tough the guy was. *Retired* Colonel Gibson. That meant... "Well, shit! You've been embedded with the Night Stalkers all this time?"

Bill nodded, his idea of being effusive.

Derek reached out and shook Bill's hand. "Knew you were good, but damn, bro."

Bill returned the handshake, then left with even fewer than a typical Bill Bruce number of words.

"What was that about?" Abby asked him from inches away. "Bill's been with us for ages."

"Colonel Gibson is beyond legend in The Unit. He's probably the best on-the-ground soldier there ever was. To have him tap Bill as his replacement? That's praise on a whole different level; like receiving a Congressional Medal of Honor but from a man who understands what The Unit means—from the inside."

Abby watched him for a long moment but kept her thoughts to herself before turning back to the planning table. Derek knew there was no way she saw that kind of potential in him—she couldn't. Could she?

18

Dilya rode Wind Runner past the "firing line." She couldn't think of them any other way. She'd pissed off Emily and they were here to make sure that Dilya never darkened the ranch's door again. They followed her into the barn.

"I know how to put a horse away, then I'll leave and you'll never have to hear from me again."

No one reacted.

A woman with long red hair stepped out of the stable office and took Wind Runner's reins. They wouldn't let her delay enough to untack and brush a horse. Dilya slid to the ground and helped Zackie out of her saddle bag. She held the dog tight to her chest, only to realize they were both shivering.

"I'm so sorry, girl," she buried her face in the Sheltie's soft fur and whispered for them alone.

"When was the last time you ate?" Claudia asked. Claudia had always been kind to her. Helped her as much as anyone except Mom with language. She also taught Dilya how to shoot a bow and arrow, still her favorite sport.

"Since forever. Wait...what?" She'd expected a tongue lashing not...

Claudia hooked an arm through hers and began guiding her out of the barn toward the big house.

"No... But..." she didn't know which way was... "What's happening?"

"You need to eat. Both of you. And get warm."

"No. Emily doesn't want me here." Dilya dug in her heels and tried to turn for her car. She escaped Claudia's grasp and ran square into Michael. It was alarming to realize they were nearly the same height, but it was still like hitting a brick wall. Zackie let out a surprised yip at being crunched between them. She'd have fallen on her ass if Michael hadn't grabbed her. Typically, he didn't say a word.

Instead it was Mark who spoke up. "Wa'll..." His fake Texas accent usually meant he was amused by something. "That there's contrarywise to what ol' Emma had to say. So, who'm I 'spposed to be trusting like? A little pip of a gal like you or the woman what I love and guv me my chill'un?" It was an awful accent, but she was in no mood to tease him about it. And she didn't think it safe to point out that *little* was a relative term. She was twenty-five and had been living with someone these last months. Though even at forty-five, Mark was still broad-shouldered enough to make his six feet seem much taller.

She opened her mouth but didn't know what to say. Emily *didn't* want her to leave?

Before she could straighten out her thoughts, they'd escorted her around the back of the main lodge and into the kitchen through the family-and-staff entrance. Zackie's nose swung away from her face to sniff the air and her own stomach growled.

The big kitchen, which could feed all the hands plus forty-odd guests, was busy with one of the chef's winter masterclasses. Ten men and women were chopping, rolling out pastries, mixing fillings, and she couldn't tell what else through her shivers. They were kicking in strongly enough to make it hard to hold onto Zackie.

Past the kitchen was a big table where she'd eaten a few meals in the past. A quarter the size of the monster out in the dining room, but still big enough for a dozen folks at a time. Beyond it was a big area of battered couches and chairs facing a stone fireplace. Emily's daughters were sitting at small desks off to the side doing homework until they spotted her.

Tessa rushed over to greet her. Little Belle flew. At eleven and nine, they were still girls, safe in their familial world. She envied them that innocence and hoped that it continued far longer than hers had. They both hugged her like a long-lost sister, then they kidnapped Zackie. Tessa at least had the awareness to offer her a smile about Belle's priorities, but she wasn't much slower; the Sheltie was a big favorite from prior visits. Most dogs at Henderson's were war dogs in training or retirement, not cute and cuddly Shelties glad for a child's attentions.

Dilya tried to imagine Tessa in one more year facing the loss of her home, her country, and the murder of both her parents. Emily and Mark dead? There was no world where that could be allowed to happen.

Once they were out of immediate earshot, she turned to Mark. "I should never have come here. I've put you all in danger."

"Something we dumb cowboys—"

"And girls," Claudia interrupted him.

"—and girls know nothing about."

She could see that Emily had filled them in on what Dilya had told her. They were each among the top warriors the US Army had ever produced. These were the very people who had taught her how to assess and survive danger. Which made Dilya feel even stupider than she already did. Who better anywhere to go to for help? And yet she hadn't, which was...depressing.

Mark handed her a big mug of butternut squash soup with tortellini and roasted red peppers in it. She wrapped her fingers around it; the warmth hurt all the way to her joints and felt lovely.

They shifted her away from the chefs and over to the fire set against the chill of November in the high plains. There was plenty of covering noise from the work in the kitchen and from the girls tossing a plushie toy for Zackie to bound after with a bright scrabble of her nails on the stone floor.

Unusually, Michael spoke first. "Describe what you saw."

This wasn't the simple answer she'd given Emily about two obvious injuries. With a pause or a raise of his eyebrows, he led her deep into the description of Miss Watson's home and what she'd seen there. She even described the scent paths that Zackie had traced both into the house and back out.

When she was done, Michael nodded. "No need to go investigate. Four attackers, one dead, one injured. Your observation skills are well honed."

Coming from Michael that was high praise indeed. Of course, he'd taught her many of those skills himself. But it didn't make her feel any better about Miss Watson.

"Now," Mark spoke softly with no hint of Texas in his voice, "we need to find out where they took her and how to get her back."

19

Derek suggested using the Fort Campbell base's very nature against itself, which Abby went along with it once he explained why. And now they were aloft to prove themselves right—or so very wrong.

Most military helo pilots flew a few hundred hours per year outside of combat to keep their skills fresh; ten to fifteen hours per month. Over dinner last night, Abby had told him that, in contrast, a Night Stalker flew a thousand; twenty a week, every week. That's what had finally registered with him about how unique they were. He understood because the three hundred operators of Delta typically shot more rounds in a year than the hundred and eighty thousand Marines—a thousand rounds a day was low-typical in a training cycle whereas a Marine might shoot that in a year. And there lay the difference between performance and mastery.

With the ninety-six helos of the two Night Stalkers battalions based at Fort Campbell and three hundred more birds of the 101st Airborne *Screaming Eagles*, there were always helos in the air. A couple more following apparently random flight paths high and well to the side of the exercise area shouldn't be noted, especially not with how low they normally flew.

They took all five of their Chinook MH-47G's aloft, but only three would be involved in the first drop.

"Ready to kick," he called to Abby over the intercom. *Charlene One* had the lead.

"In twenty." She'd already flipped the cargo bay lights to red to save their night vision.

He'd debated with himself long and hard about going in personally, but they needed an AMC. And loading the Air Mission Commander role on top of the heavy tasking Abby already carried as the flight lead wasn't a good idea. He didn't doubt she could do it, but it wasn't the best use of his resources. Yet, it meant sending his team into the fray without Derek joining in.

Bill Bruce sat at the head of the cargo bay on Abby's bird. He had a tablet computer in his hands that must connect him to the observers at each location, tipped so that Derek couldn't see it. But Bill was watching him, not his computer.

"How did you do it?" It was killing him to watch the team perform final buddy checks without him.

"I didn't."

Derek squinted at him.

"I always went in. I never took the AMC role personally."

Derek spun to look at his people. Seven guys, one woman, and a DAGOR. Team Two on the second helo would jump with silent electric motorbikes. And Team Three were going to be late arrivals, fast-roping onto the target's rooftop timed to hit the site fifteen seconds behind the first two teams to maintain the element of surprise.

Too late to switch, he could only watch as Abby's count hit Five. Then everything happened at once.

Sam had already lowered the cargo bay's rear ramp, letting in the chill swirl of the Fort Campbell training range. Derek could see the lights of the base and the surrounding suburbia in the distance, but below lay the darkness of the range. At Four, Sam tossed the drogue chute out into the wind and checked that it was drawing well. At Three, he picked up the release line and at Two climbed up into the curve of the Chinook's interior framing to get out of the way. At One, he yanked on the line. That freed the main chute, which the drogue dragged out the rear cargo hatch.

At Zero, the other crew chiefs popped the chains on the DAGOR vehicle and the big chute yanked it out of the cargo bay like a grenade out of an M32 launcher. The oversized equipment parachute caught the wind generated by the helo flying along at a hundred and fifty knots and the four tons of vehicle simply disappeared. Close on its bumper, the eight-person squad ran down the length of the cargo bay and dove off into the night. By the time they were clear, the DAGOR had slowed below fifty knots and another big chute fired out and opened to slow it further—all part of the LVAD, Low Velocity Air Drop system.

Hot Rod did a twist as his final step and saluted. That photo of a Marine doing that out a C-17 cargo lifter had already become iconic, but Hot Rod kept hoping he'd find a war photographer who wanted to take the same photo with a D-boy in the frame.

Derek raised his tablet halfway, then lowered it as if it wasn't worth his time.

The last thing he saw of Hot Rod as he fell back into the darkness was his gloved middle finger raised in salute.

Then Derek spotted Bill watching him from the head of the cargo bay's empty expanse. Derek's people were out there. Within minutes they'd be in the fight. Even a simulated one, he was supposed to be embedded in the team, not watching from on high. What was he doing up here?

He walked the thirty feet forward as Sam closed the rear

ramp and Derek sat on the opposite side of the cargo bay facing Bill.

"Different people, different choices, Derek. That's a hard one you made. Now, focus." Leave it to Bill to not comment on whether it was a good choice or bad.

Derek yanked his own tablet out while listening in on both the flight frequency—which was Night Stalker quiet—and the two jump teams—equally chill. No need for chatter if you had a clear enough plan—there wasn't any. On the tablet, he monitored the fall of the DAGOR and the team. Unguided, the truck was going to go where the wind took it and it was up to everyone else to follow it down. For that reason, air drops were typically run at a far lower elevation than strictly personnel drops under steerable chutes. But for this op, they'd decided to drop from higher up to avoid attracting attention. The unguided parachute was heading their vehicle perilously close to the trees.

"Charlie Two," he called the second helo, "this is Home Run. Shift drop two hundred meters southwest."

Bill looked up at him in surprise.

Oh, right. "Uh, make that one hundred meters." The electric motorbikes would have far less windage than the big DAGOR. Hopefully that would balance out the fall line as his main vehicle thudded down mere meters in the clear.

Bill went back to studying his own screen.

Derek went back to cursing himself for every moment of indecision, especially revealing any at all to Lt. Colonel Bill Bruce.

20

Hot Rod was first into the DAGOR while the others cleared the big chutes. He fired the engine and began counting thumps of butts in seats. At six aboard, he goosed it.

"Asshole," *Compass* cursed after he dove into the navigator's seat—seventh butt in seat. As Hot Rod's right-hand man, his task was checking the others' safety before climbing aboard, so he was always last. Compass might be his best buddy and the best map-man anywhere, but that didn't mean Hot Rod had to make it easy for him.

"Just tell me where I'm going."

"Hell!" Compass completed their ritual. "Then slide through those trees a hundred meters on the right. If you see a deer trail, that's your path."

With the infrared headlights and the night-vision goggles, he actually spotted a deer staring at them in stark terror before bolting into the woods. When Compass made no corrections, Hot Rod dropped down a gear—because automatic trannies never behaved quite the way he needed—yanked down on the console-mounted hand brake to get a four-wheel slide to make the ninety-degree turn, and gunned it into the scrub that grew along the verge. They blasted through and, sure enough, a path opened beneath the trees, straight, then curving abruptly left to avoid a massive oak Compass had failed to mention.

The plan gave him five minutes to cover three kilometers to the vehicle drop-off site. His DAGOR wasn't about running quiet, it was about getting there around, through, or over anything. They'd do the last kilometer to the target building in the required silence by hoofing it.

Compass fed him the turns he needed just as he needed them. Once they picked up a disused logging road, he eased off the gas long enough to slap from four-wheel-low to four-wheel-high and punched it again.

They made the distance with a full minute to spare. He quietly idled sixty seconds closer at a double-time jog before shutting it down. FILO, first-in/last-out, the rest of the team was on the ground and moving before the final throb of the engine. His job this time? Sit his ass in place until they needed that ride. Often times being a top driver put him at the front of the action, but sitting here alone was the ass-end of suckitude.

The others would cover the last eight hundred meters afoot in four minutes—five if they ran into any particularly unusual booby traps. Add two minutes for recon and last-minute adjustments.

He counted three-sixty and checked his watch—within two seconds.

The Number Two team would be ready on the other side of the target building on their silent electric bikes. No need for radio calls, they'd be there and all launch at the same moment.

He started the engine.

Team Three's Chinook sounded in the distance off to the South.

Into gear.

A flash lit up the trees.

He punched the gas and the DAGOR leapt forward. He covered the last kilometer in under ninety seconds.

By the time he arrived, they'd already taken the building. His team had punched in the ground-floor windows of the two-story structure on two sides. The e-bikes' crew gave the other two sides similar treatment. And the roof team had roped down from the Chinook, set grappled hooks above the windows, then leapt out and swung back to slam into the upper story in a cloud of fragmented glass.

The last flashes of simulated battle lit the windows from within as he skidded to a stop. Snipers that had landed on the roof scanned him and he waved the pre-agreed hand sign to verify his identity in addition to the infrared reflecting tabs on his shoulders.

Ninety seconds after they called the site Secure, *Charlene One* landed square in front of him. He rolled aboard. Derek and Bill Bruce the referee sat at the front of the bay, each intent on their tablets. Once chained in, Hot Rod shut down, got out, and eased himself back to stand with the crew chief Sam at the rear ramp.

Charlie Four was called in to take away the prisoners.

"Hey, they grabbed the referees too." Sam pointed at the *prisoners* with white armbands. Their hands were zip-tied behind their backs and The Unit operators escorted them in the same pack as the OPFOR prisoners.

Hot Rod couldn't help smiling. "No such thing as *Trust but verify* in The Unit's world. You are: Unit, captive, or killed. We don't want to mess with a hostage who coulda been turned or a terrorist embedded with the hostages. We disarm and bind 'em all and sort it out later. Apologies only when necessary."

They both glanced at Lt. Colonel Bruce, but he gave no sign as to his thoughts about his observation team's fate.

Once freed of the prisoners, the rest of Derek's team hustled aboard and dumped two loaded knapsacks on the tailgate.

"Sort it," he ordered.

Hot Rod and Compass were automatically handed any maps. *Grease,* who handled a submachine gun better than anyone, and *Misty,* their top sniper, received building and force plans. *X-ray* had his laptop up and running; he got all the SIGINT, signals intelligence. Derek took anything that looked like action plans. The others sorted through the leftover chaff. They'd practiced this for untold hours with everything from carefully prepped training kits to bags of civilian household garbage. Amazing what you could learn about people from their trash.

In minutes, the team had hypothesized, verified, and mapped information about a second site—underground. Direct satellite images pulled down by X-ray didn't show squat until he ran a time lapse of the last twenty-four hours of observations. Busy spot inbound and nothing outbound all afternoon up until darkness.

Derek and the seriously cute pilot cooked up an attack plan so fast that Hot Rod would have been the one left standing in the dirt if he hadn't already been aboard.

21

The debrief was more of a celebration that a formal review.

Abby watched as Bill Bruce came up, shook Derek's hand without a word, and faded away as he so often did at briefings. Derek stared down at his hand as if he was never going to wash it again. Any of the teasing or arrogance she'd felt from him the first night was no longer relevant.

It wasn't the awe he was displaying at the moment that shifted her view of him.

Nor the kiss. Though such a gentle kiss from a hard-fighting D-boy had made it twice as surprising, and that she hadn't chased him away made it damned nice beyond that.

No, the biggest change had been, actually, two changes.

First, Derek and his team hadn't treated the exercise as any more of a training op than she and hers had. Lives were on the line, the mission was real down to everything except the Simunitions and flashbangs in place of bullets and explosives. Though they hadn't been gentle. The training buildings were going to take a lot of work to put back to their normal state—

one was missing an entire wall because, *Well, it was in our way.* Damn but Derek made her laugh.

Second, he really was that good.

He—

Trisha's hand landed on her shoulder and shook Abby back and forth until she wondered if the woman was trying to make her seasick. "That so *totally* rocked."

"Worse than a lobster boat during a nor'easter," she finally snagged Trisha's wrist and lifted her hand aside. Trisha had ordered in a cooler of beer, which meant there wouldn't be any more flights for another twenty-four hours. Unlike most pilots, who were eight hours bottle-to-throttle, the Night Stalkers were twenty-four. A beer was an incredible luxury. She checked the bottle in her hand—Grolsch. A good beer. More points to Trisha. The grill full of burgers and dogs set up outside the briefing room won her everyone's vote of thanks.

"What are you looking for?" Trisha didn't clarify.

"I, uh," Abby looked at the range map spread out on the light table. Before Bill had come in and distracted Derek, the two of them had been reviewing the night's work. Though at the moment she couldn't remember why.

Each team had pushed the other to try new techniques as they hit the successive sites. Derek had even used the DAGOR to haul aboard a ton of two-man rocks. In a key attack, she'd stood the Chinook nose-to-the-sky. With its tailgate on a quick release but the DAGOR still chained down and the full team strapped in, the ton of rock had fallen from the sky. Impacting three seconds later at a hundred kmph, it had seriously flattened an armored personnel carrier—like totaled. It had definitely distracted everyone as the attack came from the opposite side of the final camp.

"Seriously?" Trisha grabbed her shoulder again, giving her just enough of a yank to force her head up.

Derek was still standing on the opposite side of the light table and staring after Bill as he flexed his hand.

"Now you're talking." Trisha stopped shaking her. Instead, Abby heard the bright tink of a beer bottle tapped against hers, making her nearly lose it to the floor.

Derek turned to look at her.

"Wha—" but Trisha was gone.

Then Derek began to smile.

Abby decided she wasn't going to ask what he was thinking.

Besides, she suspected they were the same thoughts running through her mind.

22

"Where the hell are you, Emily?"

As if she knew. It was an alien room, which she didn't recognize in the dark shadows. It was...her bathroom. Her bathroom...at home...lit by a pale blue nightlight and a slender crescent of golden moon through the skylight. Oh, right.

To preserve Mark from the worst annoyances of her command, her instincts had learned to retreat from the bedroom to the bathroom to take late night calls when she was home. Home at Henderson's Ranch. Unsure of how she came to be here, she could only picture the quiet pleasure of riding Chesapeake through the golden afternoon sunlight. Had she ridden her horse here from Fort Campbell? No effort recalled quite why she'd felt smothered by her own personal cloud of gloom while doing so.

"Emily? Earth to Emily."

"Trisha?"

"How hard did you push the limits this time? Have you been asleep for the whole twenty-four hours since you ghosted my hard-working ass?"

She knew better than to comment on that because Trisha

would then start telling her all the far more fun things *her* fine ass could have been doing in the meantime. Emily had fallen for that trap often enough to avoid it even half awake.

"What time is it?"

"Where are you?"

"Uh," she looked at the bathroom again, "Montana."

"Bitch! Is it utterly gorgeous?"

It was a bathroom. A nice one. Done in dark woods and cool tile. Hers and Mark's. Then she remembered riding across the snow-dusted foothills and breathing great lungfuls of the sharp air, which made more sense than riding thousands of kilometers across the Great Plains. "Yes."

"That makes it five a.m. My time, that is. Four a.m. yours."

That meant she'd been out for eleven hours straight; she hadn't managed even six in months.

"Tell me you didn't just go home and quit. If you did, I'm totally fucked. No way am I ready to take over this damned zoo."

Actually Trisha was more ready than she thought, but she was right, she wasn't quite there yet. "No."

"Thank you, Jesus, Buddha, Ganesha, or whoever drew the on-duty short straw tonight—Bob? Bob Marley was a music god after all. Wouldn't that make for a cool Heaven; everyone bopping along to a cool reggae beat for all eternity?"

Sounded more like Hell to her but she couldn't have slipped a word in even if she wanted to.

"So what are you doing in Montana other than catching up on your beauty sleep? Cut that out, by the way. You're already too damn gorgeous as it is. Not fair. You make it so hard for even a seriously hot redhead like me to stand out with a knockout blonde for a boss and best friend."

Trisha always produced more words than Emily could ever keep up with. "I've got a friend in trouble."

"Serious enough to drag you away from the exercise you

designed in the first place? Damn, must be ugly even by my standards."

Emily let her silence be the answer because she couldn't think of what to say.

"Anything I can do to help?"

"No... Maybe? I don't know." What had happened in the hours since she'd passed out in Mark's arms? Was Dilya even still here or had she disappeared in the night despite setting Mark to watch for her?

"Shit, Emily. That's not like you at all; you're the queen colonel in command. Gotta be a load o' seriously bad shit to mess you up. I kept the crew hopping tonight, last night, whatever this is."

"How did they do?"

"I set them up for failure in eight different ways, and none of them worked. At least not on your dynamic duo." Her patented evil-goblin laugh said that the rest of the teams hadn't fared so well. "I gave them a flight of five last night. Rose and Kylie kept all five birds and action squads alive and on the hop. I had them do a five-site roll-up maneuver. Five and five, I liked the symmetry. Even though I set them up to fail with a barren third site, Abby and Derek put their heads together and figured out the location of the fourth. My Billy was referee and he still isn't sure how they made the jump on so little data. It was so sweet. That's your new Chinook A-team."

"That's good. Keep them there until I figure out what's going on here." If she even could. "I'll let you know what's happening within twenty-four hours."

"You better, bitch." Then Trisha actually paused for a breath. "And Emily?"

"Yes?"

"Whatever dragged you away from here... Just be damned careful. Okay?"

"Yes, Trisha." But she'd already hung up as if embarrassed by showing her feelings.

It was only as she slid back into bed, hoping to curl up against Mark and pretend that she wasn't in charge of anything greater than her girls' homework, that she realized Mark wasn't there.

Instead, Tessa and Belle had slid into his place. They hadn't done that much since toddlerhood until she'd taken command of the Night Stalkers. Now it was sort of a tradition that at least one night of the typical week-per-month she managed to get home, they'd have a girl's night. Except she'd slept through this one. Well, at least they'd seen her. The phone call hadn't woken either one. Nor did brushing the hair from their faces and tucking the covers more tightly about them.

Which meant that Mark was where?

She dressed quietly and headed downstairs. The big fireplace in the lodge's main living room was unlit. The one in the kitchen sitting area was still bright with embers, but Mark wasn't asleep in his favorite chair, nor stretched out on the couch as he often was when the girls ousted him.

Check outside. The blast of frigid night at the back door sent her stumbling away until she'd donned her boots, parka, hat, and mittens. The midnight sky was crystalline. Orion the warrior stood firmly above the western ridge with his faithful dog Canis Major close beside him. The twins of Gemini lay high in the sky, watched over by the mighty bear of Ursa Major who always reminded her of the two girls protected by Mark. But it was Leo the lion who commanded the eastern sky. He'd always felt dangerous to her.

Blown snow scurried around her ankles like worried cats as she rushed to the warm barn. The horses all slept in their stalls, even Chesapeake didn't rouse at her passing. In the middle of the barn, she climbed the stairs over the tack room, which scented the air with cold leather and fresh saddle soap. In the loft, racks of old-but-not-yet-defunct gear were arrayed to the right. To the left, she swung aside the small wood panel to reveal the Tac Room's lockout mechanism. Before she could place her thumb or bend down for the retinal scan, the door swung open.

    Emily stepped into Mark's arms and let herself hide there until her heart rate settled. The tactical small room, built on the left side of the loft above the tack room, was the nerve center of their tiny intelligence service. It boasted great masses of bandwidth and connections to a lot of data architecture that would upset their owners greatly if they knew about them. It had all been arranged by President Peter Matthews before he left office—he hadn't even told his successor, though the operations run from this room had saved the current President's life several times without his knowledge.

23

DILYA KEPT HER BODY ABSOLUTELY STILL. DESPITE THE CROWDING of the room, she knew it wouldn't work but her instincts made her try. She could blend into the background in the Roosevelt Room or the Secret Service's office in the West Wing's ground floor. But the Tac Room was built for two people sitting at chairs in front of consoles—Claudia in one and Michael in the other. Though being a two-finger typist at best, Michael didn't touch a keyboard. But with Mark and now Emily in the room, Zackie had to move under the desk for them all to fit.

When she barely shifted her weight, Emily's attention snapped to her face, though her cheek still rested on Mark's shoulder.

"You sure you don't want me gone?" Dilya didn't manage more than a whisper.

"I'm sure." Then Emily turned to Claudia as if that was all that was needed. "What do we know?"

Dilya always liked watching Emily work. She'd wanted to be like her when she was young. She still did. Except when it was necessary to blend in. Emily never did that; she commanded the attention of every room she walked into. She even overshadowed Mark, which was hard to imagine yet was true every time. It was disturbing to discover things she could do that Emily couldn't.

Also to see that Emily didn't have her act completely together. Dilya saw, in retrospect, how thinly she was stretched yesterday. Even Emily Beale had limits and that uncomfortable thought made her question her own state of mind. Racing across the country had seemed the most natural thing after the collapse of her relationship with Jimmy. And yet, who did that? Certainly none of her other high school friends. They were each as settled in their choice of place as Jimmy was in New Hampshire. She was the lone vagabond of their group.

Emily might work at all of the Night Stalker bases, and their training areas spread all over the country, but she was rooted here.

Adrift. Dilya had nowhere she belonged. She'd spent half her life in the White House and most of the rest in a variety of war zones. She—

Claudia turned from her screen. "We know that due to a short runway, Choteau airport sees very few bizjets. The ones that do come in are known, mostly Hollywood and music folks coming up to their Montanan ranch-in-the-country. I reached the FBO, Choteau's fixed base operator, during dinner last night. He lives close to the field and heard a Gulfstream G650 arrive that night. Spotted it departing in the morning after Miss Watson was taken, but he didn't see the tail number."

"The 650? How far…" Dilya didn't know her nonmilitary aircraft very well. In fact, she'd rarely flown in a civilian plane.

"Far," Claudia answered her. "Moscow, Beijing, Hong Kong. Twelve hours to max range without refueling. About the only places out of direct-flight range from here are southern India or Africa, Australia, and Antarctica. It's a proper globe trotter. I've been able to backtrack enough satellite imagery to confirm there was a jet parked at Choteau during the night, but it left before full dawn, so I can't determine much more than that. Based on their departure time, their range limit would have landed them around dinner time last night."

Dilya slid down the wall until she was squatting in the corner. She was so tired. They'd all agreed to meet after six hours sleep. She'd managed three. She'd been right yesterday—they didn't have time to sleep or eat. They were too late even before they'd lost the night. Wherever Miss Watson had been taken, she'd arrived while Dilya was riding her horse back through the evening light.

"ADS-B?" Emily asked.

"I confirmed that all G650 models are equipped with the ADS broadcast system, but I have no tracking for a plane in this area at that time. They had their safety location beacon shut off or illegally spoofed as another aircraft."

Dilya was going to be sick.

"There is one odd thing."

Emily made a *Hmmm* noise.

"I did have brief satellite coverage from a Chinese surveillance bird that they don't know we're in on. Poor resolution, but it did capture a small jet thirty kilometers northeast of Choteau at the right time. If they held that precise bearing, they passed directly over a grand total of three airports of any significant size before hitting their fuel limit. Palermo in Sicily, Paris, or RAF Station Brize Norton."

Dilya looked up so quickly that she banged her head on the wall. She'd assumed it was the Russians out to grab Miss Watson. She'd been a deeply embedded spy in the Soviet Union. Though that had been forty years ago and the USSR hadn't existed for over thirty—the former KGB were now the *oligarkhiya*. No one held a grudge that long. *Don't trust your assumptions.* How many times had Miss Watson told her that?

But Italy, France, or Britain? That made even less sense.

24

WAKING WASN'T SUPPOSED TO BE PAINFUL, THOUGH AT HER AGE IT often was.

The mental haze was one she recognized. She first experienced it during her intake testing to work at the Central Intelligence Agency. Back then she'd been a naive twenty-one-year-old Yalie, months from completing a masters in Russian literature with an undergrad degree in Greek dramatic writing. At his inauguration, President Kennedy had asked what she could do for her country.

Ah, poor JFK. So much hope cut short by an assassin's bullet.

And if he'd only created the Peace Corps sooner, how different her life might have been. But he didn't do that until March and his call of January 1961 had perfectly aligned with a CIA campus recruiting drive.

Her wandering thoughts traveled back to part of the qualification testing of new agents. Could she stand up to the psychotropics without revealing what had been fed to her as critical information? The psychotropic drugs became part of agent training that was repeated and formalized over the years.

The agency's trainers held onto them much longer than the hippie counterculture.

She recalled a civilian blood donation she'd made in the seventies in which the nurse had asked her if she'd ever taken any drugs. Annoyed enough to answer, she listed them all: hash, heroin, acid, speed, and peyote. All the different forms as well: purple hearts, dexys, French blues, and black bombers for the uppers, acid on paper, in drops, as crystals...

None were on the woman's interdiction list, so they'd taken her blood. When fuzzed out as she was now, she liked to picture which of her flashbacks some poor woman was experiencing after a surgery. Staying stoned for much of her years deep undercover in North Vietnam had been a welcome escape. Those were different days. By the time she was sleeping with a Soviet two-star general, their drug of choice was vodka. Now it was usually Murchie's Earl Grey or their No. 10 black tea.

But this fog was a new one. She could happily return to sleep if the room wasn't busy doing the spins. Squinting an eye open offered only a blur of dark shapes. Interesting. Benadryl Cocktail? No one had ever hit her with the common date-rape drink before, but there was a symptomatic match. A cautious shift of her hips... She wore clothes and they felt like hers. At eighty-five, perhaps she'd lost the allure that had so often aided her work in the past.

There'd been...gunfire. A dead person? Yes. She was relatively sure of that. Another injured? Yes, she'd shot two; too bad there'd been four.

Again the body check. No feeling of unusual tightness such as a bandage or a restraint. Just the spinning nausea and the sleepies.

Her last thought was to wonder who had found her after all these years. Who had been willing to expend the manpower and take on the political risk to attack her in Montana?

25

Derek had never given any particular thought to a woman's apartment. It was a place. Some all done up girlie, some in need of a firehose washdown. Way back in high school he'd developed a standard that kept him clear of the latter type. Though clean sheets or couch was as far as his attention usually wandered.

Stepping into Abby's apartment felt more like he was entering a shrine.

Her invitation had been wordless, no more than the slightest tip of her quarter-empty beer bottle toward the door of the briefing room. Her eyes had stayed wide when he'd nodded a careful yes.

Not that her apartment was exceptional in any particular way. Standard-issue one-bedroom-apartment base housing with a sitting bar separating a small kitchen from the living room. The doors must be closet and bedroom, which meant that the bathroom was only accessible through the bedroom. Practical rather than a home for entertaining.

It was Army spotless, nothing out of place. Not even any obvious sign of its occupant's gender. A single box's worth of books on the standard-issue shelf unit, because in the Army you learned to travel light. *The Perfect Storm.* A couple books by Linda Greenlaw. Derek checked the first book, yeah, the woman who'd been the surviving swordfisher captain of that debacle. The actress who'd played her in the movie had been hot enough that he'd watched several of her flicks: *The Abyss,* Marian in *Robin Hood,* and a couple others. Kinda like Abby: slender, unconventionally pretty, screamingly competent, and —Derek kept the smile to himself—decidedly awkward socially. The actress' acerbic wit and cutting comebacks were replaced by a quirk for a smile and Abby's joy in a bad joke.

There were several more titles with keywords like Maine and lobster, or both. The expected big section of Chinook pilot memoir and well-worn Chinook helo manuals—a pilot who studied the mechanics as well as the operation. He liked that. A couple of military romance stuff, again helos. Abigail Rose was a two-track gal: Maine-style fishing and helicopters. Nothing else.

The other shelves had prop-up-frame photos of crews around helos or family aboard lobster boats; same two tracks. Always a lotta guys with Abby stuck in the middle each time, standing out because she was a half-head shorter than all the others.

A blue velvet medals' case. He glanced for permission before flipping the lid. Derek had it halfway open before Abby's expression behind that tight nod registered.

She was standing in the exact center of the living room. Her fists jammed hard enough into her pockets to overlap the front despite the open zipper. As if he'd been—

"Shit, Abby, sorry." He closed the case's lid, but not before noticing the number of awards neatly arranged across the plush interior. Or how many of them had the C or V device for combat or valor in combat. His were up on the wall in his Fort Bragg apartment for all to see. Hers were tucked away for her eyes only and he'd just... Crap! It felt like he'd just been peeping at naked photos of her. "It's..."

She remained frozen.

He wasn't used to explaining himself around women. He also wasn't used to caring about much beyond the obvious once he got alone with a woman. "You aren't like, uh, other women I've...met. It's like, I dunno." Could he sound any more inarticulate? "Like I want to understand you way better than I do." That, at least, was true.

Still no movement or change.

"Look. I'm sorry. I'll go if you want me to." Was he about to lose the scamper bet? He'd wager that, if she gave him the shuffle tonight, it might be the end of a chance of anything between them. And he didn't like the sound of that option much.

She continued to stare at him, thinking mighty hard. Was she about to think him right out of her life? Nope. Definitely not his first choice.

That's when he noticed her oversized jacket. She'd shrugged it on just before they'd stepped out into the dark from the briefing room. A classic sheepskin-lined leather bomber jacket, old, well-worn, and originally for a much bigger person. Now in the light he saw that it bore unit patches spanning decades. One bore the image of a Bell H-13 *Angels of Mercy* used for Korean War medevac missions. A Vietnam-era patch showed a skull spitting gunfire from its red eyes—1st Aviation Detachment. He didn't know who they'd been, but the twin rotors mounted on the skull said they'd flown one of the early Chinooks. Then the 176th Assault *Box Cars* he knew were another Chinook outfit. Box Cars again, but a couple decades later on, beside a Desert Storm patch. A modern screaming eagle of the 101st Airborne and finally a Night Stalkers' Pegasus patch.

He glanced back at the photos and could see the jacket's

history as it moved from one flyer to the next, finally passing to Abby. One hell of a legacy. How did a person live up to that? *He'd always liked special?* Who the hell was he kidding? Abby was in a whole different league.

His mama was a grade-school teacher and Papa was a trimming machine operator at the Georgia-Pacific paper mill—always had been, always would be. Derek had figured the Army was his only ticket out of town. That an escape route had turned into a career was a great bonus.

But still, there she stood. And here he stood. He walked away from the bookcase, circled around the couch and coffee table until he stopped directly in front of Abby. Only then did he realize that he'd copied her stance, Army boots planted shoulder wide with fists jammed into jacket pockets. His boasted only his own history: 82nd Airborne and 75th Rangers. No one wore a Delta patch, technically there wasn't one for the highly classified unit. He did have the US Army Special Operations Command flash of the knife within an arrowhead symbol laid on a map of the globe. It identified him as one of thirty thousand, not one of the three hundred most elite.

Their shared stance and posture made him smile.

Which, much to his surprise, made her own smile quirk to life. Right. Captain Abigail Rose missed nothing and would have seen that he'd echoed her without intending.

He made a shrug, not with his shoulders, but rather with his hands in his pockets, tipping them outward just enough to ask the question of what came next.

She answered with a shrug that reached her shoulders and the smile that now reached up to her eyes.

He raised an eyebrow.

She raised both and started a silent laugh.

Without removing his hands from his pockets, he leaned forward to kiss her mid-laugh.

The backs of their hands touching through the fabric of

both their jackets, they shifted together. This time their kiss was no tentative brush of the lips, at least not for long. Derek could feel Abby shift onto her toes. Not for height, but to increase the pressure between them.

She tasted vaguely of the beer she'd never finished and the char of the burger she'd eaten. But those were just notes, small accents to emphasize whatever she was. He followed the kiss along her jaw and under her chin. She tipped her head aside as he sought her collarbone. Not down her front but to where it lay hidden under the edge of her turtleneck above the nice slope of strong shoulder.

Abby tipped her forehead against his shoulder, drawing him closer. He spread his jacket open, and she slid between his pocketed hands. Easing her own jacket open, her hands rested on his hips and their bodies brushed together. Her slender figure pressed against his in the doubled cocoon of their open jackets.

Warm leather, the salt of hard-work sweat since dried, the least hint of av-gas, which added to rather than diminished the image. Instead of grabbing her, tossing her to the couch, and testing his palms against those fine curves, he pulled her tighter into his jacket until her cheek rested on his shoulder and his on her hair.

"What the hell?" They were fully dressed, his hands had yet to touch her, but he could stand like this a long time and be happy. So not his normal op.

He could feel her laugh, though it was too soft to reach his ears. "I'm as surprised as you are, if that makes you feel any better."

Derek nipped her ear in answer, which earned him a purr of contentment. Freeing his hands, he ran them over the roughness of the unit patches representing her unlikely strength. When he slid his hand up into the loose curls of her hair, she made a small *Ugh* sound.

"Ugh?"

"I desperately need a shower."

"Is that an invitation?"

Again that weird freeze. Then she shifted enough that her cheek no longer rested on his shoulder, instead her nose brushed there as if Abby was...hiding?

"Haven't showered with a guy before?"

A small headshake.

"Do you want to?"

A long pause, then an equally small nod.

This had to be the craziest seduction he'd ever been a part of. Showers together came after getting all sweaty together, not before.

"You aren't a virgin, are you?" He did his best to make it funny. She was a beautiful US Army captain but it wasn't impossible.

She kneed him dead center on the outer-thigh charley horse point, though not hard enough to hurt—much.

"I take it that's a no. Just a shower virgin. What is wrong with guys that they haven't dragged you into one?"

"It's not them." She didn't explain.

He took a hold of the shoulders of her overlarge jacket and eased her back a step so that he could look down at her. "Then what is it?"

"I..." She looked at him squarely without glancing aside but swallowed hard before continuing with what might be a subject change. "...mostly scare them off."

"Eek," he deadpanned, which earned him a smile. "Are all the men in your past idiots?"

"I've never been skilled at keeping them around for long."

"Too smart for them or is it just because you're better at everything than they are?"

"Not scaring off a D-boy?"

He studied her eyes. Nothing coy. Nor afraid. Maybe

resigned. Based on watching his own team at play in the bars, it wasn't hard to imagine guys being put off by a woman so competent. His own track record wasn't exactly stellar on that point. He traced his fingers across the Night Stalkers' Pegasus patch over her left breast. "Much to this operator's surprise, I'm finding that the more I know about you, the *more* intrigued I am."

"Not your usual ROE?" And that hint of her crazy smile teased him.

"My normal rules of engagement would not include us doing a whole lot of talking right about now."

"Or both still having our clothes on?"

"Or that."

26

ABBY STUDIED DEREK. HE LOOKED AS SURPRISED AS SHE FELT.

Even after two nights of hard flying together, which revealed his competence and clear thinking, she hadn't been ready for his intense inspection of her apartment. She'd been with guys interested in a quick tumble and a faster goodbye. Many stuck around for days, occasionally even weeks, but seldom months. Their interest only rarely extended beyond the bedroom, which was usually fine with her. Yet Derek had started here.

And he was absolutely right, the men she'd dated didn't like being outperformed by *a mere slip of a girl*—she'd heard that a thousand times too many. In high school, the strength and agility from her summers and weekends on the family lobster boat had placed her at the top of most teams. That she could outplay any of the forty-three seniors in her class—female or male—in volleyball, soccer, and softball hadn't won her a lot of good will either. When she'd graduated at the top of UMaine Orono's ROTC program and the Honors college, the instructors and professors had expressed their appreciation. Her classmates not so much.

She'd been ready for an enjoyable passage at arms with Derek; he would be shipped back to Fort Bragg soon enough as it was. But she didn't know how to react to his interest in learning more about her. Abby had still been trying to process Trisha's comment encouraging her interest in Derek. It had seemed weird, except Trisha had married a D-boy herself, so perhaps it wasn't so strange. Except it was. Picturing the woman—whose nickname among the troops was PITA, Pain in the Ass—as a matchmaker because she wanted Abby to be happy was beyond laughable.

Except with Derek's dark eyes watching her, she wasn't much in the mood for laughing. Unlike most men, he was waiting for the next cue from her. Well, she definitely needed a shower after the night's extended operation—the five-site roll-up had taken seven hours at full intensity. Especially as she'd still been ragged from the prior night's flight. As the sole female in a house of men, the shower was her private place. It was the one place she could, whether happy or needing a good cry, be truly alone. She'd never before *let* a man join her in the shower.

On the verge of overthinking everything and changing her mind about letting Derek join her, she shrugged out of her jacket and hung it on the hook by the door.

"Army spotless," Derek didn't make it a judgment.

Her boots were next, squared-up and laces untangled in case she needed to don them quickly. Sock-footed, she headed for the bedroom. A half-glance showed Derek doing the same. A part of her wanted the mayhem of clothes tossed aside in a frenzy of coming together, but a bigger part liked not only the sense of order but the sense of being ready for action. That was only emphasized when she spotted him tucking his backup piece in one coat pocket and unstrapping his ankle knife to slip it in his boot. She'd creeped out civilians when doing that herself; to a Spec Ops Forces soldier, it was very sexy—a top warrior setting aside his cherished weapons to be with her. Like being welcomed inside the careful shield, closer to the man crouched inside it.

With his back momentarily to her, she did shed one sock at the threshold to her bedroom and another just inside as a tease. Not quite a scatter of rose petals, though she doubted neither of them had romance on their minds. Her jeans and turtleneck landed either side of the bathroom doorway. As she leaned in to start the hot water, his Delta-rough palms landed on her hips. Derek's approach had been as silent as it was welcome.

He didn't slide her panties down or drag aside the sports bra that her figure only needed when working out or flying. He simply pulled her back against his still-clothed chest into an enveloping embrace. She reached to turn off the light switch that habit had turned on.

Derek blocked her and nipped her ear again. It was silly. It tickled. And…it made her want to giggle with delight in the ridiculous way she'd heard other girls do sometimes but she'd never descended to. After turning her to face him, he didn't grab between her legs or crush down on a breast. Instead, those callus-rough hands remained lightly on her hips. The slightest shift and he had her back against the glass, heated from the other side by the pounding hot water, as he picked up the earlier kiss where he'd left it at her collarbone.

It was the last time for a long while that she wasn't running short of breath.

27

EMILY TRADED SEATS WITH MICHAEL. THE TAC ROOM REMAINED quiet as she and Claudia began doing what this team did best —tracking stray threads of information. Except Emily's skills had grown rusty with disuse. She could feel Claudia racing down the data pathways while she was still trying to refresh her login credentials. Had it been so long a gap that they'd been reset? Apparently yes. Once she was in, even the screen interface was unfamiliar. She hated software updates almost as much as she hated being back here doing this. If she could teleport Lauren back from Hawaii and into the second chair, she'd do it in a heartbeat. Not that there was room in the small office for another person—one detail she'd overlooked in the design, having three observers.

What she knew was flying helicopters. Except she didn't anymore—not at the level she had as a Night Stalker or even flying to fight wildfire as she'd done for a half decade. From her first flight at sixteen, every waking minute of the next twenty years had been about flight. Well, not every minute. Mark, Tessa, and Belle had entered her life near the end of her flying career. Soon after she'd landed her last helo, the Protection Force team had spun up here at the ranch.

They'd eventually connected with Miss Watson inside the White House, which had largely been Dilya's doing. Ever since, the Protection Force had anonymously provided threat information to the US Secret Service protection details. They'd even identified and recommended recruitment of truly exceptional individuals who now filled roles such as the head driver of the President's limousine among others. Their mandate was small, focused on supporting Executive Branch protection in ways that they didn't already cover themselves.

However, with Claudia and the vacationing Lauren, backed up by Colonel Michael Gibson, Emily had become redundant. In that limbo after being done with this group but before she'd reached the decision to retire, she'd been offered command of the Night Stalkers.

After a year, she almost had a handle on running the three thousand personnel and two hundred aircraft of the 160th. But she didn't have a whole lot of—

Someone nudged her shoulder.

Finally logged in, Emily focused on—

The next nudge was harder, enough to twist her chair. She spun to face Dilya. "*What?*"

This time Dilya pushed against her shoulder with a single finger. Finally catching up with the message, she rose to stand shoulder-to-shoulder with Mark and Michael as Dilya slid into her seat.

"I may have grown up in the pre-tech world as a Southwest Asian war orphan," Dilya didn't turn as she began poking through the data structures. "But being inside the White House bubble for a decade, I caught up a bit."

Emily tried not to think about just what systems Dilya would have the opportunity to infiltrate during her years there. If she didn't know that Dilya would never do anything to hurt her adopted parents, adopted country, and the First Families, she'd be scared stiff. Should she be anyway?

In under a minute, she was having trouble following the threads Dilya chased and lost track entirely within two. By three, Dilya was trading one-word sentences with Claudia about which ideas they were each chasing.

"Dilya. You shouldn't…"

Mark placed a finger on the bottom of her chin and pushed her jaw closed. When she glared at him, he opened the door and gestured for her to lead the way out. Old habits, left over from when he'd been her commanding officer and later the wildfire Incident Commander, made her step out of the room. Mark closed the door behind them.

He nudged her toward the stairs.

"But…"

"We need to wake the girls for breakfast and school soon." Taking her hand at the bottom of the stairs, he led her out of the barn into the November darkness. "I was thinking of giving them a sick day to see you, but I don't know how long you'll be here this time, so we'll play it by ear."

"The Lieutenant Colonel Mark Henderson I knew was never one for *playing it by ear*."

"Accept that perhaps I learned a few things watching you."

"Watching me?" Emily didn't know what anyone could learn by watching her. "What? Lessons in how to screw up your life?"

He stopped her a foot from the broad steps up to the lodge's porch by the simple expedient of picking her up by the shoulders of her coat and turning her to face him before plopping her back down onto her own two feet. "Don't try to piss me off, Emma. It doesn't suit you."

"No, but it *does* seem to suit me. I'm running so hard that I slept right through the girls crawling in bed with me. But, oh sure, I spring out of bed when duty calls." She slapped a pocket but couldn't find her phone. She could picture it on the nightstand beside the girls. She hoped no one else had called to wake them.

"So quit." When she couldn't answer, Mark nodded to himself. "Didn't think so. You've still got good work to do, honey. Hold that focus and get it done. We'll still be here."

"You make it sound so simple."

"I wish." His low chuckle made her feel better. "But we'll get through it. They..." he nodded toward the barn hidden by the darkness "...will have answers soon enough if there are any to be found. Now let's go roust the girls. I'm thinking they've already had too much beauty sleep."

28

QUESTIONS.

Varied accents. Both genders.

Most were obvious voice changers, others might be AI-generated. A few felt real but she had no way to judge.

They addressed her by a variety of names. "Miss Watson" was among them, though no one was supposed to know that name. Others were names she'd used, but most weren't—and never had been. Though she certainly knew to whom those belonged. She couldn't decide if she should feel honored that they thought she had personally handled quite so many undercover missions. It would have meant she was an even busier woman than she had been.

The drugs still wrapped around her brain. There was no such thing as a functional truth serum, but there were disinhibitors that left one open to suggestion.

But she'd thought up her own strategy for withholding vital information during interrogation way back during that wintery edge of the Cold War of 1961. Perhaps it was the advantage of a Yale education. It had worked and she'd cultivated it over the years until it was fully automatic.

She answered every question—at length. She buried the bits of truth under a Midas-sized gold mountain of prevarications, misdirections, fibs, and outright lies. Her favorite resources were Aeschylus and Aristophanes, such a way with words. Plato's rendering of Socrates were always too heavy-handed for her taste, but Homer's *Iliad* was another favorite that served her well. *Beowulf,* Confucius, Lao Tzu all worked well, though she'd never been able to sufficiently unravel the *Mahabharata* to make it a part of the game.

They worked especially well as none of those contained concepts like Russia, CIA, modern technology, or anything else from the last several thousand years.

"You were the lover of the KGB's Lieutenant General Sergei Kulakov from—"

"—the time that ships set out upon the wine dark sea." The opening image of her favorite translation of the *Iliad*. "There was a woman of exceeding beauty." Her then-persona of Emmaline Trask—or had she been Erika Iliana at the time?—might not prevail in a contest with that flighty little bitch Helen of Troy, but she'd certainly garnered Sergei's attention when it mattered.

She slid into Aramaic, which, while popular in the same era as Homeric Greek, had nothing to do with the *Iliad*. Nor the *Odyssey* if one was going to be a linguistic nitpicker. But as her interrogators were unlikely to comprehend either one, especially not with a Jamaican Patois accent, she plunged ahead.

"She be renowned, bra, crost the many states of Greece and the Middle Kingdom." Xi Shi was of the same era as both Homer and Aramaic, sixth century BCE, just forty-five thousand *stadia* to the east of Athens. Or was that fifteen thousand *ri* to the west. She tried to remember when that would be by the Chinese calendar, but the drugs were fuzzing her mind too much. But... "It came to pass in 3161 by the

Hebrew calendar that the little slut decided to spread her legs for a mere boy of a man." Paris' fling—which she narrated at length, embellished with the raciest bits of Danielle Steele, and translated into ancient Hebrew—had started the Trojan War. But the Greeks had launched a thousand ships and settled it once and for all, even salting the earth upon which the city had maintained its fields. Only Paris and a few of the women escaped, including the slut Helen, of course. She herself had happily spread her legs for her Russian general. He'd been everything a man and a lover should be, in addition to providing copious intelligence from behind the Iron Curtain.

"We were asking about—"

"—why the female troops led a rebellion. Fair Lysistrata was a great leader. She did not desire sex less than her comrades in connubial abeyance, but she detested war far more."

And as Aramaic slid once more into the foggy depths of Homeric Greek, she wept for the final madness of Cassandra of Troy—blessed with true prophetic vision yet cursed by Apollo to never be believed.

Like Cassandra, she also knew too many truths.

The questions being asked by the voices had no hint of archaic Greek syntax, but they also bore no trademarks of inverted German verbs or Russian didacticism. No gendered nouns or articles.

"Evandra." That finally snared a segment of her slewing attention. An old Greek name. Meaning good woman. Which told her into whose hands she'd fallen.

Of all the people who could have grabbed her, of ones willing to permanently expend manpower to do so, why had it been these people?

29

"We can confirm the English have her," Claudia started the report as they convened once more in the Tac Room. She and Mark had a lovely couple hours with the girls before the school bus arrived and even had time for a very pleasant shower together before the guilt drove her back to the crisis.

"Seriously?" Emily didn't doubt their work. But that didn't shift the fact from the realm of the inexplicable.

"Seriously," Dilya confirmed. "We were able to spot the aircraft by satellite over Greenland shortly prior to sunset. That's exactly when we'd expect it based on their departure time and direction from here. At 2300 hours, a plane fitting the description landed at RAF Brize Norton. But as it was the middle of the night there, we couldn't fully confirm it. We only managed a glimpse under the runway lights."

"We also," Claudia continued, "waited to confirm that no other plane of that description landed at any successive airport along that flightpath. We can confirm at least Miss Watson's arrival there with a reasonably high degree of confidence."

"Well, that's weird as shit," Mark grumbled.

"Any particular reason?"

He looked at her with that evil smile he used at a particularly good joke. If he'd had his mirrored shades with him, he'd have pulled them down despite the darkened room. Noticing her glance at the top of his head, he fished into the inner pocket of his jacket and slid them on. Now she and the lit monitors were reflected back to her.

"What? Did you take a lot of the base commander's money at poker?"

"Nah. Fay was never big on poker. Though her Number Two has a real weak spot for it. Might have earned myself a couple fistfuls of pounds sterling the times I've passed through there."

"We have to go get her!" Dilya jumped to her feet, waking Zackie, who gave a surprised bark from under the desk.

Emily put a hand on her shoulder and pressed her back into the chair. "It's not that simple." She glanced at Michael.

He spoke without hesitation. "Logistics first, plans later." Oh God, that meant they were going to do this Delta Force style. Emily's gut hurt. It didn't mean he was wrong, but now the planner instilled in her by her present command warred with the reaction-based tactician of her piloting career.

Claudia had flown with and then been married to Michael long enough to require no explanation. She tapped in a set of orders and sent them to the Secretary of Defense. He'd learned to simply approve whatever the Protection Force sent him. "That's a C-5M Super Galaxy transport on the move from Westover Air Reserve Base in Massachusetts. They're the closest asset at the moment and the reservists will be so happy for a chance to fly that they won't ask a lot of questions."

Emily called Trisha and received a *mumph* in a sleep-slurred tone. Late morning here in Montana meant noon in Fort Campbell, which was Trisha's midnight as she'd been overseeing night operations. Turnabout was fair play.

"I need the top three Chinooks stripped down in prep for C-

5M transport. It's already en route." It was a several-hour task for a top crew to remove the rotor blades and heads to fit aboard even the largest of the military transports. C-5M Super Galaxies were huge aircraft, but Chinooks were not small either. Three at once was a serious ask.

"Fuck!" Trisha dropped the phone twice in her sudden scramble before answering more lucidly. "With or without the Delta teams?"

Emily glanced at Michael and received a nod. "With."

"On it." And Trisha was gone. She didn't even slow down long enough to dump any imprecations upon Emily's head. When action was called for, there were few better than Trisha O'Malley.

"Okay, now what's the plan? The last I checked, the UK was still a friendly power."

"*That*, we'll have to figure out on the way." Mark pulled out his phone. "Just texting the kids to hang with Julie for the next couple days. They'll all love it. Her Jared is seven and has a super crush on Belle. Belle eats it up and Tessa gets to roll her eyes at both of them, then hang with Julie. Sweetest thing you ever saw."

Great, another piece of her family's life she was missing. Then it registered. Did she have such a sleep deficit that a full night wasn't enough? It seemed so. "Wait, you're coming with us. No, you're staying at the ranch."

"Someone has to make sure Dilya stays out of trouble."

"Hey!"

They both ignored her.

"Seriously, Emma. Unknowns grab Miss Watson, there's got to be heavy shit going down. I can't run any interference if I'm off riding my horse across the wide prairie."

She glanced at the others.

Michael nodded that he was aboard as well.

Claudia hid her smile as she turned back to the screens.

"Y'all—" she gave it Mark's full-on bad Texas. She was from a tiny desert town in Arizona. "—best git you'selfs a-movin'. That Galaxy aerioplane is prolly already off'n that there Yankee runway."

Emily gave her a kiss on top of the head and followed Mark out the door with Dilya close on her heels. When Michael tried to immediately follow, Emily pointed at Claudia's back.

Michael did a double take, circled back, and kissed Claudia very soundly before joining them. Emily knew that once mentally in mission mode, the rest of the world ceased to exist for him. She would have laughed in his face if he wasn't so sweet about it when reminded.

30

Abby woke to two simultaneous sounds: a very loud ringing phone, and a very male curse. She went for the more predictable one first.

"Uh-huh."

"Captain Abigail Rose?"

"Uh-huh." Then the voice clicked into her brain. "PITA O'Malley." Oh, shit. Not the thing to call your commanding officer, even if everyone did behind her back. She wasn't strict, Abby might even like her. But that didn't begin to mitigate what a pain in the ass the lieutenant colonel could be when she set her mind to it.

Trisha laughed. "Proud to be. And don't you forget it!"

"Not a chance, ma'am." Abby rubbed at her eyes.

"Sorry for the midday call-up."

Abby had failed to lower the blackout curtains last night and the noontime sun lit her bedroom with a painful brightness. "How long do I have?"

"You're about an hour late."

"How can I be an hour late when you only just called me?"

"There's a FRED on the way to load your helo as fast as you

can break it down. Need two more hooks of your choice." A FRED. A C-5M Super Galaxy—aka a Fucking Ridiculous Economic Disaster. Or Environmental Disaster, take your pick. The C-5Ms, the largest transports in the US military, were finally hitting their stride. However, the name had stuck as the original C-5As built in the 1960s had created a budgetary overrun unequaled for decades to come, had miserable reliability, and chewed fuel like it was free. A dozen generations later, it was a halfway decent aircraft.

"Roust *Charlie Two* and *Four*. They both kicked ass last night."

"Done. So…" Trisha managed to draw out the two-letter word enough to make it sound positively salacious, "…do you happen to know the whereabouts of Captain Derek Kylie?"

Abby blinked. She did!

Sitting up, she spotted the empty pillow beside her. The empty, undented pillow with the sheet and blanket neatly arranged as if that side of the bed had been unused. That wasn't right. She recalled it being very well used.

Then she remembered the male curse and spotted Derek standing still in the bedroom doorway as if trapped there—a fully clothed Derek. With his back to her, but looking at her over his shoulder. His expression was very careful.

"E-yup, I've got eyes on him," her tone even sharper than she intended.

"Uh-oh," Trisha sounded sympathetic. "Well, he and his team are on call-up too. Do you want to tell him or shall I call him separately?"

"I've got this." She hung up. Setting her phone calmly on the nightstand to avoid heaving it in his face. She resisted picking up the firearm she'd left beside it. Instead, Abby folded her arms below her bare breasts. No way would she be the embarrassed one here. "Well?"

"Uh, this looks kinda bad."

"At least he got something right."

"I—"

She decided she didn't want to hear it. Pushing out of bed, she snapped the covers into place. She walked past him to the bathroom. "You'd better hurry. We have an immediate call-up. You and your teams—three birds' worth. Full loadout, no details."

He tried to speak again.

She rerouted to her bedroom door. He started to turn but, half through his turn, she straight-armed his shoulder hard enough to send him tumbling sideways into the back of the couch. "You'd better be gone by the time I'm showered. FYI, that'll be under two minutes." She closed the bedroom door and headed for the bathroom.

Another one-night stand. She sighed. Even with her lousy metrics, that was still going to drop her success-with-men average.

31

Trisha was right, they were an hour behind before they even started; even with the improvements since the Chinook F variant, it still took a great deal of work to prep one for transport. Abby shadowed her crew chief Sam as they worked on *Charlene One*, handing him tools or lending a hand as needed to speed him along.

Pulling the Chinook's six thirty-foot-long rotor blades required care and a skilled forklift operator as each weighed three hundred and fifty pounds. Removing the two rotor heads that raised the blades well above the fuselage was a much bigger task. Even the monster FRED couldn't swallow a Chinook with the rotor heads still mounted—seventeen feet of helicopter height didn't come close to slipping into a thirteen-and-a-half-foot-high cargo bay.

Helping out kept her mechanical skills at least somewhat current. Most crew chiefs wouldn't trust a pilot to hold a flashlight on their birds, but Abby had fixed plenty of lobster pot hoists, bilge pumps, and boat engines over the years. Under Sam's watchful eye, she at least *felt* useful. *Charlie Two* and *Four* were going through the same dance, but without their pilots pitching in beyond the simplest steps.

It also gave her a good excuse for avoiding Derek. Once he and his teams showed up at the loading site, he'd tried to approach her several times. Sam, reading the situation easily, brushed him away twice, then almost dropped a rotor blade on his head (purely accidentally, of course). Derek finally got the message.

The dodge and avoidance routine wasn't going to work if they were flying on a mission together, but it sufficed for the moment.

Trisha strolled through the orchestrated mayhem just like the old hand she was.ABby would bet good money on Trisha's unpleasant reaction to an *old* tag in any form, so she swore to keep that to herself.

"So, Mr. D-boy put himself in the doghouse."

She left Abby time for half a nod.

"You have the duration of this teardown and loading cycle to fix it."

Abby could only gawk at her.

"The C-5 will be here in an hour. Emily's plane lands about two hours after that, just as we finish loading these birds. I don't want *your* shit in *her* lap. She's got enough of her own going on. Clear?"

"Uh, clear, ma'am." Abby saluted because she figured it was better than punching a superior officer in the nose for pushing it into the wreckage that so often defined Abby's personal life.

Then Trisha offered a rare, non-evil smile. "It probably doesn't sound like it, but trust me, I'm doing you a favor. Billy and me? Holy fuck we were such a mess. We wasted weeks, months—I've blocked it out of all memory." She waved her hand like a windshield wiper in front of her face. "Nearly got my fine ass thrown out of the regiment as part of it—as if that wouldn't have been a Shakespearean tragedy of sufficiently grand proportions. And ixnay on comments about any grandness of my ass, I already know it's awesome. Go fix this—now!" Then she walked away.

Abby looked at Sam, who remained very focused on the driveshaft he was disconnecting. She looked at Trisha's retreating ass and considered tossing out a few uncouth observations anyway—ones that would be sure to put her on disciplinary action.

"Could you hand me the thirty?" Sam asked as if he hadn't heard a thing.

She picked up the arm-long thirty-millimeter wrench and contemplated how best to apply its hefty weight to Derek. Instead, she handed it off to Sam. "I've gotta go deal with a rabid piece of shit."

Sam nodded, then whispered. "I liked the guy, but give him hell, sister."

"Yeah, I liked him too—and I will."

32

"Incoming." Hot Rod's gaze locked in, close off Derek's left shoulder.

Derek leaned away to the right, bending down for the blade in his right calf sheath. They'd set up a squat just inside the big hangar where the three Chinooks were being disassembled. A chill afternoon wind had risen, curling the crisp wind in around the edge, but it wasn't worth the energy to move their setup.

Any spare tables were being used by the helicopter teams to sort parts, so Delta had set up on low crates and sat on ammo cases as they sorted and stowed gear. Not knowing the assignment, they were assembling two complete inventories—training and live mission. It meant meticulously sorting weapons and ammo—twice. Once done, setting up survival packs, without knowing the kind of environment they were headed into, became the next split task.

All of which meant that his position sucked to deal with whatever was coming his way. Even before he turned, he knew he was moving too slowly.

The point was proved when a boot connected with his left butt cheek hard enough to knock him aside—and to hurt. He let it carry him through a roll before popping to his feet. Or trying to. One foot landed fine on the concrete floor. The other landed on a fifty-round cardboard box of 7.62mm ammo, which busted open and the cartridges rolled beneath his foot. That pitched him into a pile of halfway repackaged MREs. Field rations could be made a third less weight and half the size with the judicious application of a knife and a fourteen-inch strip of hundred-mile-per-hour duct tape. A necessity if they'd be hauling a week of supplies around in a field pack. The ultimate indignity, he finally came to a stop with his head resting on Misty's boots—the only woman in the squad.

"Bootlicker," Hot Rod teased him.

"You never do that for me," Compass moaned with mock envy.

Misty just put her other boot on his shoulder and gave a shove, tumbling him into a shipping crate that didn't budge one bit when he slammed into it. "What did you do this time, boss?" She didn't usually say even that much, but she'd made it through Delta qualification, so she didn't need to.

"What makes you think I—" Then he focused on his attacker. "Hey, Abby."

All she did was point out the open hangar door before turning on her heel and stalking away. He followed her out into the weakening sunshine, shaking out his hip where her boot had connected. On top of the wind, the air temperature was dropping—not as fast as it had in Abby's apartment this morning, but close. The thickening cloud cover had him wagering on precipitation by sunset. He hoped that it would be cold enough to snow, or that they'd be gone to wherever they were headed. Freezing rain was the worst.

Abby stopped well away from the others, with her hands

once again fisted in her jacket pockets. If only... Yeah. Not a whole lot of utility thinking about where that had ultimately led last night. Nothing coy or cute in her present stance; she was one pissed-off woman—he'd faced enough of them to have no doubt on that score.

"My commanding officer is inbound."

He'd seen Lt. Colonel O'Malley drift through, so Abby must mean Colonel Beale. He'd never met the legendary officer, and by the sound of Abby's voice, shouldn't want to. But she'd flown with Colonel Gibson and he wanted to see what she was like. He'd never met Gibson either. He'd commanded all of Delta when Derek had qualified, and retired about the time he came out of the two-year training pipeline.

He waited for Abby to have her say. Along the way he'd also learned that interrupting pissed-off women never worked well.

"I've been ordered to keep whatever mess this is out of the colonel's face. That means you're going to behave like absolutely nothing happened between us. You clear?"

"Abby, I wasn't—"

"Good. Glad that's settled." She turned back toward the hangar.

He grabbed her by her jacket's shoulder. There wasn't time to block the fist headed for his solar plexus, but he did manage to tighten his guts before it landed. Though not quite enough.

Derek could breathe, if he was careful, but he couldn't keep a hold of her.

"Anything else? No? Good." And she was gone.

A shadow loomed over him.

"Billy. Great. Exactly. What I. Need." Breathing was still being a challenge.

Bill Bruce didn't answer. Instead, he grabbed Derek's arm, turned him precisely in Abby's direction like he was aiming a weapon, then flat-palmed Derek hard enough in the center of his back that he could either stumble into a fast trot or plant his face on the tarmac. He went for the shambling trot.

Sensing it wasn't over, Abby didn't return to her crew or head toward his crew. Instead, she headed around the hangar corner out of sight.

33

Halfway down the side of the hangar, Abby stumbled to a halt. She lay her shoulder, then her head against the corrugated steel. The cold did nothing to ease the heat of...hurt, rage, embarrassment? She didn't even know. Could it be all of them at once? She could certainly identify with each individually. And they each were plenty painful in their own right.

Closing her eyes didn't help. All it did was focus her attention on the sound of impact wrenches extracting bolts, forklifts running fast errands, and a soft laugh from the Delta team transmitted straight through the metal.

Opening her eyes was even worse. Directly in front of her, Derek Kylie leaned against the same siding, facing her.

"What part of go away... Never mind." She closed her eyes again.

"This morning...night...whatever you Night Stalkers call the middle of the day when you're supposed to be sleeping, I wasn't walking out on you."

She opened one eye enough to glare at him.

"Okay, I was. But not because I didn't want to stay beside you."

She opened the other eye. But if it was a lie, she couldn't see it. Of course she'd never been good at that. Her personal style included falling for every straight line that came her way. If it was a joke, she could always follow what was going on. When it involved her emotions, none of it made any sense.

"Look, this," he waved a hand around, "Fort Campbell. This is *your* home. Your world. I didn't want everyone to think that I came in and took advantage of their top Chinook pilot."

"So, you were going to sneak out without saying a word." If she barfed up her pain on his boots, would he leave her alone? Too bad she hadn't stopped for a midday meal—her midnight—before hurrying out to prep her helo for transport. Not much in her system right now worth throwing up.

"I was going to leave a note." He grimaced. "Okay, I like to think that I'd have thought to leave a note once I was clear of the bedroom without waking you."

"I'm guessing that you're not big on that after you slide away from a woman's bed."

His grimace, shifting to a look of pain, answered that well enough.

"But..." She didn't know why she prompted him. Maybe to see how deep a hole he could dig.

"This is your home. I wanted to give you the option of how you dealt with things. Last night was great." His shift to a happy smile came close to earning him severely barked shins. "Okay, now I'm lying. It was better than that. But if you wanted to treat it as a single night of fun and keep it just between us, I was willing to support that. I wanted it to be your choice."

Last night hadn't been great, it had been the best time she'd had in way, way too long—like ever. One soldier to another... No, one *warrior* to another, had made it even better than that. There were a hundred things that required no explanation. No need to explain why she served. Being a D-boy and a Night Stalker, especially after a pair of highly successful missions together, there'd been no need to explain anything about internal drive to be the best—both of their motivations were built that way.

No need to explain the sidearm they'd each dropped on the nightstands rather than hiding under a pillow. Not even why she had plenty of protection beside the bed. Not that she'd used it recently—having to break the seal on the box had demonstrated that—but she would, of course, be prepared. And once committed to action, there'd been no holdback or acting by either of them. It was the freest she'd ever felt in a man's arms.

His words slowly sank in. What if he was telling the truth? Had he been trying to protect her reputation or had he been slinking away like an asshole who didn't want to wake up with a woman once he'd screwed her? The latter thought hurt like hell but the former made more sense. In their two nights of operations together, Derek had run dead clean. Even the way he worked with his team didn't have a single fault she could pick out.

Protecting her made more sense. She closed her eyes and began thumping the side of her head against the metal siding.

He slipped his hand between her head and the metal, so she whacked it hard one more time and he jerked his fingers away.

"What?" He asked as he shook his hand out.

"Think there's a single person on either of our teams who doesn't now know we were together last night?"

He glanced over her shoulder, then shook his head. Shook his head and smiled—on the verge of an outright laugh.

She got the joke but wasn't feeling it. "My team likely has you labeled as a *persona non grata*. And I could go ya twenty bucks easy that your team has tagged me as a notional bitch."

"That depends."

"On what?"

"Is a *notional bitch* like a *national*-level tier of bitchdom? If so, I don't think you qualify, sorry."

"You *are* from away. If you go Downeast, *notional* means stubborn."

"Was that an invitation to meet your folks?"

"Speaking of stubborn. No. Ma died when I was three." And why did she feel it was necessary to throw that in?

Derek reached out to tap the Desert Storm patch on her jacket. "If your Pop is still around, I'll *go ya* that twenty that he's right proud of you."

"He's about. Back on the boats after doing his twenty years." And how happy would he be at how she'd handled this whole situation? She'd always been a Daddy's girl, didn't have a whole lot of choice in the matter with a single male parent. In turn, his idea of parental protection had to do with her being untouched by mere mortal men—ever. Even her rare *good* boyfriends had left him bewildered about how to react, not that he talked about anything other than helos and lobster, but she could see it in his face. She thumped her head a couple more times against the metal siding.

"What?" Derek looked concerned.

"Once, just once, I'd like to handle a situation with a man without messing it all up."

"Personally, I think that last night we handled each other just fine. And it wasn't you who messed up this morning. I should have stuck and explained myself rather than leaving when you told me to go."

"I doubt I would have listened." Abby knew that too was true.

"Notional much?" Derek grinned.

He had no idea. Though maybe he did. To make the grade for the Night Stalkers required an exceptional supply of stubborn tenacity. It probably took much the same to be a Delta operator.

Now if she only knew whether that made them a good match or one doomed before they really began.

34

EMILY SAT IN THE RIGHT-HAND COPILOT'S SEAT OF THE RANCH'S King Air twin-engine turboprop plane. They were flying over Nebraska before they even came close to having a plan to go with the three helicopters they had on the move. The task was twice as hard as they had to plan over the intercom because Mark was flying. Michael, Dilya, and Zackie were in the first of two clusters of four luxury seats.

Mark had purchased the same model of airplane that he'd flown as the Incident Commander – Air during their years flying against wildfires for Mount Hood Aviation. He'd bought it so that he and the girls could come visit her at Fort Campbell at least once a month. She also worked a week per month from home, gaining her two more weekends with the girls. Not this time.

"It's the best we've got so far," Mark pointed out.

When neither Michael nor Dilya made any further comments, Emily sighed. She'd welcome an idea from the dog right about now, but Zackie was probably napping. She checked the autopilot and area radar before telling him, "Do it!"

Michael called Claudia to send another request to the Secretary of Defense, this time asking a favor of His Majesty's Royal Air Force.

Mark nodded that she had command of the plane, pulled out his phone, and dialed. "Howdy, Fay... Yeah, it's me. How've you been doin'?" No need to introduce himself to the UK base commander.

Emily scowled at him and he paused long enough to lean over the radio console and kiss her on the nose before continuing. There was plenty of his history she didn't know, but it didn't mean that she had to like it.

"Had me this itch of a notion."

She poked him sharply in the ribs to knock the Texas out of him. It didn't work, of course.

"My Emily has a small flock of Hook helos she wants to give a bit of special training to. Also wants to be staged for a possible something I'm no longer cleared to know a thing about over to the continent. Mind us dropping in for a spell?"

He glanced over at her. If Trisha had done her job, which she always exceeded, it would be... *Nine hours,* she mouthed.

"Grand. That's grand. We'll pop round over in close about nine hours from now if you don't mind setting up a bit of clearance for us. Tell old Ralph to warm up the cards and have his cash handy." Mark winked at her though Emily couldn't figure out why until he said the next line. He was a step ahead of what the Brits would say. "Oh, right. That'll be close on 0600 your time. Well, mayhaps we'll be a-catchin' up over morning chow. See you soon." Mark hung up. "I have control."

Not that there was anything to do, the autopilot probably flew better than she would over the big stretches of the Great Plains—she'd never been a fixed-wing gal. But his grin said the King Air wasn't all he was pleased to have control of. He may have retired after doing his twenty years, but he still enjoyed the game—especially when he was the one dealing the cards.

35

Derek wished he bumped shoulders with Abby a little less often; the woman was incredibly distracting. He'd be down in mission-prep mindset and she'd go striding across the hangar like a self-guided missile. Even if she was targeting nothing fancier than a screwdriver or a bottle of water, his attention auto-locked and tracked until she was gone again—or Misty "accidentally" dropped the butt of her carbine on his foot.

Abby's earlier assessment had proven a hundred percent accurate. Every time he came near her crew, a low and feral growl of incipient rage crystallized in the chill air. Each time she came near his D-boys, their already low and sparse conversation faded faster than the daylight behind the thick clouds of the approaching storm.

But circumstances didn't let them remain separate for long. Three CH-47F Chinooks filled a C-5 Galaxy cargo bay. So, a trio of Night Stalker-modified MH-47Gs absolutely packed it solid —though the bay stretched longer than the Wright Brothers' first flight. Each helo's double-size extended-range fuel tanks bulged outward along either side, making for a very tight fit.

Then there was the loadout inside the birds, packed solid

with Delta vehicles and gear for the flight. *Charlene One* had reloaded one of the nine-man DAGORs. That had placed her crew and Derek's in close quarters as they debated which gear to take.

Abby cursed. "It would help if we knew where we were going and what utter moose's mess we were about to step in."

Derek was about to correct her that it was moose *shit* when a voice behind them answered, "England. And we have no idea."

Abby spun on her heel, then saluted sharply.

Derek turned to face the oddest-looking group. He saluted the blonde colonel who must be Emily Beale. He'd heard she was tough as hell; he hadn't expected her to be knockout gorgeous as well. Colonel meant mid-forties at a minimum and this slender blonde wasn't showing a bit of that. A big man in a sheepskin-lined denim jacket loomed close behind her. His jet-black hair was as straight and almost as long. As he didn't remove his mirrored shades, it was a mystery how he saw crap halfway up the Chinook's ramp, inside the C-5's cargo bay, under a heavy overcast sky. To Beale's other side stood a pretty girl wearing a hot-pink parka and lime-green scarf that made it hard to focus on her face. Once he did, she looked to be mid-twenties with Southwest Asian dark skin and brilliant green eyes. She had a Sheltie dog close by her heel but off lead.

The last person…

One warrior recognized another. He wore a black turtleneck and a non-descript jacket, and his face said he'd spent years living outdoors. Older was irrelevant upon seeing the deep skills inherent in his stance and assessing gaze. Though Derek knew they'd never met, there was no mistaking the man from the stories about him.

Derek drew up to parade-ground attention and saluted. "Colonel Gibson. An honor, sir."

He nodded, then barely ticked his temple with a loose-handed salute in return.

"Funny how some of us don't rate anymore, isn't it?" the big guy commented to Colonel Gibson like it was a great joke.

Abby gasped, "The Majors." Then she saluted the big guy.

"Lt. colonel (retired) but, yep, that was me 'n' Emma. Had us some serious fun." He left Abby hanging with her salute up long enough to make it a tease before returning the gesture.

Derek risked a glance over at Abby.

"Legendary inside the Night Stalkers," she whispered. "I'll explain later."

"Legendary," the big man must have exceptional hearing. He tested the word, "Legendary... I like that one. Whaddya think, Dilya? Do Emma and I rate as legendary?" He struck a pose with his hand over his heart and his head turned up and to the side.

Derek couldn't stop the laugh—which was at least half nerves at meeting Colonel Gibson.

"Not so much?" The guy gave up the pose with an easy shrug. "Y'all ready to get this here hoss into the air?"

"England, ma'am?" Abby asked. "We loaded both training and battle kit. Should we dump the latter?"

Colonel Beale shook her head. "I wish we knew but we don't. Keep it."

"Then we're ready to go."

"What's the full complement?"

"Three Chinooks. We have six crew per bird—total of eighteen." Abby glanced at Derek.

"I've set up a mixed force. A pair of Polaris four-man MRZRs in *Charlie Two*—each with three Delta and a 24th STS comm specialist I kept on loan from the Air Force. Five SilentHawk hybrid-electric bikes with operators are stowed in *Charlie Four*." He hooked a thumb to indicate Abby's bird. "I loaded a single DAGOR in favor of fitting more gear options aboard *Charlene One*. Nine seats but it's running light with myself and three other Delta knowing there were more personnel inbound. I loaded the .50 cal Browning for good measure."

"Christ, Emma, the Brits are going to think we're invading. Should I warn Fay?" The big LC-retired guy looked worried.

Colonel Beale glanced at Gibson, who reacted by not reacting. She nodded as if that meant something.

"Saddle up. Captain Kylie, seat all but you and your best three at the front. Captain Rose, just you at the back."

Before Abby could protest about leaving her crew in the wind, Beale turned on her heel and headed for the outside passenger stairs. The inside steps to the passenger seating area embedded in the top curve of the cargo bay couldn't be lowered with the third Chinook in the way.

Derek waited until they were the last two in the cargo bay. "Are legends always kinda spooky?"

"Yes," the girl Dilya answered from close behind them. Even his Delta-trained situational awareness had missed her remaining. "Of course, that's only because you can see them. I prefer being invisible." Even with her dog, she *had* been invisible.

"How much training has the pup had?"

Dilya's smile was radiant. "Zackie is ten, so not a pup. And a lot. Mostly by the Secret Service dog teams."

Derek finally caught on that he was in over his head—again —and called out to the crew to load up. By the time they were all aboard, the four massive engines had already spun to life.

The upstairs rear passenger cabin on a C-5 looked just like any commercial airplane that had seen too many years of service. Seventy-odd seats, three to either side of a central aisle, all facing backward. There were no windows anyway and, being seated backward, it was far safer in case of a crash— never a cheery thought.

Derek was unsure who to select. Even with Delta training, you couldn't be a specialist in everything. They'd been using the DAGORs a lot. And if the action team included any of these supposed legends, they'd need the seating capacity.

That meant Hot Rod, possibly the best driver in the whole Unit, definitely the best in a DAGOR. And if he took one of that fireteam, he needed the other, because Compass could find anything anywhere. He also could work strange and interesting magic with a block of C4 or a thermite torch. And, as much as he hated to admit it, Misty could outshoot Derek on his best day.

He kept it simple. First, he chased everyone to the far front of the cabin. "Hit the galley. Get sleep. Great job on the loading."

A few minutes later he signaled to his three choices. The rest of the crews spread out a bit as there were plenty of extra seats, but that still left a six-row gap to the huddled group of people and one dog at the very rear of the upstairs seating area. With the noise level of a C-5 cabin, they were huddled to hear each other, not over any fear of being overheard by the others.

36

"Who's going to say it? Not my job anymore."
Dilya rolled her eyes at Lt. Colonel Henderson.
"Hey, I'm retired, squirt. That has to come with a few perks. One is not giving that damned speech."

No one had explained who she was, but Abby noted Dilya was completely comfortable with the Three Colonels—which sounded even scarier than the Two Majors. Back when Henderson and Beale had led the 5th Battalion D Company, they'd become the best team in SOAR history. The advanced techniques they developed were still top-of-the-textbook a decade later. Dilya was certainly more comfortable than Abby would ever be around Colonel Beale. Still, it was damned weird to have a civilian and her pet dog along for the ride.

Beale looked at Colonel Gibson, who shrugged his discomfort with doing whatever the task was. Or perhaps he embraced being the role model for Unit operators never speaking. Thankfully Derek didn't hold to that model, at least not completely. Though it would have saved himself and Abby a lot of trouble if he'd spoken up this morning; their respective crews weren't exactly buddying up just yet.

"Fine," Dilya huffed out. She turned to face Abby and Derek's four-person team. "There may or may not be a load of heavy shit about to go down. If it does, you're not allowed to talk about it—ever. If it isn't one of these people—" she indicated the circle of people leaning forward to hear "—this never happened." She turned to Colonel Beale. "You sure about this, Emily? This has to be the biggest group ever in on one of these things. Your biggest was what, five plus me? Claudia's was four, I think."

Colonel Gibson scowled at her.

"Hey, not deaf or blind. I may not know what happened, but I sure know who was in it."

Beale shook her head. "You forgot about Mark's bird on that one when you stowed away. And you're missing three people on Claudia's. And no, I'm not saying who. Get on with it."

Dilya pouted for all of about three seconds. She was clearly a girl who liked to know things. Girl? She was probably all of three years younger than Abby herself. Which, she now understood, was part of her disguise. *I'm just a kid, so it's like totally safe to ignore me.* Probably not.

"Okay. If the Chairman of the Joint Chiefs asks, you tell him you wanted to go to England in November to work on your tan because Scotland has such fine and sunny beaches. You can't even tell Peter or Zack. Not if they ask nice. Not if they corner you in the Oval Office and make it a Presidential order. No how. No way."

"Oh." Abby, finally having a frame of reference, recognized the dog, which led her to the girl.

"Oh?" Derek asked.

Abby pointed. "This is the First Dog, Zackie." The dog popped her head up and wagged her tail at being named.

Derek's eyes shot wide even as he reached down to scratch behind her ear. "Which makes you the First Dog Sitter and First Kids' Nanny."

"*Was* the first dog," Dilya replied. "Anne gave her to me when I quit because she's the awesomest other than Emily or either of my moms."

"*Either* of your moms?"

"The first was a war refugee murdered in the Hindu Kush," Dilya waved a hand at her own face. Her darker complexion and bright eyes now made sense. She made the gesture as if that was a completely normal background for a girl, a young woman, to have. "The second rescued me. She's the Army's top sniper."

This time it was Derek who flinched in surprise. "Kee Stevenson? I've shot against her."

"Did your D-boy ego survive when she kicked your ass?" Dilya leaned close, eager for the answer.

"She didn't kick my ass."

Misty rolled her eyes at him.

"...but she did beat on it some." He shot a grin at Abby for using *some* all wrong.

"She did beat-some on it," she whispered the correction.

"Whupped his behind *ba-ad*. Did a number on mine too. Damn but your mom is seriously chill." Which was more words than Abby had heard Misty string together in the last two days.

Dilya looked as if she was going to burst with pride. None of which explained why she was here. Or why it fell to her to do the talking with the Three Colonels in attendance.

"So anyway, these kind of missions are so secret, they don't even get code-word classified. No need as there will never be a file about them. Uh, what comes next?" She blinked her eyes at Emily twice before she nodded to herself and continued, "Oh, yeah. This is your chance to bug out. No bad marks on your report card if you have the common sense to run away. So, who's out?" She didn't even wait for an answer. "Has *anyone* ever bailed on one of these things?"

Beale shook her head, "No one has been that smart on any

I've been involved with." Then she turned colonel-serious. "Just because she's young and funny—"

"I'm funny? Cool!"

Beale ignored her. "—don't doubt Dilya's words. A black-in-black operation will push you to the limits. I've never lost anyone in ten of these, but others have been far less fortunate."

"Ten?" The other two colonels twisted around to look at her in shock. "Nobody survives ten. Two, maybe three." Her husband's darker complexion turned almost as pale as Beale's fair skin.

She just raised her eyebrow as if to say, *You aren't the only one with a past.*

"Damn it." Henderson shoved his mirrored shades atop his head and stared at his wife before turning to Colonel Gibson. "Can you believe that I was naive enough to think she was merely the best pilot I've ever flown with?"

Gibson was very slow to respond. When he did, rather than answering Henderson's question, he held out a hand and shook Beale's once before again disappearing into his Delta-silent bubble.

Abby wondered what it would take to have someone talk about her like that. That's when she noticed that Derek wasn't staring at Beale or Henderson. She remained very careful to not turn and acknowledge that he was looking at her.

37

Derek waited until the others had dispersed to hit the galley or stretch out to sleep across a couple of seats. No one intentionally sat next to the interior stairs on a C-5, it was the coldest place in the passenger compartment as the cargo bay below was only marginally heated and the steel stairs didn't create a tight thermal seal. Staying there offered him and Abby a degree of privacy.

She heated a breakfast burrito, hash browns, and poured a cup of hot chocolate. He did the same except with black coffee.

"The Three Colonels?" She made it both a title and a question as soon as they settled.

Derek started a review of what little they knew. "Means it's as real as hell. Colonel Gibson? There's never been a better soldier. He, all three of them I guess, have a real penchant for surviving. Must say I like that."

She nodded her agreement. "Dilya?"

"You're the one who recognized her."

"Don't know much, but did you see her badge?"

He shook his head. After tugging off the hot-pink parka, she'd tucked it away before he could see it clearly. No... "She purposely held it so that you could see it. Didn't look like an accident now that I think of it. She must have some reason she wanted you to know."

Abby shrugged. "She's Yankee White. Cleared to be armed around the President. Which means…" she thought about it a bit "…she wanted one of us to know not to underestimate her."

Neither of them had that level of clearance, not that they had any need for it. But between that and Dilya being with the Three Colonels, it brushed aside any doubts that something heavy was going on. So, he moved on from the players to the objective they'd just been briefed on.

"All this because of one woman? A rescue?" That's what they said, but it didn't sit well enough to not be questioned.

"Or are we kidnapping her?" Abby must be feeling the same uncertainty.

"They're not going to bring along a civilian and her dog, no matter who she is, if it's an execution."

"So, when they said rescue, we should probably trust them on that."

"For now."

Derek liked the easy synchronicity of their thoughts. Yet another thing to like about Abby, as if he needed more.

"A test?"

He should have thought of that one. He inspected the plane, the scale of the crew they'd brought aboard, and that the colonels had come themselves despite two of them being retired. He shook his head. It didn't fit. "The last two nights…"

"Those were our tests." Abby finished the thought for him. "Unknown objective. Unknown opposing forces."

"How do we plan when we don't know anything. Yeah, I hear you."

They sat through half a burrito each but neither of them had anything to add.

He tipped his head back, indicating the front of the plane

behind them. "We've got a large crew here, but only a few of us in the know for what little bit of good that's doing us. Security could be a real issue. Unless we use them…"

"…without using them," Abby nodded slowly at first but then offered him the first real smile since they'd passed out in each other's arms last night.

"A full-on Delta/Night Stalkers demonstration over here…"

"…so that no one notices whatever our small team is doing over there. I wish we had Trisha along."

"Why?"

"The way she thinks is pure, out-of-the-box evil."

Derek smiled. "Oh, I think the 1st Special Operations Force Detachment-Delta might be up to doing a little of that."

38

"Have you decided if you trust us yet?" Colonel Beale sat in the airplane seat to Derek's other side.

Abby took a careful breath before answering with, "No. At least not completely. Though it's not like you gave us a lot of choice."

"Or actual information," Derek added.

Beale rubbed at her eyes. "I've never known so little going in. In the past there has always been a precise military objective. Rescue of a single civilian is not our normal bill of fare. Stopping a war or an attack with a weapon of mass destruction is more typical. Stopped a few presidential assassination attempts."

She and Derek glanced at each other. There'd been a spectacular debacle a few years back in Colorado when every post analysis newscast said the President should have died—but he hadn't. Had Beale been a part of that? No way to ask. Time taught a lot of lessons and they exchanged a nod confirming that Beale just might be what she seemed. She certainly *seemed* as authentic as anyone Abby had ever met. Still, she'd like more than a feeling to go on.

"Why her? Who is Miss Watson anyway? Why did the Brits grab her? Are we about to start a war with one of our closest allies because of her? Without knowing any of this, it's hard to know what to think. Colonel, not to put too fine a point on it, but you sure you folks've got both your oars in the water? We can't imagine the only other thing that fits, you three colonels all going rogue."

That last evoked enough surprise on Beale's features that Abby believed it caught her out.

Beale stared at the rear bulkhead of the C-5's passenger cabin close in front of them. "Going rogue? I've been accused of many things, but that was never one of them. Trisha came close a couple times—very effectively I might add—but I never had the knack for that. That's one of the reasons I chose her as my second in command, she doesn't instinctively adhere to the rules and regulations the way I do. Mark too. We're both creative in flight, but we like our boundaries. It's hard to tell what Michael is thinking at the best of times. Asking his wife doesn't help much. Though she's a Night Stalker and is one of my closest friends, she's as conversational as any Delta operator."

Abby felt the shock all the way down to her boots. Trisha had married Bill Bruce, a D-boy. Colonel Gibson had married a Night Stalker. Sure, the two teams worked together, but this was ridiculous.

Derek was grinning at her until she thudded a bootheel down on his toes. She didn't bother being subtle about it.

"Miss Watson," Beale might have smiled at Abby's action, but it was too brief to be sure, "is a national-level intelligence asset. No one except her, and perhaps Dilya, knows what she's been into."

"Dilya?"

"Uh-huh." A voice said from close behind her.

Abby twisted around enough to spot Dilya peeking between her and Derek's seats from the next row behind them.

Emily waved her to circle around to join them. "Don't underestimate Dilya based on her age or appearance. She's as highly trained in clandestine services as you two are in military ones."

"Except I started learning those skills when I was eleven and never stopped." Dilya didn't bother to blush or shrug as she sat cross-legged in the aisle beside Emily. Zackie climbed into her lap, licked Dilya's face, then settled.

"She's also thoroughly annoying. Never assume a conversation is private if she's around—even if you think she isn't."

Dilya simply smiled at Emily's scowl. "Or if Zackie's around. I haven't fitted her with a microphone but—" Dilya covered the dog's ears "—for a Sheltie—" she uncovered them "—she's plenty skilled."

"Explosives or people?" Derek asked. "Or a bit of both?"

"People."

Abby wondered just how expert the fluffy little dog needed to be to belong in this crowd.

"What Emily said about Miss Watson is a bit of an understatement. She carries the history of every major spy or spy ring, on any side, in her brain. All their techniques, most of what they knew, and much of what they learned. She's as close to an encyclopedia of international spycraft as there is. At least we hope so. They took her by force: one dead, one casualty." She looked down at Zackie long enough to dig her hands deep into the dog's fur before continuing in a tight voice. "What were they after that they couldn't just ask? All I know is that we need to get her back."

Emily nodded. "At any cost."

"Oh...wonderful." Abby wondered if it was too late to sign aboard Ricky's lobster boat for a quick career change.

39

Kentucky to England was a long eight hours. Once Beale and Dilya had stopped asking all of their hard questions, they'd left the two of them alone.

Abby wanted to talk to Ethan and Sam but both her copilot and her crew chief were crashed out. Almost everyone was. They'd been rousted before noon, the middle of their night, and done three hours of hard work in the bitter cold.

She and Derek moved a row farther away from the chill rising along the folded stairs but remained well clear of the others.

"Talk about something. *Anything.*" She couldn't sleep. Abby knew she should but couldn't. There were too many unanswered questions on every front—both professional and personal. She was worn out by thinking about the former with too little information and didn't exactly want to jump into the latter, also with too little information.

"Well, let me see." It was nice of Derek to not ask about what. "The first girl I ever kissed—"

"That's where you start?"

"If we're going to get to know each other, there are probably stories worth telling, leastwise that's how I figure it."

Abby leaned her head back against the worn seat and closed her eyes. It's not as if the cabin had any windows to distract her except for the tiny circular inspection port in the door. She flapped a hand to indicate her submission to his lack of logic.

"—was a total fiasco. Her papa caught me at it and whupped my behind good enough you can probably still see the handprints on my behind."

"On your— How old were you?"

"I was seven if I was a day. The saucy minx who'd enticed me out behind the shed was six and cute as a newborn calf."

"You grew up on a farm?"

"Nah, I grew up in town. Tight squeeze getting behind the garden shed. We probably shouldn't have giggled so loud as her papa was just inside working on a broken lawn mower. What was yours?"

Abby was surprised to notice that she'd rested her hand on his forearm in sympathy. Even through the warm coat and thick shirt, she could feel the shape of his muscles. Derek had a very solid feel to him.

"Well, I've bared my deepest darkest secret. Your turn to give, girl from Downeast."

"My cousin Ricky. On a lobster boat. We were both nine, I think."

"Was he a good kisser?"

"At nine, how would we know?"

"Your papa catch you at it?"

"No, but a good-sized wave did. Knocked us both breathless against the side of the cabin. Chipped his tooth." She opened her mouth and tapped one tooth in from her right upper incisor. "Did it with the top of my head. Still has the chip as far as I know."

"You marked him for life."

"Yep. He never recovered. Married and two kids, but I'm the one who marked him."

They talked of high school sports and Spec Ops Forces testing. Somewhere around favorite foods she felt herself drifting off. When Derek offered his shoulder, leaning against him seemed the most natural thing in the world.

40

Every one of Derek's instincts were ringing alarm bells.

Abby's last sigh of contentment before her breath evened out into the lazy song of sleep told a whole story. Whatever her conscious mind thought, her subconscious had made a definite decision about him. One that apparently included sleepy, cozy thoughts.

Personally, his inner dial was set to run for the trees, except there were none to run to high over the Atlantic. No matter what she thought, it wasn't a *guy* thing. There was no Y-chromosome gene that said *screw 'em and get out*. It was just the safest reality.

He wasn't even one of those guys who claimed they just wanted to spare the women future pain. Fighting as a D-boy ranked as one of the ultimate high-risk occupations, and ending up injured or dead had accounted for too many of his teammates. Photos with a D-boy's face were never published until after they died, because the crazies hated Delta operators even more than Navy SEALs. Once revealed, they would be personally hunted. But Derek always figured that if a woman fell in with a D-boy, and he made damn sure she knew what she was signing up for, then it was the woman's choice.

No one could know the risks better than a person like Abby. How many missions had she run with her helo filled with the dead and dying? The downing of *Extortion 17* and *Turbine 33*—two Chinooks that went down hard during the War in Afghanistan—would have both been before her time, but he'd wager she'd flown with plenty of people who'd lost friends among those fifty-six. Henderson, Beale, and Gibson would definitely have lost friends among them.

All three had served at the highest levels to go beyond the front lines in the Iraq and Afghanistan Wars. The only explanation for the Three Colonels' presence was the *importance* of this Miss Watson. Must be a hell of a lady.

He rested his cheek on Abby's hair.

What the hell was he doing? The soft feel of it almost had him bolting upright. But…he didn't.

What the hell had happened to him? Forty-eight hours ago he'd rolled onto her helo and gone forward to check in with the pilot. Now he was flying off to invade a friendly country. Yet that wasn't the weird part of the scenario.

Derek had always favored a be-here-now mindset. It served him well as a Delta Force operator. Women had always been the ultimate iteration of the mindset. Delta trained constantly, often on a thoroughly chaotic schedule just to keep them on their toes. And being the nation's top counterterrorism unit, they were on call-up at all times.

They often launched with no time for even a phone call. His folks had gotten used to it. They knew that if they didn't hear from the chaplain or his commanding officer, they should always assume that he was fine. His friends were either in the field with him or had long since lost touch. Connections with women? When a dinner date could easily be blown off for a month spent incommunicado while crawling through Burmese jungle? That didn't work so well. What did work was if his attachments didn't...well, attach.

Somehow, slipping past all his guards, Abby had undone that in a single night. He'd *wanted* to stay with her. Wanted to watch her wake up and have sex before the new day started.

And he definitely shouldn't have started trading stories with her. Because the more he found out, the more he wanted to know. She made him want to be with her. She made him...laugh.

Most women, truth be told, made him want to leave.

Not this one.

41

"Why do I get the feeling that I'm not done with her?" Derek had tried to find the center of the rain shadow cast by the monstrous airplane without much luck. Technically ten degrees above freezing, the English air didn't feel that warm for a second.

The Brits had cleared one end of the massive Base Hangar for them—being British they'd named it for exactly what it was, the base's primary hangar. A quarter-mile of contiguous open space, it covered over five acres. Further down the row it had swallowed a pair of C-17 cargo planes getting fresh tires and an Airbus A-400M in the middle of an engine replacement. No one working on them yet, but the day was still early by anyone's standards except the Night Stalkers.

Most of the crews had sought refuge from the chill rain inside the hangar while the C-5's loadmasters pulled out *Charlene One*. Because that was Abby's and—what he was coming to think of as *his* bird—he'd stayed by the ramp to watch the process. Abby and her senior crew chief Sam ignored the slashing ice water as they monitored the loadmasters' every step. His best move was to stay out of the way, but the added bonus of watching Abby had been enough to keep him out here alone.

Except he wasn't alone. Dilya and her dog had retreated from the rain by heading for the hangar at a dead run. He confirmed twice that he could see her hot-pink parka there. The way she could slip up to his elbow was still unnerving more often than not.

But at that elbow instead stood Colonel Gibson as if it was a sunny day in August.

"Uh, sir?"

Gibson gave no sign that he heard Derek's question or whether he'd been there long enough to hear Derek's first question to himself about being in a relationship with Abby.

His attention was most of the way back to watching Abby—which he realized he could do just as well from the far drier refuge of the open hangar—before Gibson spoke.

"There is another option."

Derek pictured Emily saying that this Miss Watson woman must be recovered *at any cost*. That phrase meant that standard safety protocols were of little concern in this extraction. And he pictured Dilya's beseeching look when she declared, *we need to get her back.*

He closed his eyes but answered, "Yes, there is another option." He and Misty were top snipers even among Delta. They were both expert with weapons that could kill out past two kilometers. Gibson would be as well.

If needed, he'd just been given clearance to exercise the ultimate solution to protect the woman's secrets. A sniper was often said to be the most personal of hunters. Not only did they hunt a specific person and see the target clearly as they shot, but they often studied their habits in detail to ensure proper identification at extreme distances. He'd never been part of an assassination squad, though he'd fought in war zones where he'd hunted other snipers.

But Miss Watson was someone that the people around him knew and deeply respected—even loved. Would they ever forgive him if he had to shoot her to keep her knowledge out of others' hands? Would Abby?

Colonel Gibson no longer stood beside him to answer these questions.

42

The drugs were a warm blanket, familiar in their weight upon her thoughts and the soft foggy cocoon they wrapped around her. She'd been trained in many of these types of scenarios. Imagined a myriad of others over the years as mental exercises. Still, over sixty years of spycraft should have prepared her better for this moment.

Or, better yet, avoided it to begin with; she'd turned lazy in her dotage.

The North Vietnamese had never known how deeply she'd infiltrated their territory, for all the good it hadn't done during the American War, as the Vietnamese called it. The Soviets hadn't existed for thirty years and to their knowledge she'd been blown up five years before their fall—yet their former KGB's throttlehold on Russia was worse than ever before.

She'd later arranged to die so that even the CIA lost her trail when they'd decided she knew too much, had outlived her usefulness, and needed removal for security reasons. And then, after years of protecting the residents of the White House, foolish old woman that she was, she'd thought that quitting and retiring to Montana had been a sufficient final covering of her trail.

She supposed it had been. The long roster of enemies she'd confronted were gone. But instead of fading away, the list of new nation-states with a grudge against America had multiplied like the Hydra, sprouting two heads for each cut off. And she'd been no Hercules with goddess-given swords and poison-tipped arrows to defeat the beast.

Yes, she'd guarded herself sufficiently against enemies both foreign and domestic. What she hadn't done well enough was protect herself against allies.

The English.

She supposed it was both the best and worst that could have happened. Mossad would have already given up and killed her by now. The French DGSE would at least have fed her decently. The English were going to polite her to death. All understated. All apologetic. They were going to kill her with deep regrets and far too much hesitancy.

There was only one hope.

Please let them have hidden their trail well enough that Dilya did not come looking for her. The girl had such gifts. They must be saved for the future. Dilya didn't know her own powers yet. But she had the basis now; she would grow into them on her own. The US was swinging the wrong way and it was only people like herself and Dilya who had a chance of swinging it back.

People like Dilya anyway.

Her own dance might not last out the day.

43

"Howdy, Fay. What has you out and about at this early hour?"

Emily turned to see a tall brunette climbing down from her vehicle. It was hard to see more until she circled clear of her Land Rover's headlights. She wore standard camouflage in the UK's multi-terrain pattern. The rank pennant revealed at the front of her blouse by her unzipped jacket bore the four thin blue stripes over wider black stripes of a group captain. Definitely the commander of RAF Brize Norton.

"This certainly looks like a Yankee invasion."

"We aren't invading, Fay. Honest. And you know about me, I hail from half of everywhere, but Yankee isn't on that list. You'll find me in Montana these days."

"Except you aren't in Montana. Neither are you over to Credenhill." Fay squared off in front of him.

"How's your dad?"

"Retired," she relaxed a little. "And hating it. Otherwise he's fine. How's yours?"

"Retired and appears to be enjoying himself. If yours likes horses, he should come visit the ranch."

"Hates them."

Mark shook his head sadly at such a travesty before looking over at Emily. "My dad was stationed over at RAF Credenhill for a piece. While Dad was doing cross-training with Fay's dad at the SAS, we did half a year of high school together."

"Yet here you are." Fay did *not* sound pleased at Mark's sudden appearance. "I thought you'd retired. In fact, I recall stories about a hell of a retirement party out on that ranch of yours."

Emily liked that Fay hadn't so much as shaken Mark's hand yet.

"Just a small gathering. Nothing much, but we had us a load of fun. Didn't we, Emma? Fay, this is my Emily. Emma, my old friend Fay."

Her grip was firm and friendly enough under the circumstances. "Are you the one staging a Yankee invasion?"

"I'm from DC, Montana, and temporarily Kentucky. All outside New England."

"You're all from the US, which makes you Yankees."

"Not bona fides," Abby joined them now that her helo had been rolled into the hangar and her crew had set to work on it. "They're all from away. Yankees," she tapped her chest, "only hail from the greatest state in the country."

Derek had followed her over. "Listen to her and you'd think the rest of us never did a useful thing in all our days."

"Might be. Might be," Abby agreed. Then her crew chief called out for a hand and they both moved off.

"She's from Maine," Emily explained. "Nobody understands them in the US either."

Fay looked toward *Charlene One* now under the bright lights inside the hangar and then the two more helos revealed in the C-5's cargo bay. "Those Hooks are black."

"They are?" Mark continued playing it coy for reasons only he would think were funny. "Oh right. Didn't I mention that

Emma here is Colonel Emily Beale, commander of the 160th SOAR Night Stalkers Regiment? How silly of me."

"*Your Emily,*" Fay sighed. "You think I'd have learned by now that you never deal a straight hand."

Mark slapped his palm to his chest as if mortally offended. He was overplaying the whole...

Emily finally caught on. Mark was never a goofball unless he was teasing someone or there was a reason. His fake Texan accent was mostly for the former and it was nowhere in sight, or hearing. Which meant he had a reason for doing this. He was dragging out the moment so that Emily could make her own assessment of Group Captain Fay Cutcher. Mark trusted Cutcher. Had kept up with her and not because she was an old high school girlfriend. No, it was because they could be useful to each other. But he knew he wasn't a regimental commander and he wouldn't make decisions for Emily herself.

Still, it wasn't much to go on. This was a black-on-black operation they could never admit to. On the other side, grabbing Miss Watson was something the Brits could never admit to either.

The question became, was it the British establishment that had grabbed her or had someone *gone rogue* as Abby and Derek had labeled it? If the latter, perhaps she could trust Mark's old friend. If the former, not at all.

44

"What did you think of her?"

"She dissed Yankees," Abby sniffed at the air. "Not even worthy of my consideration. If she—"

"No, Abby, be real." Derek cut her off as they steadied one of the big rotor blades until it settled cleanly on the forklift's tines. "She's the commander of the Royal Air Force's largest base. She could lead us to the kidnappers—or be in cahoots with them."

Abby glanced over to where Beale and Henderson were still talking with the Brit. "Snap judgment, I haven't a clue. But we had less time with her than folks from away have with rational thought."

"Hey, I'm from away."

"Like I said." She loved it when others made her point for her. "Honestly though, how do you judge that?" Then she focused on his face. There was something bothering him, deeply.

A quick look around and she could picture Derek and Colonel Gibson standing together in the rain watching her. Talking about her or talking options? Guessing about Colonel

Gibson, probably the latter. Her breath caught as she remembered her earlier conversation with Derek on the plane. Derek was a top marksman, but that didn't mean he'd necessarily be shooting at a British soldier. Execute Miss Watson if they couldn't rescue her? How cold-blooded was the silent colonel? Probably not for her to judge after his decades of service but that was a puddle far deeper than the ducks.

She couldn't seem to stop keeping track of Derek. It was ridiculous that a single night with a man could let him slip so deeply into her thoughts. Well, it had been three nights: two simulated battles, with a very pleasant aftermath to the second, and sleeping on his shoulder.

"Did he—" She shook her head. Oh, he absolutely had. "Never mind. Not my business."

"You're a part of..." Derek flapped his hand helplessly, in no particular direction that she could discern. In her brief experience, he was, atypically for a D-boy, rarely at a loss for words. Something major was bothering him.

She stepped up close to him while the forklift was holding the blade aloft so that Sam and his team could bolt it into place. The hand she rested on the center of his chest found damp cloth, a warm heat, and contours that had been burned into her memory in a single night. Being a Spec Ops warrior, he had an exceptionally nice chest that she'd deeply enjoyed.

"Derek. We're both SOCOM. You don't get here without facing a lot of harsh realities. Just because we didn't think of it, doesn't mean Gibson is wrong. If it comes down to it, trust his judgment and your own about taking the shot."

He laid his hand over hers, pinning it to his chest. Then he closed his eyes as if her touch and approval were far more important than she knew them to be. "You're the absolute best, Abby."

"So, I guess that leads me to an even harder question." She needed a joke before everything turned entirely too serious.

Derek opened one eye to look at her.

"How do we judge something like us?" Except it didn't come out funny, not like she'd intended. Instead it was all too real.

"Us." Derek opened the other eye, saying it without any indication of an emotion. "You asking seriously?"

Then the forklift almost ran them over as it backed away from the blade and departed to fetch the next one.

She waited while it rolled to the C-5 to fetch the next blade. Then decided what the hell, she'd already put her boot in it. "I'm asking because what with Trisha being a mass-hole—"

"A what?" Derek laughed.

"She from Boston. Makes her a flatlander from Massachusetts. Anyway, she's all married to a D-boy and has been pushing us together with the subtlety of a bull moose testing out his new antler growth. Your beloved Colonel Gibson married a Night Stalker, too, for good measure. And because you grinned at me worse than a hyena on a Thursday when you found that out."

"They have hyenas in Maine?" He was definitely dodging the question. Which reminded her all too well of his face when she'd caught him slinking out of her bedroom.

"Okay, fine! You looked happier than a mudflat clam curled up in its shell. Is that better?"

"Much." Derek helped her flip over the next rotor blade resting on the forklift's tines as soon as it rolled up, then ease it back against the stops for more secure handling.

"Seriously, Derek. Be real. It was one night and not even that because you tried to scoot away."

"Are we back to that?" he groaned.

"Hey, I may forgive you, you know, eventually, possibly. If the mood strikes me. And I might actually understand-some that you had good intent no matter how you bungled it. Doesn't mean I don't get to hold it over your head forever and ever." That was closer to the funny she'd intended in the first place.

Now he *was* smiling at her. "The only way you get to do that is if we're around each other that long." His shock at his own words caught up with him about the same time it slammed into her.

"Oh Jeezum Crow. You're definitely more trouble than you're worth." *Forever and ever?* What in the world had made her say it that way?

"I probably am." Derek waited until they'd prepped the next blade for lifting before continuing—very softly. "But I think you're worth finding out if that's true."

"You twisting that one around on me. You're the one who's trouble."

"Says who?"

Abby wanted to bury her face in her hands. She also wanted to drag him into a dark corner of the hangar and see if even half of her memories from last night were real. Too bad the lights didn't leave any dark corners in the vastness of the echoing Base Hangar. Every noise was amplified by the steel walls and they'd discovered that neither of them were particularly quiet while in the throes of ecstasy. She wished she had another, lesser word for how he felt inside her, but she didn't. And that, Abby supposed, was that.

Waking up on his shoulder, with his cheek resting against the top of her head had left her with shivers, good ones. Ones that the mere memory of warmed her insides on this bitter British morning.

"What am I going to do with you, Derek?"

"I'm thinking that's a straight line you don't want to leave hanging out around me."

She studied him for a long moment before answering. "You're probably right." But maybe not.

45

"What do you think they're not telling us?" Misty risked asking Sam.

Hot Rod and Compass had been useless as always. *She's way cute. I see why Derek is into that.* Utterly useless. With the DAGOR still loaded inside *Charlene One* and her sniper rifle checked twice, she had nothing to do. Waiting for the Go on a mission, that was fine. Sitting around while everyone else was on the hustle, not so much.

Abby's crew chief was checking the last hydraulic connections inside the aft rotor head on *Charlene One*. The other two helos were unloaded and well on the way to being reassembled. The C-5 Galaxy had been towed away to a parking area. In addition to being useless, she felt exposed—not a comfortable position for a Delta operator.

Sam tugged on each quick disconnect in turn, making sure all held fast before closing the service access. He then turned to inspect her just as carefully. "Are we talking about Abby and Derek, or the mission?"

"I think the first is pretty damned obvious, don't you? Deeper than either of them sees it."

That earned her a smile. "I'm glad someone else thinks so."

"Last time Derek didn't hang with the crew during a flight..." She couldn't even remember when.

"Same, same." Then Sam's gaze swept over the three aircraft. "A bad thing happened. No warning. They grabbed us based on the last two nights' exercises and they're praying that it works."

"Shit!" Misty wished she'd asked someone else. Confirmation of her own guesses didn't feel any better than hanging around being useless. "Thoughts?"

He shrugged uncomfortably. "Stay ready?"

"Yeah, stay ready." *For anything!* She knew from her years as a sniper that fifteen minutes was about the max on full alert. After that, your shooting percentage plummeted. It was one of the services provided by the spotter: keep an eye on the ball so that the shooter didn't have to until the time for the shot came. She'd done her rooftop tours at the White House; Delta snipers up top any time that POTUS was transiting past the box of the thick walls and windows. They followed strict time rules for switchover, even spotter to spotter.

"Ready but not too ready?"

She offered Sam a nod. He understood that fine line. Spec Ops to Spec Ops made the world an easier place.

Then she caught sight of Abby and Derek. They were leaning close to talk, but they didn't have their mission faces on. They were just...talking, all private-like. Spec Ops to Spec Ops? She eyed Sam. She could see bits of the attraction drawing Derek to the Night Stalker.

Then her possible interest in Sam dried up and blew away. Would attraction turn into *dis*traction at the wrong moment during the mission? That would be bad. Seriously bad. Now she had yet another thing to watch out for.

Shit!

46

EMILY COULDN'T FIND A WAY TO DUCK OUT WHEN GROUP CAPTAIN Fay Cutcher suggested they all get breakfast together. *A chance to talk without distractions.*

Fay had a private dining room in the officers' mess hall, and soon she, Mark, and Michael were tucked away in it. It offered a clear view of the main runway. Mark, accepting her decision to not inform Fay about their true mission, started the meal by catching up on various personnel whom Emily had never met. All very civil and so British that she felt as if she'd stumbled into a sitcom.

However, the underlying tension was palpable.

If they translated their ranks to NATO standards, Emily was technically a rank above the British base commander. And Fay, not being stupid, not only knew that but knew that Emily had a deeper agenda. Flying in on no notice with a trio of Night Stalker Chinooks had probably set off alarm bells all the way to the RAF headquarters at High Wycombe. Perhaps it would even appear in this morning's briefing for their prime minister. No question of Captain Cutcher sleeping last night.

"He didn't!" Mark exclaimed as a large pot of tea arrived at the table.

"He did." Fay nodded. "Even a simulated munition will crack out a Rolls Royce's windshield at five paces."

As they launched into a new story, Emily took the opportunity to text Abby. *Need to keep the RAF busy. Get C 2&4 airborne fast. Local practice runs. Testing. Don't care. Make it look good. C 1 stay ready.* She didn't want the RAF thinking too deeply.

47

Once the three helos were reassembled and run through short flight tests, everyone headed to the chow hall. But Derek's nerves hadn't let him sit. Instead, he'd gotten his breakfast to go. When Abby did the same, the rest of both crews—Night Stalkers and Delta—followed their lead. Soon, they were all sitting in the hangar under one of the area heaters that did little to cut the wet chill.

No one had a lot to say but at least sitting in a group put a halt to whatever was happening between him and Abby. Derek didn't know how he'd gotten into that conversation with her, but could definitely do with a way out—a *fast* way out. Long-term thinking wasn't a D-boy's forte. Long-term thinking about a woman had no place in a D-boy's or in Derek's personal world.

Impossibly, he thought it might be fun to go out on one of her family's small fleet of lobster boats. Physical labor didn't faze him and it would be a chance to see how she'd lived. Learn about her childhood, too, which sounded far more exciting than his own.

His speed and agility had made him a striker and co-captain on the Muskogee High soccer team. Football had tried to recruit him and he'd started training. But when his best friend's brother got brain damaged on the field, he'd quit. And that was about the only noteworthy thing he'd done prior to joining the Army. No college valedictorian straight to officer like Abby. He'd been plucked from the ranks and sent to Officer Candidate School for his leadership skills. Command liked that he'd brought his entire squad intact through three tours in the dustbowl wars including that disastrous final withdrawal and several undocumented forays into Syria.

The nerves were coming back. Everyone was done eating and starting to fidget when Abby's phone chimed. She showed him Beale's message.

About time.

"*Charlie Two* and *Four*," she called out, "spin it up. Full drill razzle dazzle. Get on with the Tower. Clog up their pattern as much as they'll let you, then do a little more. Arrange a practice zone for hot LZ unloads and retrievals. Exchange Delta teams back and forth. Stage attacks against each other. Let's show the Brits what our birds can do."

Glad of something to do, they didn't run to their birds—they sprinted.

Once they were on the move, Abby glanced at him and raised an eyebrow. *Charlene One's* team were up on their toes, just waiting for an assignment. Abby wasn't ordering, she was asking. Damned decent of her.

"Uh," officer training had taught him that you could hesitate for data and recon, but you didn't hesitate in making decisions once it was all in hand. "Okay, this team is going to look just as busy, but we're going to stay low profile. We don't want the *Charlene* to grab the Brit's attention. Stay here in the hangar?"

Abby shook her head. "We'll roll out into the open and spin up the rotors. But we stay on ground."

"Excellent. DAGOR team, switch it up. Compass, you drive. Hot Rod, you're in the nav seat. Cross train each other in high-speed load and unload. The key is never be more than twenty seconds from ready for action—immediate departure or attack. This is the action team. For now, those folks," he waved at the other two birds already loaded up and rolling out of the hangar, "are just a distraction from us. Go! Go! Go!"

Abby pulled Misty aside and Derek shuffled close enough to overhear. "You do everything you can to screw them up—both your team and mine. Steal a chain. Be a prisoner, but escape when they least expect it. Grab one of those small cargo trailers and load it in the bird when they aren't paying attention, whatever you can think of."

Misty's grin almost matched the evil redhead's back at SOAR headquarters. Then she too took off.

"Damn but I like the way you think, Captain Rose."

"Right back at you, Captain Kylie."

"You two are so cute together," Dilya effused from, again, close by his elbow.

Derek jumped in surprise. D-boys never flinched. "Goddamn it, Dilya. You're messing with my cool."

"You aren't cool, so don't worry about it. But you are good. Michael would approve."

That took his breath away. To earn praise from Colonel Gibson, even secondhand, was a big deal. The colonel's reputation said he wasn't known for doing much of that.

"And what are you doing? Why didn't you fade in with the others?"

"Because Captain Cutcher may not know about Miss Watson, which means she can't help us. Or she does know, and would never lead us to her. Either way, I'm better off staying close by the two of you if I want to find her."

"Oh joy," he teased her.

Her smile said she fully understood the joke.

"Look, Dilya. I don't know all your skills. But if things go dynamic, I'm going to look for you one step behind me and a half step to my left. Clear?"

The young woman turned instantly serious, almost looking as if she was going to cry. Instead, she rested a hand on his arm and whispered, "Thank you." Then she and her dog hurried to the wet line that the rain painted on the lip of the hangar's open door where she stood facing out into the predawn light.

"What did I say?" Derek looked to Abby because it wasn't the reaction he'd expected.

Abby rested her hand gently on his other arm. "You honestly don't know?"

He shook his head. Sass. An argument. A scoff. Any of those he'd have expected. Not the shock.

Abby went up on her toes and kissed him...then cursed him. "Damn you for being a decent man, Captain Kylie. It would be much easier to dismiss you if all you wanted was sex."

"That *is* all I want."

Her crooked smile called it a lie. Which it was. Because if it was a lie, any future sex wouldn't have to be with Abby. But she was the only woman he wanted in his bed—which wasn't like him. Which only made the whole conversation about the chance of something longer term happening between them worse. It wouldn't be freaking him out if it didn't feel so real. With all that mushed together in his aching head, the one thing he knew for certain was that he absolutely didn't want the conversation to go any farther down that mine-strewn road.

"So, what did I say?" He could see he hadn't fooled Abby. Well, as long as he kept fooling himself, that would have to be enough.

"Dilya is a girl, a young woman out on the edge of a clandestine world beyond our imagining. On the edge where people die suddenly and unexpectedly. You didn't shut her out or treat her as if she was a newborn fawn not worthy of note.

You just said that you expected her in the action and then offered to protect her."

"Well, sure. It's what we do, protect civilians."

"You heard Beale. Dilya is no more a civilian than we are. And you just acknowledged that. That's something I expect she doesn't get to hear very often. That girl is seriously alone in the world. Like recognizes like, except I have family and the Night Stalkers. I'm guessing she doesn't." Abby turned back to watch his team racing the DAGOR backward onto her helo.

Derek studied her. If he wanted to keep Dilya safe, who he barely knew, where the hell did that leave him with Abby? Protect her? No, far more than that. He'd guard her with his life.

48

A SHOT WITH A PNEUMATIC INJECTOR MADE HER HEART physically hurt as the drug slammed into her system.

At least for now they must have finished with the psychedelics and other disinhibitors. This was a dose of pure adrenaline to snap her awake. She was impressed that it didn't kill her as the shock of it convulsed her body.

Her vision cleared even as the male nurse turned away from making sure he hadn't stopped her heart.

She looked at her hands in surprise, they weren't secured to the table. While drugged out, apparently it hadn't been an issue.

Well, that was damned sloppy. What are we going to do now, Miss Watson?

On the nurse's table, there was another air injector.

Loaded.

She grabbed it. Pressed it to the nurse's neck. Thumbed the trigger.

Psychedelic or more adrenaline?

Either way, it should be interesting...

By the way he dropped to the floor and began shaking, she'd go with adrenaline.

A man to the other side of the bed had one arm in a sling. He reached inside his jacket with the other. The nurse's tray had several interesting items. A bottle of hydrogen peroxide came easily to hand. She managed to loosen the cap as she grabbed it. Just as he pulled a sidearm out of his shoulder holster, she used the power of the adrenaline still surging through her and squeezed it hard with both hands.

The cap blew off and a pint of H_2O_2 sprayed into his face. He dropped the gun to claw at his eyes; she managed to grab the gun as it fell. She looked at the bottle in surprise.

"Thirty percent solution?" Lab grade, ten times the concentration of the commercial product. Well, at least they were keeping whatever they were up to well sterilized. She tossed it aside as the door to the room opened. Guns were tactless and very impersonal. At the moment she didn't care and shot the two people rushing into the room in the face.

The echo of the gunshots slapped hard off the white tile walls. Not an operating theater, but not far from it. An interrogation infirmary with everything needed to keep the subject alive after the application of overzealous methods. She'd caught and questioned enough spies and high-value personnel herself to recognize most of the methods on display.

Mr. Screamy Face blindly tried to throw himself clear of the gunfire, which wasn't aimed in his direction at all. Instead, he leapt full force into a concrete wall, the impact almost as loud as the two gunshots, and collapsed to the floor.

With his hands fallen away from his face, she recognized him. One of the people she'd shot when they kidnapped her in Montana. That explained the sling. If it wouldn't waste the bullet, she'd put one in his brain.

She hopped off the bed. Or she tried to. Either her body had been abused past reason by the drugs, or her advanced years were catching up with her. She was only eighty-five, so she'd go with the drugs.

For kidnapping her, she kicked him firmly in the face, which hurt her toes badly—next time shoes first, then kick. His nose didn't resist. The blood followed rapidly. Too rapidly, he must have busted it when he hit the floor and even her barefooted kick had driven it into something critical. Not her problem, other than her aching toes.

Once clear of the fast-spreading blood pool and stable on her feet, she looked through the drug vials laid out. No anesthetic or other knockout drug. She loaded the bottle of lysergic acid diethylamide solution into an injector and gave the nurse a dose of LSD. She administered it directly over his spinal cord at the base of his skull. Intrathecal injection took under a minute for onset; it also provided a far more intense ride in her experience. She gave him a second and third dose for good measure—there were no recorded deaths from an LSD overdose.

"Enjoy your trip." He'd be completely useless for a long while.

One of the dead people at the door had managed to splatter their brains out into the hall and not all over his dark suit. Lean and close enough to her height. She could feel the clock ticking as she stripped him and pulled on his clothes.

The nurse had the smallest feet, though even tied tightly, the shoes gave her clown feet. Neither of the dead men had been hat people; she tucked her long silver fall of hair inside the back of the jacket. Both the dead men's IDs went into her pocket. Knife and sidearm with an extra magazine, but she left their phones. She didn't have time to try unlocking them with whichever face or finger—besides, they were too traceable.

Mr. Screamy Face's body had gone slack in that most final of ways. The nurse was the only one left to enjoy the situation.

Three observation cameras, which she smashed.

"Now. Where are we?" She dragged the other two bodies far enough into the room to close the door. For good measure, she spread plain petroleum jelly on the outside door handle. Anyone who tried to enter the room might panic at the unexpected sensation and assume they were now poisoned. If she was lucky, it would create more delay before anyone entered to see she was gone.

She considered breaking off a couple of scalpel blades and embedding them in the jelly on the underside of the knob but that would take too much time and wouldn't cause much additional delay. A quick scouting of the outer guard station scared up two sets of keys for the door lock. She tossed them into the room.

The dead bolt was keyed inside and out. Lock prisoners in. Lock the unauthorized out. She retrieved one of the keys and slid it into the inside lock. Then she took a length of silk suture thread and wrapped it around the key. After closing the door, a quick tug locked the bolt from the inside. A harder tug and she snapped the suture off at the door jamb. Back at the observer station, she found a laptop with a screen of three cameras showing nothing but black. She smashed it on the corner of the desk until she could recover the small hard drive, which she tucked in her pocket.

Her next best action? Motion. Still shaky didn't matter. It was time to be elsewhere.

49

Nothing resolved, the breakfast with Fay Cutcher never moved past the remotely polite. Mark appeared to be running low on things to talk about and they'd only just been served.

Emily added stories when she could think of one, but her attention remained almost entirely on watching the Chinooks flying exercises through the dawning light. The two backup helos were doing an impressive job of it. Flying sideways, even backward through the airspace. Teams dumped in the middle of the runway only to have the other helo snatch them aloft with long lines. It was definitely a spectacle. Michael, predictably, spoke as little as ever.

An orderly came rushing in and handed Cutcher a note.

Fay read it at a glance. "What in tarnation?" Then she read it again before turning back to the table. "Please enjoy your meals. This orderly will return you to Base Hangar when you're done. Excuse me, this requires my personal attention. I'll see you at the hangar as soon as this is resolved. I look forward to discussing joint exercises between our teams while you're here, though I think you'll find more interesting challenges with our SAS at RAF Credenhill." She said the last as the sort of suggestion one made to avoid saying it as a direct order. Basically, *Get the hell off my base!*

Emily kept her silence until Cutcher and the orderly had left them with their meals.

"She doesn't know whether to get rid of us as quickly as she can or to keep us close so that she can see what we're up to." Michael spoke for the first time.

"I don't care what she's up to," Mark blew out a hard breath. "If I had to come up with one more story, I'd have been a dead man. Been a long time since Fay and I did more than pass each other by or have a quick chat in the officer's mess. I'm tapped out."

Emily kissed him on the cheek. "You did great. I'd love to know what called her away from our meeting so suddenly."

If someone at High Wycombe headquarters decided they shouldn't be here, how hard would the Brits be throwing them out?

50

"What do you mean it's locked and we don't have the key? Who is in that room?" Fay could see the brain spatter on the wall and the bloody stripe indicating that a body had been dragged into the room—a very dead one by the volume of red. No, too much. There must be two bodies. It was the blood, spotted by a janitor, who had escalated the initial find, which rose rapidly all the way to her attention. She'd have to remember to compliment the chain of command on its efficiency—later.

"You aren't authorized to know that." A man who'd been trying to open the door upon her arrival did his best to block her approach. "I need a medic!" He kept scrubbing at his hand with a bit of toweling, which looked to glisten under the fluorescent lights. He reached for the door knob again, but jerked his hand away as if acid there burned him.

Fay tapped her group captain pennant. "This gives me—"

"Absolutely no authorization here."

She nodded to the flight sergeant and lance corporal she'd gathered on her way here. Fay had been in this building but hadn't been aware of it having a basement. She'd only been assigned here three months ago and was far from knowing all the ins and outs of this sprawling base. They grabbed the man and made quick work of stripping his weapons and tossed her his ID.

"Agent John Brown. So, you're Queen Victoria's lover. I must say you look surprisingly healthy for being a century and a half dead. No ministry listed, makes you a special agent of MI5 or MI6. I don't know or care to discover your real name. Toss him in lockup, no calls in or out. I'll deal with him later."

His protests escalated until he attacked the sergeant. The lance corporal was military police and used to such problems—he dropped the man with a single blow of his fighting baton. Silence. They wouldn't be getting any more answers from him for a while. She hoped that his headache was epic—once he regained consciousness. She hated spooks.

"Get this door open." It was heavy steel. She was on the verge of calling for one of Mark's Delta operators by the time an armorer finally arrived. A strip of C4 excised the lock and left her ears ringing despite evacuating to a safe distance and donning hearing protection.

Raymond, her second in command, came in just as the armorer finished checking for booby traps, and swung the door open.

"What is this place?"

Which was all Fay needed to know from him at the moment.

Two dead men lay close inside the door: one in uniform, one in his skivvies. No ID on either one. Two other men by a surgical bed. One's eyes and face were burned red and he lay in a pool of blood that wasn't expanding. The other wore medical dress and was pacing rapidly around the room—barefooted. The crisscrossing lines of bloody prints showed he'd been at it a while and not conscious of walking through the pooled blood.

When she touched him, he screamed. His pupils were shot wide and his entire body jittered. A quick inspection of the supply table told her why—she didn't need to read the labels to recognize that there was a large array of drugs here. Whatever had been administered to him had left the man mentally incapacitated.

"This one needs medical attention—after he's locked up. Not where he can speak to anyone else."

Raymond nodded and pulled out a radio.

The bed. The last remaining clue. Someone had been here, more than briefly by the impressions and rumpling of the sheet and thin pillow. Straps hung loosely to either side of the table.

"Someone got out. Commander Raymond, find him and detain for questioning. Use any means necessary. I don't like the idea of a rogue agent on my base. Assume armed and dangerous."

Raymond glanced down at the three corpses. "I dare say."

A secret basement interrogation room on her base. An escaped prisoner. And—

Fay looked up and to the southeast.

And the sudden arrival of a large contingent of American military.

She ran a hand over the sheet one last time.

Who was here that MI6 had and the Americans wanted badly enough to stage what amounted to an invasion of British soil? A Russian defector? A North Korean spy? The head of China's weapons program?

Had the Americans already grabbed their target and were preparing to race out of the country? No, they still had the C-5 Galaxy parked on her runway.

Fay called the field's control tower as she hurried out of the room. "Are the Americans showing any signs of leaving?"

"No, can't say as they are, ma'am. And ma'am?"

"Yes?"

"They're pretty darned fine at flying those Hooks, if I may say so, ma'am. Our boys could take lessons from these folks."

"Just keep them here. As long as that C-5 Galaxy stays here, they won't go anywhere. On the quiet."

"We're refueling them now. I'll just make sure those chaps and their trucks happen to park in the way."

"Excellent. No departure clearance without my personal say-so."

"Yes, ma'am."

51

When Derek started talking to Dilya about her dog, Abby checked out. She'd always been more of a cat person. It was hard to be a dog person when out on the sea for unpredictable hours. Having a warm cat waiting for your lap at home was always a pleasant thing. Of course, being in the Night Stalkers, she couldn't have either, but she enjoyed them whenever she took leave.

Grabbing a radio, Abby stepped out of the hangar and onto the tarmac. With the morning light and the rain clearing off, she could see the helo operations clearly. As they worked different techniques, she called up tips and corrections to hone their skills. With the chance to offer immediate feedback, rather than the usual after-action reports, she could watch them improve.

It also let her call in a few twists of her own, then watch their responses. That short-cycle feedback loop provided instant, quantifiable results. She'd definitely be implementing this type of training more widely in the teams when she reached home.

Group Captain Cutcher rolled her Land Rover straight into

the hangar, but she was the only one to get out. The DAGOR passed by outside and Abby could see through the glass that there were no other occupants in the vehicle. She would feel sick to her stomach—later. For the moment, she wished that her carbine rifle was not in the door clip on her helo. She turned away enough to hide the motion as she placed her hand on her sidearm.

Because this was the UK, Cutcher exited to Abby's side of the vehicle. Abby glanced over the hood of the vehicle that now separated her from Derek. From his angle, he saw her motion and gathered his rifle from where he'd leaned it beside him. After signaling Dilya to stay put, he hot-footed it around the back of the vehicle.

"Where are your commanders?" Cutcher faced her squarely.

Abby almost stumbled forward in her shock. "They departed with you. What did *you* do with them?"

"I was called away at breakfast." She glanced at her watch. "Only seventeen minutes ago. They must still be there." Cutcher rubbed at her forehead as if that couldn't be possible. It didn't sound like a ploy.

Abby eased her stance as Derek came around behind Cutcher and slowed at her signal. Dilya remained in place—but Zackie didn't.

The little dog trotted straight toward Cutcher despite a soft hiss from Dilya.

The sound had Cutcher twisting to face Dilya just as Zackie sat directly in front of her and began happily wagging her tail. She was focused on one of Cutcher's hands.

"Hey!" This time Dilya shouted.

Derek glanced her way. In answer, Dilya nodded toward the dog.

Derek looked at Zackie, then shifted from a covering position to standing close behind Cutcher. Once there, he rested the barrel of his rifle against the small of Cutcher's back.

Abby stepped in front of her. "You will want to think about your next actions very, very carefully, Group Captain Cutcher."

"This is outrageou—"

"Zackie doesn't make mistakes. There are only a few smells she'd react to like that." Dilya stormed up to face her. So much for staying safely in Derek's shadow.

"What are you talking about?" Cutcher scowled at her.

"Where is she?"

"I told you, they're at breakfast."

"Not them. Miss Watson!"

Abby held up a hand to stop Dilya physically throwing herself at Cutcher. The hand Dilya had placed inside the cuff of her opposite sleeve was a motion that no one had missed. "No, Dilya."

A group of early-arriving mechanics at the planes farther along the big hangar noticed trouble brewing. They gathered up some heavy tools and rushed in their direction.

Abby knew it was getting out of hand, but didn't know how to stop it. Overwhelming force seemed the best option—her only option. She managed to catch Misty's attention out by *Charlene One* and gave a simple upsweep of her arm, the military hand sign for *Come*. Then she fisted her hand and pumped the arm for *Hurry!*

Misty stepped on the running board of the DAGOR, shouted something to Compass, and the vehicle raced across the fifty meters from their practice area in seconds. Her own crew, led by Sam, arrived at a sprint less than ten seconds later.

The line of Delta operators and Night Stalkers with their carbines at the ready had the Brit mechanics skidding to a halt.

Once they all stopped moving, Abby waved for her people to lower their weapons. Everyone did—except Derek. He kept his rifle against the small of Cutcher's back.

"Our dog…"

Cutcher looked down at the small Sheltie like it was an alien.

"…has traced a unique scent to your hand."

Abby glanced at Dilya for confirmation and received an emphatic nod.

"This means you have been in recent contact with a forcibly kidnapped US citizen. One who is a very high-value asset." Or at least Abby hoped that's what was going on.

"I haven't been in contact with anyone."

Derek nudged Group Captain Cutcher's spine enough to remind her this was not a good time for a lie.

She raised her hand as if to look at it, and Zackie's gaze tracked it up. "I…brushed it over a, uh, hospital bed."

Dilya whimpered.

52

A KLAXON RATTLED ALONG THE HANGAR AND WAS MIMICKED FROM the next building over. Farther down the service bay, a smarty-pants had punched the alarm. Derek didn't dare turn, he just hoped to hell that someone had his back.

Misty's shoulder brushed against his to declare he was covered. Good. Now he wished he dared a sigh of relief. He didn't.

"World of hurt inbound," he informed Abby.

As calm as could be Abby lifted her radio. "*Charlie Two. Charlie Four.* Full guard on our position. Do not, I repeat, *not* fire without specific command. No one in or out. Confirm."

"*Charlie Two.* Guard only. Weapons *not* free." *Charlie Four* echoed the call. Within moments, the two Chinooks had settled to a high hover just outside the Hangar Bay doors. The hot wind of the exhaust driven downward by their rotors hammered into the hangar. Enough of the noise remained outside that they could speak by raising their voices.

Derek risked a glance out and upward. Both helos' miniguns were fully manned, crew chiefs at each one with helmets on and visors down. Rear ramps were lowered and he knew his Delta snipers would be covering angles from there as well.

Already there was the whooping *nee-naw* of approaching RMPs. How soon would American forces be shooting up Royal Mounted Police cars? You didn't fire warning shots with M134 Miniguns, you laid swaths of unfriendlies to waste.

"Your move," Abby didn't look away from Cutcher.

Cutcher assessed Abby for five long seconds while the *nee-naws* grew loud enough to overwhelm the whine of the hovering Chinooks' big turbines. Then Cutcher reached for her belt.

Derek flipped the safety on then off again with a loud click to remind her to try no tricks. Cutcher's fingers shook for a moment before she managed to steady them and pull her radio from her belt rather than reaching for her sidearm. They were dead steady as she dialed in a frequency. Almost as chill as Abby—but not quite to her high standard.

"This is Group Captain Cutcher. Form a perimeter. Do not approach. Acknowledge."

"Are you sure, Captain?"

"That's an order."

The irritating *nee-naw,* which had been escalating to painful as the open front of the hangar captured and focused the sound, faded away. But the flashing blue lights continued to paint the walls and everyone inside.

"Captain Rose," one of the helos reported. "We can see a non-RMP vehicle at the perimeter. Colonels are getting out."

Abby confirmed the radio call then nodded to Derek.

He took a careful breath, safetied his weapon, and took a single step back.

Cutcher again waited the count of five before keying her radio. "Three Americans at the perimeter. Let them through."

Nobody spoke. Nobody moved. Except Zackie when Dilya

whispered, "Treat." She raced to her mistress, terribly pleased with herself.

"Sorry we're late to the party," Mark drawled out as they drew close. "Couldn't pass up that fine sticky toffee pudding for dessert. Always did like that."

He rocked back and forth on his heels for a moment as if just noticing the situation. His smile said he was enjoying the moment though Derek couldn't imagine why.

"Well, this is quite the change. What did you do this time, Fay? You didn't brick over Principal Humphrey's office door with him in it again, did you?"

"No! She—"

Abby's glare stopped Dilya cold.

Which impressed Derek no end. After even his few minutes' talking with her, he knew that silencing Dilya wasn't as easy as Abby made it look. In fact, she made the whole FUBARed situation look easy and smooth. If he was ever going to choose a woman to follow, he'd never find one better.

She addressed the colonels without looking away from Cutcher. "Zackie has identified a scent on Captain Cutcher's hand, apparently from contact with a hospital bed."

Oddly, Mark and Emily stayed silent. It was Colonel Gibson who moved forward. Rather than facing Cutcher or even Dilya, he squatted in front of Zackie, keeping one hand in his jacket pocket. The dog stretched out her neck to sniff at the pocket, gave a happy wag, but stayed where she was.

Derek guessed at what the man was up to. "Under half the reaction she had to Captain Cutcher, sir. And she broke away from Dilya the instant she picked up the scent."

Michael didn't turn, though he nodded, then looked up at Dilya. "Who else?"

"Only three that she'll rush to greet. She forgets *heel* or *stay* around her hero, a German Shepherd named Rex who works at

NASA. Also around First Lady Anne and Miss Watson. That's it."

Michael petted Zackie. "And you."

Dilya blinked, then nodded. "Okay, four. Except we're rarely apart, so she doesn't get a chance to show it much."

Michael stood, pulling out his hand and showed everyone that he had several slices of crispy bacon wrapped in a paper napkin. Then he handed it to Dilya.

Derek laughed. "Like a war dog?" They were trained to only accept food from their handlers to reduce the risk of poisoning. War dogs were highly valuable assets with bounties equivalent to a decade's income in some zones, typically double the bounty of their handlers.

"Mostly it's Secret Service trainers rather than war dog handlers," Dilya broke off a piece and fed it to Zackie. "She'll also accept food from Anne or dog biscuits from Miss Watson. But, yes, that's it. Not even the President."

Cutcher was staring so wide-eyed at the girl and dog that Derek wanted to laugh.

Michael turned to look at Cutcher. "I accept Dilya's assessment. Where is she?"

Derek couldn't see her face, but he could see Cutcher's confused shrug. "Where is *who*?"

53

She'd ducked out of sight at the sound of running feet. Her escape had been discovered too fast. When she sorely needed the speed and agility of her youth, not even the shot of adrenaline, which still had her heart pounding, provided it.

The labyrinthine basement led her past offices unpeopled at this hour, dark storerooms, and mechanical utility rooms. The last made her smile—briefly. How many years had she squatted in the White House basement in Mechanical Room 043, like a spider working the many threads of information that flowed through the building?

Not like Moriarity, but rather Sherlock's brother Mycroft. Collecting rumors, formulating plans, and implementing solutions through shadowed nudges, anonymous hints to others, and tips to his famous brother. All in defense of a country that had, in the foggy view of imperfect hindsight, abused her. Her own government had been willing to throw her life away by assigning her to the riskiest of objectives. Even decades later, she was an object still worth hunting.

Too many years buried in the darkness had taught her that everything was a conspiracy. Henderson's Ranch had been too abrupt a change, but the small town of Choteau had reminded, no, *re-taught* her about sunshine and fresh air. She'd almost forgotten about those. Her past forays into the twisty streets and convoluted secrets of DC, typically under cover of darkness, didn't make for a generally optimistic frame of mind.

Over the last few years, Dilya and her own eventual peregrination to Montana had turned that around.

Turned it around—and made her lower her guard.

She stumbled into a lunchroom. Big enough for a couple score of people. Not a full-on cookline, instead set up with a steam table line and rolling racks. The main cafeteria must deliver pre-made meals to here. A chalkboard announced the day's specials—which were enough to make her stomach growl without bothering to read them. How long since they'd last fed her?

A scrounged energy bar and a box of orange juice made her feel much better. A banner told her, finally, where she was— RAF Brize Norton. It confirmed what she already knew but that didn't make her feel much better. An interrogation black site, directly under the UK's largest Air Force base, explained why she wasn't dead yet. The Brits were too polite, too careful.

There was also a narrow window high on the wall. Too small to exit, but it showed hints of daylight—and the flashing blue of police lights.

Time to move.

She glanced again at the window. They weren't converging on this building; they were passing by at speed. A crisis elsewhere on the base might buy her more time. She was almost out into the hall before her fogged thoughts wondered about what that crisis might be.

Praying she was wrong, she doubled back, scrounged a piece of chalk from the kitchen drawers, then moved to the menu board.

54

"I'll take you there if it resolves this mess." Captain Cutcher was looking back and forth between her and the three colonels.

Abby looked to Colonel Beale, but she shook her head.

"What?"

"Not a wrong step yet, Captain. Keep going."

If Group Captain Cutcher and half a brigade of Royal Military Police weren't gathered about, she'd... Abby didn't know what. Scream? Shoot the colonel? In the foot maybe, but still! *Keep going?* Like that made any kind of sense.

Probably the same kind of sense as holding a Group Captain at gunpoint on British soil. It was more normal than finding an orange-and-black lobster—about one-in-fifty-million chance—but not by much. Yet here she stood in command of a team doing just that. She remembered one of Pa's favorite sayings: *Horse sense is what horses have to keep them from betting on people.* Which was odd as the family had never owned horses that she knew of. At the moment none of this made a lick of sense but she couldn't see any exit from the path they were on.

Derek offered an infinitesimal shrug and flicked a thumb's-up of encouragement over the barrel of his rifle. Some big help. Yet he raised no questions. Made no complaints, instead stepping straight into the fray on no more than her say-so. Whatever else he was thinking, he trusted her and, at the moment, that was a prize of immense value.

Abby turned to the Brit. "Captain Cutcher. Would you be so kind as to lead us to that hospital bed?"

Cutcher was so calmly British that all she did was turn slowly to glance over her shoulder at Derek.

Abby waved for him to lower his rifle.

Once he did, Cutcher nodded. When she turned for her Land Rover, Abby shook her head. She had hanging-by-fingernails control of the situation and refused to give up any of her advantages. Colonel Beale had made it clear that this was Abby's to solve.

Well, she couldn't do that from the air. She was no ground pounder, but Derek was. She remembered his comments during the debrief from the second night's exercise, making the hard choice to be the mission commander in the air rather than going in with his team. He'd stayed in the sky, now it was her turn to come to Earth.

"We'll take my vehicle," she pointed at the DAGOR. "Colonel Beale, you will board *Charlene One* and assist Captain Ethan Merced as copilot. I want you aloft inside sixty seconds and flying overwatch on us. Keep birds *Two* and *Four* on perimeter patrol. If the Tower argues, drop a Delta team on their roof. Derek, load 'em up. Dilya, you two are with us. But goddamn it, stay behind us this time."

Derek must have been issuing his own orders. Just as she and Dilya finished herding Cutcher and Zackie into the DAGOR behind Hot Rod and Compass, *Charlie Four* grounded. One of the hybrid motorcycles was rolled down the rear ramp. Derek climbed aboard and *Four* was airborne before Abby could decide if that was an improvement. Misty climbed on behind him. Abby also noted that in addition to the carbine hung across the front of her uniform, Misty's long sniper rifle now hung crosswise over her shoulder—its muzzle sticking a good foot above her head.

As they raced through the base with Derek and Misty as flankers, she wondered who would play her in the movie version. With her luck, probably some white guy over twice her age like Tom Cruise. No, he'd play Derek. She'd be replaced by a blonde with a massive cleavage—the kind who didn't wear a t-shirt under her deeply unzipped flight suit.

Abby slapped her hand against her forehead and thanked God that Cutcher and Dilya sat in front of her and couldn't see the gesture. She considered doing it again to knock the image out of her head.

Derek spotted it, of course. Only a few arm lengths separated them, and both his electric motorcycle and the DAGOR were quiet enough to speak over. However, her Chinook flying overwatch above them—without her at the helm, which counted as beyond weird—and the phalanx of RMP vehicles close behind them made speech impossible.

She was on her own. Except she wasn't. Derek was right there beside her, even if they couldn't speak at the moment. His proximity was a comfort.

Not something to expect from men in her experience. Yet here he—not some movie hero—rode beside her, Captain Abigail Rose. That image sustained her through the next ninety seconds until they reached a remote building along the north side of the base.

55

No one had cleaned up the scene in the interrogation room. Derek read the blood spatter patterns easily from experience.

Too much to do. Too little of him. Derek shards: that's what he needed. But he'd left Hot Rod and Compass outside with the vehicles, bringing only Misty with him as backup.

If there were multiples of himself, one could confer with Abby about the best way to de-escalate what they'd escalated in the first place. Or did it need to be taken up another level?

Another could be at point, keeping everyone safe. A third running a deep site assessment. A fourth...

But since there was only one of him, he stayed close behind Cutcher. If Cutcher had to be put down, he didn't want it to be one of his team. A senior officer of one of the country's closest allies... There were certain tasks you didn't delegate.

"What's he still doing here, Raymond?" Cutcher asked a man wearing the three stripes of a wing commander. No question who she was talking about. The room's only other bloodied occupant—still on his bare feet—paced intently about the room, adjusting a stethoscope on a shelf, then carried a box of bandages across the room and back before placing it exactly where it had started. Then he turned it around three-sixty and that satisfied him before he moved to the next object.

Two med techs were hard pressed to keep him from treading on the swathes of blood on the floor or tripping over the two RMP investigators photographing the corpses.

Raymond held up an injector. "LSD. Carl thinks it was a massive dose." One of the med techs nodded, then blocked the man's effort to get by him. Raymond continued, "He says we probably won't get anything rational from him for at least ten hours, possibly longer. This keeps him calm. Any attempt to get him out of the room—" The wing commander shuddered.

The drugged man crossed close by him, circled back, straightened the collar of Derek's jacket, then moved on. His pupils were fully dilated. While he was close, Derek could hear him mumbling to himself. He appeared to be caught up in a disjointed recitation of...*Hamlet*. With the dead around him, that wasn't much of a surprise.

He'd been in the grisly aftermath of battles. Walked through homes where his team had to gun down fathers, mothers, and even underage sons when they grabbed for weapons. Dinner still steaming on the table. But under the bright fluorescent lights, this was one of the worst.

"Uh, Commander Raymond, could you turn on the small lamp by the nurse's station?"

When he did, Derek switched off the overhead. It was like he flipped the switch on the drugged man as well. He let the med techs guide him to a chair, where they quickly strapped him in.

Abby squinted her question at him.

"Dilated pupils, bright lights, witness to three ugly deaths, and drugged out of his mind on acid. I figured he might be just a touch overstimulated."

The smile she shot him ranked even better than the *carry-*

on nod he'd received from Colonel Gibson back in the hangar. She turned to Dilya. "You and Zackie are up."

He noticed that Dilya reacted to the blood or corpses even less than Abby or any of the Brits. Whatever the girl had been through inured her to such sights.

All she did was say, "Miss Watson, *faigh*."

"Fog?"

"More like f-a-gh, where you swallow the *gh* sound. Scots Gaelic for *seek*."

"Zackie speaks Gaelic?"

"Of course she does. She's a Shetland sheepdog." Dilya's smile would befit a merry imp as she waved a hand to prove her point. The dog tracked from the hospital bed, trotted twice about the room, lingered by the corpse wearing only his underwear, then headed out the door.

After a similar close inspection of a shattered laptop, she turned left, then doubled back and took the right-hand hallway at a brisk trot. That meant the scent trail was still strong, at least to Zackie's nose.

Misty gave him a small nod indicating she could take the guard position on Cutcher, but Derek waved her to run point beside Dilya. He kept behind Cutcher and Abby, watching their six to make sure the others didn't follow.

Then he let out a bark of laughter.

Abby had fallen back to trot beside him, "What's so damn funny this time?"

"Nothing much, I admit. But no one is coming hot from behind. I realized that we gave no indication we—" he nodded at Cutcher's back.

"—had taken the base commander by force." Cutcher could obviously hear him better than he'd intended. "Let's keep it that way and get this resolved."

Twisting aside only a few times, Zackie had shifted up to an eager run, then did an all-claws slide as she attempted to turn a one-eighty on the slick linoleum. She led them into a kitchen where a person had turned on a few lights and was priming a large heating urn with water. At having his lunchroom invaded by an armed squad of American soldiers—and a dog—he barely blinked as if he'd seen it all. Then he spotted his commander and froze.

56

"Anyone come through here?" Abby asked the person holding aloft a half-emptied water pitcher as if carved from marble in that position.

He set it down so abruptly it was surprising that it didn't shatter. He jerked to attention and saluted Cutcher. "I was first in, Group Captain."

"At ease."

"See if anything's missing," Abby told him.

He glanced at his commander.

"Do it."

Zackie was zigzagging back and forth across the kitchen. Miss Watson must have spent time here.

"Two knives and—" the server held up a half-empty packet of cookies. "Right on the center of the counter so as I couldn't have missed it."

Zackie sat and stared up at the chalkboard.

She, Derek, Cutcher, and Dilya circled up close behind the dog. The dog remained focused on the very left end of the chalk tray, with good reason. "We found your cookies."

"Biscuits," the server corrected her. "Digestives." There was a stack of four of them barely on the tray.

"Digestives. They look as dry as a—" now it was Abby's turn for an inappropriate laugh.

"—as a dog biscuit?" Derek finished for her, nudging his shoulder against hers.

"Miss Watson guessed you were on her trail, Dilya. And, of course, you'd have Zackie with you."

But Dilya was busy pushing Cutcher out of her way. She inspected the chalkboard, the tray, the underside of the tray, and where it attached to the wall. When a tug wouldn't free it, she ran her fingers along the edge.

"She must have left a message other than biscuits." Dilya's motions became more and more frantic as her search turned up nothing of interest.

That's when Abby spotted the chalk on the back of Dilya's left knuckles. She grabbed Dilya's wrist and checked her other hand. No chalk marks. Picturing Dilya's motions…

"Miss Watson is a very smart woman."

"She is. Why do *you* say that?" Dilya inspected her own knuckles.

"The biscuits were teetering on the edge, as if telling us to look beyond the edge." She slapped a thigh pocket of her flightsuit and extracted a small flashlight but it didn't show anything when she shone it at the white-painted cinderblock wall. "Kill the lights."

Someone did.

Abby shifted the flashlight to strike the wall beside the chalkboard at a grazing angle. The paint was a gloss white but, with just the right angle of light, she could see that non-reflective areas had been chalked to form letters.

"White chalk on a white wall. As I said, very smart."

Derek's hand clamped firmly on Abby's shoulder. "Speaking of…" He whispered to her as he squatted beside her.

All her life, her brains had pushed men away. Derek didn't let go and his training meant he didn't need contact with her to keep his balance. Instead he squeezed her shoulder for a long moment as he picked up a piece of chalk and began recreating the message on the lower corner of the chalkboard. It required shifting the light several times and making a few guesses, but the message finally came clear.

D, Run! No follow. W.

"What in the world could ever make her think I'd listen to that?" Dilya stood with both fists on her hips.

"Maybe she didn't think we'd be with you," Derek teased her.

That earned him a quirky smile, "Or she did and still thinks we should run. Who knows how deep the danger goes?" She said the last in sepulchral tones and made a creepy fingers-wiggling gesture.

"Only comes up to here on the ducks," Abby held a hand to her hip just as Ricky would when describing the dangerous ocean out on his lobster boat.

Derek's laugh echoed off the hard walls. The rest just looked at her like she was crazy. Nobody from away understood a Mainiac's sense of humor—except Derek.

"So, give Zackie a biscuit and then tell her to Seek again."

Dilya did, and said, *"Faigh"* again.

She sniffed in a circle. Stopped and tilted her head a couple of different ways before looking at Dilya with what even a non-dog person like Abby could read as confused.

"Try starting her out in the hall again."

Dilya led her out, called out the Seek command, and Zackie came straight back into the lunchroom.

"She follows the freshest scent, right?" Abby asked as they all watched Zackie crisscrossing the room.

Dilya nodded. "Or the strongest."

"Which means that either way, it isn't out in the hall."

"But—" Dilya waved a hand to indicate the four walls of the lunchroom. There were no places to hide.

Abby took a cue from Colonel Gibson and watched Zackie instead of her own intuition—especially as the latter wasn't leading her anywhere.

Behind the counter, refrigerator, trash can, halfway to the door, back to the supply drawers behind the counter, over to the chalkboard... Then Zackie's puzzled look again. The Sheltie appeared to get the paths mixed up from there.

Chalkboard to middle of the room, over into the servers' side of the counter.

Abby's eyes tracked to the answer mere steps ahead of Zackie.

"The dumbwaiter. We're in the basement. She took the dumbwaiter where food supplies must be delivered from a service truck up at street level."

It wasn't big enough for even Dilya and Zackie together, though Derek had to physically force Dilya not to ride up into the unknown alone.

57

Miss Watson hated being right. That it was a skill that had kept her alive all these decades didn't make her feel any better at the moment.

She sat in a tan TUL—Truck Utility Light, the military version of a Land Rover Defender 90 compact SUV—that she'd liberated. She'd also borrowed the driver's parka after knocking him out.

After capturing the truck from three buildings over, she'd parked close by the building she'd been incarcerated in. The low sun, having cleared most of the roof line, would stop people from looking her way or seeing into the hard shadows cast over the vehicle.

Unless they found its driver where she'd left him tied up and knocked out sooner than she expected, everyone would assume this vehicle was hers. The most basic place to hide, in plain sight. Wearing a military parka over a plain clothes suit inside the base's security perimeter also marked her as a person worth avoiding. She could do with a little less attention for a while.

A dozen RMP cars remained down by the monstrous Base

Hangar, blasting the area with flashing blue lights. A pair of Chinook helos circled above them in a way they made look aggressive rather than merely an exercise. A third hovered above the far side of the building she'd escaped from less than half an hour ago. The helos were all black and had long refueling probes. Only the 160th Night Stalkers flew their birds that way.

Well, at least that meant, if Dilya was indeed here, she wasn't alone. Emily Beale or her people must be here as well. No, Emily would see to Dilya's safety personally; the colonel was here as well.

Dogs were out on ground patrols, but they didn't worry her. They'd be explosive sniffers, and she had none on her to attract their attention. As long as she didn't run, she wouldn't do so either. People-tracking dogs were far rarer. If there were even any on base, they were unlikely to be trained to hunt a specific human, most of those were body-finders rather than trackers. However, that meant the alerts were out and she wouldn't be slipping out the front gate to stroll the English countryside any time soon.

But Zackie had always been trained in finding people, not explosives or drugs. And she wouldn't need a sample scent. That dog, like its owner, was too smart. If they'd found the Digestives, and she had little doubt Zackie would, they'd continue hot on her trail. Her chalk handiwork had been completely futile.

"Getting old, girl." She realized that her message was not only futile, but would intensify Dilya's search.

So, Dilya and a rescue team were coming.

Except she couldn't risk that, because she'd been right. Dilya's greatest asset at this time in her career was in so few recognizing her skills. Unlike herself, the girl remained an unknown.

The proof of danger to her protégé raced over the perimeter

fence. A pair of Dauphin helicopters caught the eastern sunrise until they glowed like a pair of shivs right before someone slid them between your ribs. If they'd been Army Air Corps blue-and-white or UK Ministry of Defence white-with-red-stripe livery, she'd have been less worried. At the worst, those would deliver a half dozen SAS warriors each. There were straightforward ways of dealing with the British equivalent of Delta Force.

Instead, these birds wore plain white along with their tail number. She pulled the IDs out of her pocket; the ones she hadn't had time to look at since she'd taken them off the dead bodies. Face, name, scannable code, and the coat of arms. No need of a flashy title like *MI6* or *Secret Intelligence Service* splashed across the front. The coat of arms with an English lion and Scottish unicorn rampant said more than enough.

They were the ones after her and they were going to be very upset that she'd killed one of their agents in the US and three more less than an hour ago. Those weren't the sort of reports that the PM wanted during her daily briefings. Which, she glanced at the low sun, would be happening within another hour.

MI6 had sent in a double flight of black ops agents to get this, her existence, "resolved" before they had to report it.

She too wanted to resolve this quickly—before Dilya landed in their sights.

But how?

58

"Well, that's interesting." Abby hung by her fingertips clamped around cold metal with her toes perched on the low rail. She peered over the edge and looked down at what Zackie had found. In a demolition dumpster big enough to toss a couple of jet engines, lay a man with his hands and feet bound and duct tape over his mouth.

"He's breathing." Derek took a step back.

Without needing to be told, Misty dropped to one knee, planting the other firmly in front of her close to the dustbin. Derek used it as a launch point and cleared the edge like he was hurdling over a foot-tall tree stump, not the lip of a giant steel box that she had to cling onto to see inside. Yet for all the height of his vault, he landed quietly, absorbing the shock easily. He extended a finger to the man's neck. "Good pulse. No signs of blood."

At Derek's last word, the bound man's eyes cracked open, and he struggled to focus. His scream was sufficiently muted by the gag that all it did was rattle around the inside the dustbin. Very little of it managed to spill over the edges.

"Thoughts?" Abby didn't have time for this. She'd seen the

unmarked helos come in for a landing down at the Base Hangar. Not a good sign. The nearest US military force lay just fifteen kilometers away at RAF Fairford. Being Air Force, they might know about the C-5 Galaxy transport's arrival but not about Abby's Army team. Getting any useful form of support from them would probably require hours and bucking much farther up the command chain than she had time for.

Fine! The Three Colonels could delay them as long as possible to keep them from noticing what Abby was doing under their very noses. But the tide had turned and was beginning to run hard in the wrong direction.

Misty moved out of the way and Derek swung out of the dumpster as lightly as he'd swung in.

"You'll have to teach me how to do that. Who knows when it might come in handy," Abby told him.

"Do what?" The man didn't have a straight face to save his life.

"Also, how you did that without stinking of garbage at the end." She sniffed the air near his shoulder and got a snootful of a reminder of having him in her bed. "Oh, you didn't."

He opened his mouth to—

"What do we do about him?" She nodded toward the man grunting ineffectually against his bonds. Miss Watson had hogtied him so he couldn't even kick the side of the bin to draw attention.

"I think we should leave him because—"

He agreed with her assessment and that's all she needed to know. Abby twisted on her heel to face Dilya. "Keep Zackie going."

They'd come up on the far side of the building from her team's vehicles and she hadn't bothered to call them in. They were afoot for now.

Dilya was watching Zackie and chewing on her lower lip. The Sheltie kept ranging back and forth around the dumpster, but the scent trail obviously ended in the middle of the pavement.

"She drove that man's car away." Dilya hauled herself up on tiptoes to peer down into the dustbin. "Did you have a vehicle?" Abby joined her.

He nodded, then winced. Miss Watson had probably left him with a severe headache and Derek's intrusion hadn't let him sleep off the worst of it.

"What was it?"

He grunted against the gag then rolled his eyes. The latter action made him wince again.

Derek was scanning the base, turning a slow circle. Misty raised her rifle and did the same thing through her scope in the opposite direction. Being Delta, they undoubtedly noticed and processed a thousand details she would miss. But Dilya had the skill.

Abby nudged Dilya, then nodded toward Derek. It only took her seconds before she too was doing the slow turn.

"If she's watching us, she's well hidden," Dilya concluded.

"I don't even know her, but trust me, she's watching us." Abbey knew it for a fact.

"Leaving Zackie the clue of the cookies, means she either knew or guessed that you were here." Derek continued the thought.

"Then," Abby nodded to herself, "she decided that warning you off wasn't enough—which it obviously wasn't, we're here—and so needed to break the scent trail."

"Which means we've lost her." Dilya scooped up the dog and hugged her hard. Zackie must be used to this and snuggled her head tight against Dilya's shoulder.

"Not...quite." Misty spoke so rarely that it was startling every time.

Abby glanced at her to see if she'd spotted Miss Watson's

hiding place, but she was looking at the other end of the field. Abby turned and looked at the Base Hangar.

"It means," Abby knew, "that the trouble is only just beginning."

They'd left the DAGOR behind when they'd started following Zackie's nose.

Abby didn't break into a run, she broke into a sprint. Not for the DAGOR, but straight for the far end of the hangar.

59

THINK, WOMAN. THINK!

She'd had too many drugs, too little sleep and food, and far too many fears for clear cognition.

Dilya and Zackie, accompanied by a trio of soldiers, two women and one man by their sizes and gaits. All three highly trained, but none of them were Emily Beale or Michael Gibson. Not even Mark Henderson. She'd know their strides. Where were they when she needed them?

At least they were headed *toward* the real problem. Except they were taking Dilya with them—straight toward the MI6 teams that had arrived by helo. The Chinooks had forced them to land well clear of the hangar, but once on the ground, those agents aboard would be numerous and well versed at hiding their movements.

And once they recognized Dilya for what she was—they'd never forget.

She knew what to do.

Miss Watson shoved the Land Rover into gear.

This was going to get very ugly—very fast.

She jammed the accelerator down to the floorboards.

60

Zackie glanced aside, drawing Dilya's attention to a bright chirp of car tires and a racing engine. She stopped and spun to look. Abby and Derek followed so closely that they nearly flattened her on the spot. Only their hands clamping hard on her shoulders kept them from all tumbling to the ground. Misty and Group Captain Cutcher ran just far enough behind to stop without adding to the pile-up.

A beige Land Rover jerked out of a line of the vehicles parked beside the building Miss Watson had been imprisoned in.

"Of course," Abby cursed. "No one would expect her to hide in plain sight of the building she'd just escaped."

"That must be her!" Dilya waved.

But the car wasn't racing toward them. It was racing down the wide taxiway in front of the massive hangar. It didn't appear to be aiming for the crowd of people there that included the colonels. Instead she was aimed directly at the two MI6 helicopters only now taxiing toward the hangar.

"She's going to ram them." Once Derek said it, Dilya knew

he was right. Whoever was aboard those helos was a greater threat than—

Miss Watson would die as assuredly as those still in the helos.

"No!" The scream ripped at her throat. Just as it had when the renegades had put their guns to her parents' foreheads and pulled the triggers.

61

ALOFT OVER THE BASE IN ABBY'S HELICOPTER, EMILY'S ROLE AS Overwatch—given her by Abby with excellent decisiveness under pressure—meant that she and the crew chiefs were wholly focused on the safety of the ground team. As pilot, Ethan would keep the bird aloft. Her role constituted maintaining situational awareness.

It was hard to keep her attention on the wider goings-on because the team of Abby and Derek formed such a wonderful distraction. Could it have been only three days? She recalled the battles of Trisha and Bill as they'd negotiated how to work together as a team. Trisha seemed born to battle against everything around her just on principle. The whole team had nearly broken around her before she and Bill had resolved their path together. And they'd both brushed close to death so many times in that period that Emily could almost believe in miracles at their survival.

Abby and Derek were already as smooth in operation together as any she'd seen. Too easy. Now she must guard against whatever might break them apart.

For ten minutes Emily had scouted and hovered over the

building and become none the wiser. When they all reemerged from the building, racing along behind Zackie, the relief nearly swamped her. She could do nothing to protect them while they'd been inside . And their race across the airport field behind the dog told her that Miss Watson was indeed alive and had freed herself.

She had Ethan swing over the dumpster once Derek had jumped out. He coughed out a brief laugh on spotting the man bound there. Definitely Miss Watson's work. Following their careful scan of the area, she still spotted nothing out of place, not that she'd expected to.

Emily could only curse when, after a moment's conference, they all began running down the long taxiway toward the far end of the Base Hangar. They paid no heed as they raced in front of a taxiing Airbus A330 aerial tanker. Whatever they'd figured out, it must be bad. The one in British uniform, which must be Group Captain Cutcher, pulled out a radio, said something, and hung it back on her belt without pausing. The A330 stayed where it was.

"Hey!" Sam the crew chief called out. "On our six, ground level."

Ethan didn't wait to find out what it was, he spun the helo hard counterclockwise so that he opened the view to the side gunners and herself.

Emily managed a breath. It wasn't a tank or technical—a pickup truck with an anti-aircraft gun mounted on the bed. It wasn't even a phalanx of crazed Royal Marines, if Britain ever allowed such transgressions of emotion, with machine guns and RPGs.

It was a lone Land Rover, racing down the taxiway. Not toward Dilya and the other runners, but aimed past them toward the—

Emily began issuing orders.

62

Miss Watson heard the heavy beat of the Chinook's rotors passing overhead. At first she cringed every time they'd done so, afraid of being discovered. She'd taken enough money from her jailers' wallets that she could get to London. There she kept several sets of identity carefully hidden in various secure drops. After that, she could leave the country cleanly and no one, not even that sweet girl Dilya, would ever find her again.

Except Dilya's presence had foiled that plan.

Now, she aimed the Land Rover toward the MI6 operatives dispatched to recapture her. MI6 had run into a contingent of American soldiers. Could the Americans take care of themselves? With Emily Beale here, she'd bet on them over the Brits. But Dilya and her dog would stand out like sore thumbs. She'd be a flashing sign in her pink parka saying, *Look at this girl. She's incredibly important.* And as much as Miss Watson didn't trust them, not for a split millisecond, the Brits weren't stupid.

A massive shadow swept over the Land Rover as she crossed the tarmac at a hundred kmph.

Mere feet off her nose, the flying Chinook descended with its rear ramp down. They scraped it on the pavement, kicking sparks in a bright spray that caused her to blink.

They slowed abruptly.

To veer aside would roll the vehicle.

Before she could think to jam on the brakes, a hard jounce threw her painfully against the seatbelt. The Land Rover shot up the loading ramp and into the cargo bay. Her headlights came on automatically in the dim interior and a crew chief was waving her ahead as calmly as if guiding her to the correct position for an oil change.

The instant he gave her the Stop signal, others appeared from the shadows to wrap chains over the tires. In the rearview mirror, the day disappeared with the closing of the rear ramp. Then she could feel the Chinook lift back into the skies.

Someone rapped their knuckles on her driver's window.

She pushed the button to lower it.

"Engine please."

She pressed the Stop button, put it in Park, and stepped on the emergency brake, not that the Rover could so much as wiggle against the chains.

"I'm Sam, crew chief of *Charlene One*. Welcome aboard, ma'am. She wants to talk to you." The man hooked a thumb toward the cockpit.

Miss Watson eased the door open, careful not to bang it on the side of the helicopter's hull, and slid out of her seat. There was no question about who awaited her.

The crew chief followed close behind, as if he didn't trust her to walk the twenty feet. But when Sam folded down the jump seat for her before returning aft, she felt a little more kindly toward him.

"Hello, my dear girl."

Emily peeled off her helmet and turned to face her. "Only *you* get to call me that."

"I might have heard it from your father a time or two." She'd met FBI Director Beale several times, though never in Emily's presence. The girl was sharp enough to figure that out before she spoke.

"So," Emily took a careful breath, "why are the Brits trying to kill you?"

"Kill me? Oh no, they're too polite for that. They simply want access to everything I know. But we have a far more immediate problem." She pointed out the window to where the small group, easily identifiable by their four-footed companion, had resumed their journey toward the Base Hangar, though at a more sedate pace. "MI6 can *not* be allowed to see or meet Dilya."

63

Derek had watched the Chinook collect the Land Rover with awe. He'd known they were good. But to *forcibly* pick up three tons of speeding SUV and rebalance the load on the fly wasn't merely good, it was magic.

"Ethan's getting there," was Abby's observation.

Derek wondered what the hell she'd have done differently. Flying upside down while doing it, perhaps?

Colonel Beale's voice, there was no mistaking it, snapped out over his radio's headset. He glanced aloft as she spoke, "Surround Dilya and Zackie. Block all visual to downfield."

He clicked his mike in reply, then signaled Abby by pointing to his side as he turned to face Dilya. The girl, he couldn't stop thinking of her that way, had dropped back to try and coax words out of Misty. He would wish her luck, except she appeared to be already having some success. Damn but she was good. What knowledge was she adding to the curious collection she kept in her head?

Misty, seeing his change of demeanor, clammed up and scanned three-sixty around.

He pointed at the ground directly in front of him and said, "Sit."

"I'm guessing you don't mean me." Then Dilya looked down as Zackie sat exactly where she was told. "Why did she listen to you?"

"Because I'm listenable."

Rather than the expected eyeroll, it earned him a puzzled expression. Or rather, it earned her dog one. It was silly, but having the dog listen to him felt as if he'd crossed a significant threshold. Seriously lame but still...he liked it.

The moment had placed everyone where he wanted them: he and Abby blocking any downfield view of Zackie or Dilya, Misty on guard, and Group Captain Cutcher standing around as well. She squinted her question at him but he didn't have any answers.

Not until the Chinook helicopter landed nearly on top of them—with its airframe between them and the group still several hundred meters away—did he catch on. Dilya wasn't special. Probably much the way Abby wasn't special. In their very rarified specialties, they were exceptional.

The rear ramp dropped and an elderly woman in an ill-fitting man's suit was standing on the threshold of the cargo bay. He doubted his entire team could have stopped Dilya and Zackie as they raced aboard to hug her. The woman, slender and still beautiful despite her age, hugged her back just as fiercely.

It was impossible to see them together and not smile. Even when Dilya burst into tears—whether of relief or another origin, they were beautiful together. He glanced at Abby, wanting to share the moment with her too, but she was studiously facing away. When he rested his hand on her shoulder, she shrugged it off—like she would throw it across the English Channel if she could.

Oh Gods, he was such an idiot. Her mother and

grandmother dead while she was still a toddler. And here was Dilya hugging this woman like a child, and the parent who couldn't be close enough. He wanted to comfort Abby. To wrap his arms around her and hold her tight.

And that thought froze him in place. A crying woman? Him wanting to get closer rather than run farther away? Would offering comfort move them from an awesome one-night—so far—fling into uncharted *relationship* territory? That was a terrain he swore never to navigate until he'd retired from The Unit.

He'd seen the mayhem wrought on teammates' psyches when their civilian homelife, confronted by Delta realities, went sideways under the pressure. How many times had he been forced to shift his primary action team because at the last minute someone's life collapsed under his feet and distracted his mind. The field that The Unit played upon didn't allow for less than one hundred percent concentration. A quick inventory and he knew he was right. His top three, Misty, Hot Rod, and Compass were single. The rest of his primary team were single or divorced. Sacrifices were necessary to serve at the top level of The Unit.

From the darkness within the Chinook, Colonel Beale stepped around Miss Watson and Dilya and headed down the ramp.

Except being single hadn't stopped Beale. Or Gibson. Or Bill Bruce. *Shit!* He didn't know what to do except warn Abby. He whispered to her, "Incoming. Beale."

She nodded but didn't turn as she wiped at her eyes.

Beale stopped square in front of him and didn't face Abby. Instead she watched him. Attempts to read the cool blonde's expression led nowhere. Anger for his too-obvious interest in Abby? Condemnation for not comforting her when she was clearly in pain despite the shrug-off? Nothing. There was nothing there on her face to read.

Instead, Beale simply stood, watching him and waiting. Waiting for…Abby? Beale was probably the one person she least wanted to show any weakness to, and he'd done nothing to shield her from that. Shifting him from unwelcome to disappointing.

And still Beale waited as if she had nothing more important to do. Misty called in Hot Rod and the DAGOR from where they'd still be waiting. Misty then took up a circling patrol. As if he needed a refresher course in his own rules. Worrying about a woman? Talk about distracted. *Sheesh.* Time to get her out of his head. If only it was that easy. To borrow from the SEALs, as much as he hated on principle to do that, the only easy day was yesterday.

Group Captain Cutcher began to circle the Chinook to continue back toward her people. But Ms. Chill Beale simply held up a single finger, stopping Cutcher in her tracks—without ever looking away from him.

"What?" It came out harsher than he intended but she didn't react. It was like being the inevitable loser in a staring contest with a blue-eyed cat who didn't ever blink.

And that earned him a frown, then a sigh. "I had hoped it would be easy, for once." Her shrug said that she wasn't about to explain.

"What's next, Colonel?" Abby turned and stepped into their small circle. Her voice was military perfect.

"We have a dozen MI6 field agents, probably highly skilled—"

"Lethally skilled," Miss Watson joined them with Dilya hovering at her side. "Hopefully they didn't get a good look at Dilya. They can *not* be allowed to identify her."

"Why were they hunting you?" Cutcher pushed forward. "Who the hell are you that MI6 is after you?"

"Would you like to know which of your MPs are currently being blackmailed by foreign powers—and I'm not only talking about by Russia, the EU, and the US? Or perhaps you'd be interested in the identity of the UK's top hacker for hire? GCHQ doesn't know his identity, but I do and, frankly, your people are far too trusting."

"Kwan?" Dilya asked.

Miss Watson shook her head.

"Oh," Dilya nodded. "I should have seen that. Yes, that is a *very* risky choice."

That simple comment finally wiped *girl* out of his vocabulary for Dilya. Delta knew a *lot* about the forces that opposed them—pre-engagement. More than the OPFOR would like, often more about their structure and assets than they knew about themselves. Of all the hackers for hire in the world, a world he knew existed but didn't understand beyond annoying emails and scary headlines, Dilya had just connected how many disparate threads of information to figure out who the UK would hire?

"How smart are you?" He didn't mean to blurt it out like that.

"Smarter than the average bear."

"I'll be sure to protect my pic-i-nic basket."

"It won't save you," she grinned at him.

He returned the grin and tapped his finger on his sidearm in its holster.

She shrugged a *maybe yes / maybe no*. Then she slid up her sleeve to reveal a Benchmade black-anodized foldable Mediator knife in a wrist sheath. Even the simple gesture told him she knew how to handle it like a pro. At this distance, she'd damage him, even if he shot her first. Definitely not *girl*. They traded smiles once more.

"So," Abby stayed focused on the colonel. "Do we drop their bodies down a crab hole to stop them?"

"What's a crab hole?"

She didn't answer, but he'd apparently now made himself a

target for Dilya. "It's a depression in the seabed floor where dead stuff tends to accumulate." A flick of her eyebrows suggested that perhaps his body belonged there. "Crabs go there to feed. It's the best spot to drop your crab pot. Most are closely guarded secrets."

"Give me a break, Dilya, I'm from Oklahoma. Crab pots aren't exactly our thing."

"Still, if you're going after—" she cast her voice so that no one else noticed. The slightest shift of her eyes indicated Abby.

Abby, who was still refusing to look at him.

Yeah, she heard your thoughts, buddy boy. You're now off *the reservation but good.*

It was a good thing. He didn't want a woman in his life anyway.

64

Abby couldn't stand to look at any of them other than Colonel Beale. If she looked at Group Captain Cutcher, she'd freak out. Her job was to be a pilot, not try to answer impossible questions about the proper action against an ally's foreign intelligence service. If she looked at Dilya or Miss Watson, well, she'd barely kept the tears at bay the first time.

And Derek? He had her in such a jumble inside that she didn't know which way was up. His touch, probably meant to soothe, had risked tipping her over the edge into hysterical weeping, which she would *not* do in front of her commander. No one, man or woman, had ever had that effect on her, that deep connection. He embodied new territory she was in no way equipped to navigate. So, like an LZ that was truly too hot to land in, she'd avoid the whole zone.

If she looked at the dog… It was Dilya's dog, so who knew what its superpower might be.

Focus on Beale. "Awaiting orders, Colonel."

"I don't have answers, Captain. And," she stepped back to peer around the side of the helo toward the Base Hangar, "I'd estimate we have about thirty seconds to come up with a plan."

Abby swallowed hard to keep the churning knot in her gut down where it belonged. All she could think to do was shoot them. This was getting far too real. Unless—

"Shoot them, ma'am."

"Now just a moment, young lady," Captain Cutcher reached for her sidearm and suddenly Misty's long rifle was poking against her back.

"Two nights of practice..." Abby let it hang in the air.

"Ha!" Derek selected a frequency and clicked his radio's mike. "Double-check your weapons. Sims only. I repeat, Sims only. Take the Brits down Delta style in sixty."

Abby called her own team and began issuing orders. No need to confer; they were in such synchronicity. As soon as they finished, she had a horrid thought. "But they'll have live weapons. When they fire back at your men—"

"If we give them a chance!" Then Derek laughed as he grabbed her hand. "C'mon! You wanta see the fun up close, don't you?"

Hot Rod was just rolling up in the DAGOR with Compass beside him.

"You," Derek beeped Dilya on the nose and got his hand swatted. Oddly, she caught him with her wrist rather than her hand and he reacted as if it truly stung.

Abby wanted to give her a cheer.

"Stay the hell out of sight. You too." He pointed at the dog, then shifted to point into the Chinook's cargo bay. The dog went and, after a confused scowl at Derek, Dilya followed.

"Misty. Up." Derek called out as he dragged Abby toward the DAGOR.

Misty slung her sniper rifle over her back and vaulted up to the .50 cal Browning machine gun that had been mounted on the turret. "Only got live rounds here, boss."

"Then don't hit anyone."

"That's against my nature." She grinned as she faced

forward. She stood on the middle seat of the row behind the driver and navigator. That raised her upper torso above the roll bars, but placed her hands on the handles of the big machine gun mounted on a turret. It could swivel three hundred and sixty degrees around her.

Derek boosted Abby onto the tailgate. "Hang on!"

The extra heartbeat that he spent with his hands around her waist as if relishing the memory—which she did as well—and almost left him behind.

Hot Rod did his usual bolting toward the action before everyone was fully aboard.

65

CRAP! THE HAND THAT DILYA HAD SLAPPED WITH HER KNIFE'S wrist sheath was all Derek could use to leverage himself aboard the racing DAGOR. And it hurt! He'd have to find a way to pay the twerp back—like teach her dog a new trick since Zackie listened to him now. It would fluster Dilya even more.

"Straight at them, Hot Rod. Misty, do not destroy their helos—at least not unless absolutely necessary."

He flipped up one of the rear side-seats in the DAGOR's truck bed. From the storage beneath, he extracted a blue-painted sidearm. "Don't say I never gave you anything." He dropped it, along with a single blue magazine, in Abby's lap. "Don't shoot them in the face. They won't necessarily have goggles on to protect their eyes. Even if they do, it's just plain nasty."

"Only one mag?"

"I like your style, but this won't take long enough to do any reloading." He took a pair of altered Glocks himself and then passed more up to the others. Simunitions rounds fired like the real thing, flew about a hundred feet, and stung if they caught you. No paintball, but still nonlethal. Live rounds couldn't fire

Hold the West Line

in blue guns; they had smaller barrel sizes by a few crucial caliber. The blues, however, could fire in a standard weapon, which could be severely embarrassing—or worse, as they gummed up the works or caused jams without doing more than annoying the enemy.

Before every mission, a Delta operator scrounged through their entire kit to purge the blues. Carrying both at once was against all the rules. Of course, D-boys and girls weren't exactly big on rules.

"Rev it loud!"

Hot Rod yanked the shifter down a gear and punched the accelerator. The engine roared.

Derek popped his head up to check the MI6 team's reactions.

As he'd hoped, every head was facing their way but he could see beyond them that his guys had gotten into it. Sixty seconds warning had been plenty.

Charlie Two and *Four* had initially climbed high. An MH-47G was a hella powerful bird with a ten-meter-per-second climb rate. In thirty seconds, they'd popped up to a thousand feet and kicked out their cargo.

It began raining D-boys. The pair of four-man MRZRs and two bikes fluttered down to either side of the DAGOR's central path with a driver parachuting down so close behind that they were mounted in seconds. One of the guys tried to land directly into the MRZR's driver's seat but missed and ended up on the passenger side with his weapon at the ready. Though no one else seemed to notice, Derek would tease him about it later. Maybe change his tag to *Wrong Side* or *Passenger*. Not *Shotgun* —the dude would enjoy that too much.

Hot Rod slammed the DAGOR into a four-wheel spinning slide that finished with Abby's and Derek's toes a bare meter from the leader's knees.

The MI6 boys couldn't look away as he and Abby were slid

off the tailgate and onto their feet together by the last of the momentum like a movie scene.

Because behind the MI6ers, the two Chinooks had plummeted back to Earth as only a Night Stalker could do. They'd been doing such antics long enough that none of the Brits thought anything of the overhead noise and didn't even look up. Pity, the maneuver was an amazing thing to witness. Fifty feet and twenty tons of helo had stood on its nose and fallen out of the sky, only to swing flat and slam into a hover at ten meters up.

There they kicked out FAST ropes. Within seconds, it was raining more D-boys. His team slid down the ropes so close together that their feet were practically touching the next man's hands below him.

They landed silently and raced up behind the Brits.

At a nod from Derek, they all took the final step and pressed a blue sidearm up against the base of each man's skull. Eyes that had been squinted at Abby and Derek all shot wide.

Only one decided to fight back. He spun to slap-grab the weapon against his skull, not realizing it wasn't lethal, but taking a huge risk if it was. One of the boys on an electric motorcycle goosed silently forward. Seeing what he was up to, his teammate released the sidearm, dumping the magazine as he did so, and dodged out of the way. The bike's front wheel scooped up the attacker between his legs. When the biker jammed on the brakes, the fool landed face down on the pavement, not even hanging onto the empty weapon. The driver eased the bike up beside him and casually planted a boot on his neck.

Misty fired a single round. The big Browning barked hard and the round screamed between his and Abby's shoulders before punching a hole in the pavement between the leader's feet. Once she aimed it at the leader's face, she didn't need to ask if there were any other heroes.

No one wiggled so much as a finger while they were stripped of their weapons, zip-tied wrist and ankle, and left to squirm on their faces.

"I see what the Tower meant when they said we had something to learn from you folks." Group Captain Cutcher and Colonel Beale had come up close behind them.

"Just having a little fun, ma'am." Derek had a dozen prisoners, very angry prisoners. But he had no idea what to do with them. "Uh, got any LSD handy?"

Cutcher didn't look amused.

66

Sir James Alfred Lloyd III didn't in the least appreciate being called onto the Prime Minister's Ardabil Persian carpet at 10 Downing Street. That it was merely a copy only made it worse. And to top that off, she'd done it in front of a passel of Americans: most in uniform, but a scant handful of civilians as well. They all stood well back. As the Foreign Secretary, he deserved respect, not this preemptive summons before he'd even finished breakfast.

"An item has come to my attention, James." PM Leith's accent didn't include the least bit of breeding. Yorkshire. Since when had anyone useful been born of Yorkshire? The next PM would probably be Scottish or, even worse, Welsh with a ridiculously unpronounceable name, at least by civilized people.

"Oh, and what pray tell is that, Prime Minister?" She didn't even have the wherewithal to scowl at the dropping of her surname in his address.

She tapped a button on her keyboard and the large screen to the side of her desk lit up. A dozen men in camouflage were hog-tied on the tarmac. A female group captain was standing over them. RAF Brize Norton. He'd already been informed that the teams he'd sent in had gone silent. At least now he knew why.

"I have no idea what this is. An exercise?"

"Apparently one in futility." The PM sighed. She tapped the screen again.

And there, impossibly, was bank documentation of the payoff of the numerous debts of the family estate—by the House of Saud. They had saved him from being evicted due to his mother's gambling debts and his own failed investment strategies. Tens of millions pounds sterling had simply appeared in his accounts. And they'd asked for so little in return: favorable intervention on BP contracts, a relaxing of criteria for military export sales, and the like. All of which would probably have been granted through normal channels anyway. He had simply made it easier—in most cases.

There were a few however, that it would be better if no one ever...

The PM tapped the button once more, and there on the screen was what he'd been promised would never come to light.

She pressed a button on her phone, but said nothing.

The doors behind him swung open, though he couldn't look away as the PM rose to her feet. She was too tall and brittle to be womanly.

"James Alfred Lloyd III, you are to be tried for high treason. Pending trial, you are removed from your role as Foreign Secretary. You will be held in His Majesty's Prison Belmarsh without possibility of release. All of your accounts and assets, both domestic and foreign, are hereby frozen. Officers," she looked past his shoulders, "please read him The Caution and get him out of my office."

He stood numbly as they bound his wrists behind him and informed him of his right to silence. All he could see was his wife's and her mum's faces when they were ejected from their ancestral home. The estate had come down their matriarchal line since a grant from King Henry IV. He was the interloper, the one who'd "married up" in the world.

Somewhere he found the words to admit he understood his rights—none.

When they turned him about, the Americans were still there. Four military...officers. He knew the stance on even the plain-clothed one from the time he'd served. And, if he imagined her younger...

"Evandra?" Unlike the PM, she was still lovely. Her long blonde hair gone silver. The men's suit didn't mask that she remained slender. Her eyes were still the same bright blue of the spring sky that lit her lovely face.

"Rather than kidnapping and drugging me to find out what I knew, you should have had your men kill me outright, James."

He nodded. "As always, you are correct. I should have." Then he glanced at the two officers. They hadn't missed that for a second. One whispered the date and time, they must have a recorder running. Another nail in his already sealed coffin couldn't matter. He knew that no secrets survived long around Evandra.

As they led him from the room, he nearly fell over a Sheltie who'd fallen asleep by the door. He hadn't known that the PM had a Sheltie, too. He'd always liked them and saw no reason to hold their origin—or their owners, he risked a glance over his shoulder and saw nothing but sorrow—against the cheery animals. For his last step of free choice, he circled quietly around the dog so as not to wake her.

67

"Evandra?" Dilya had materialized at her side as soon as James was escorted out. She had blended in so well that even her own honed skills had missed the girl's presence. Now they all rode back in the midst of a police escort racing from 10 Downing Street to the London Heliport. Apparently, the PM couldn't get rid of them fast enough and Miss Watson found no reason for complaint.

"An old name, my dear. One that should have remained lost in time. There's no other threat now. That name only ever led to James." She would contract the hacker that the GCHQ trusted and have him verify that the PM had all records of herself and this incident purged as promised. As to the dead agents in Choteau and Brize Norton, sadly it was nothing that a fabricated *training exercise* couldn't account for. Such was the clandestine world.

Hopefully she was at long last rid of it. She could feel her shoulders sag with relief as she settled into the plush leather of the up-armored SUV.

Although there was a chance that the Saudis could trace their paid lackey's demise to her, they knew better than to come after her if they wished to retain control of their bit of desert. Their secrets ran as deep and dark as the oil under their sand. Of course, James, too, should have known better. Perhaps she'd send the Saudi Crown Prince a little reminder. He was a man with even greater pride than James and, as such, could be manipulated with so little effort. She could also ruin him with a flick of her wrist, but such power had never interested her.

"What would *you* have done with James Lloyd?" She looked at Dilya. The girl never seemed to seek power. Yet Miss Watson had searched so long for a replacement that she second-guessed every decision. Though she'd recruited Dilya a decade ago, she still had doubts that she'd found a proper heir. Dilya's skills were so advanced at such a young age that there would be no controlling her if she went off the reservation, so to speak. If that happened, Miss Watson knew there were those who would take care of the problem, and she hated the mere thought. Did Dilya want power or—

"Nothing. He'll never live to be tried. Between MI6 and the Saudis, he knows that and will most likely kill himself to hide everything. Tonight if he can—before his arrest is made public so that it can be covered up. Knowing his own life is lost, he'll protect his family."

Sadly, she was right. But it was also comforting. There were a dozen obvious ways to manipulate this situation to her advantage and Dilya had thought of none of those. That was a good sign for future—

"Of course, if I wanted to shift the balance of power in the Five Eyes Intelligence Alliance, I would…"

Miss Watson twisted to face her…and was greeted by a seraphic smile. She forced herself to return the gesture. Now she'd have to keep a closer eye on the girl…if she could. That thought made her smile genuine, and gave her hope for the future.

68

Abby had made a simple decision at Brize Norton—to keep her mouth shut.

They needed to take down the MI6 team? No problem.

The colonels and Miss Watson decided it was urgent that they fly into the heart of London and land at a heliport along the Thames that was barely bigger than her Chinook? Fine, she flew them there.

Colonel Beale wanted her along for some reason? She went.

The PM decided on a public...well, internationally shared with a select few Americans, evisceration of their Foreign Secretary? She stood witness.

Time to fly back to RAF Brize Norton and fly home? She could do that too.

Charlie Two and *Four* were already half broken down to repack in the C-5 Galaxy by the time she landed by the Base Hangar. As far as the other teams knew, they'd been brought here on a perplexing mission to fly around RAF Brize Norton for a few hours and take down a bunch of suits as a demonstration. They'd be shaking their heads at this one for years. They'd met Dilya and Zackie aboard the C-5 during the trip over from the States but didn't know anything about them. Not one of them had so much as seen Miss Watson.

Her own crew knew about teaming up with a civilian and her dog as they rescued an old woman—but nothing of who or why. Inside the black-in-black core of the operation, only the colonels, Dilya, Derek, Miss Watson, and herself knew all of what had happened. Derek's team didn't know the who, the why, or Dilya's role in it all.

She jolted when the tower mentioned the time. It wasn't even noon yet. Everything had happened in the last six hours, including the dismissal and arrest of one of the most powerful cabinet members of the UK government, based on actions *she'd* taken. There was no way to comprehend that. Though a part of her mind kept attempting to, it failed miserably.

Once they had the bird shut down, Abby shed her helmet, closed her eyes, and lay her head against the pilot seat's back. Midday. Midnight her time. Except Fort Campbell was six hours earlier. She should only be going to sleep now. Twenty-four hours ago, she'd taken Captain Derek Kylie to her bed. It was impossible, but the math worked out...which made no sense whatsoever.

She opened one eye at a sound. Ethan had gone out his side door—and Beale was climbing in. Beale, rather obviously, wasn't used to the feel of a Chinook seat as she kept shifting about.

"Do they always happen in layers like that?" Abby closed her eyes again. Had she ever been so tired in her life?

"No. I've always had, or been, peripheral help. But like this, no."

"Is it over?"

"The operation."

"What else is there?"

When Beale didn't answer, Abby looked over at her. She sat

in the copilot's seat staring out the windshield with her hands resting lightly on the unpowered controls.

"Like the feel?"

"This was never my bird," Beale said softly. "MH-60 Black Hawk, then a too-short five years in a Night Stalkers DAP Hawk. After that came the Firehawk, the wildland firefighting config. Still the same bird."

"Front of the fight."

"Not anymore." Beale's voice was so wistful it almost hurt.

Abby looked ahead. She couldn't imagine a day when she wasn't flying. Could Derek imagine a someday without The Unit filling every available moment? Probably no more than she could.

Still Beale hadn't moved, but Abby didn't want to simply abandon her.

"I'd better go find Derek and have him load up his gear before we start taking my baby apart," she reached out to pat the console.

"He's not here." Beale said it like the sky is blue.

"When will he be back?" Abby sat up straight and fully turned to study Beale's profile.

She didn't say a word.

Abby slammed against the back of her seat at that gut punch. It knocked the wind out of her more thoroughly than being butted by a full lobster trap swinging in a rough sea. Yes, it had been a crazy mixed-up couple of days. His not joining Miss Watson's trip to 10 Downing Street had simply struck her as Derek keeping a Delta-low profile. Honestly, she'd been so careful to keep inside her military box after the takedown of the MI6 team that she hadn't noticed him missing from the group.

But that he was gone?

Without a word?

"Where the hell did he go?"

Beale still didn't look her way as she said, "Stirling Lines in Credenhill, Herefordshire. The British SAS base."

Perhaps an emergency call for assistance as the Delta teams were already local? It didn't seem likely.

A cooperative training exercise? Arranged on no notice like their own journey to RAF Brize Norton. And she knew only two people who could have arranged it.

"Gibson?" Though she already knew the answer.

Beale simply shook her head.

Derek! He was suddenly avoiding her. "Didn't he see how transparent that was?"

This time Colonel Beale turned to look at her. "He's male. Therefore I'm guessing...nope." Damned woman was smiling at her own joke.

She hadn't chased Derek away like so many men before him. She'd seen the look in his eyes after they took down the MI6 team. They'd operated together tighter than any transmission's synchromesh. He had...

"No." She couldn't believe it.

"Yes." Beale said with that same damn smile.

"He turned chicken on me?"

Beale's look said plenty.

Abby slapped on *Charlene One's* electronics and tapped the screen for the Warm Start Checklist. With a flick, she routed it in front of Beale. "Read!"

Beale began reading down the list almost as fast as Abby was doing the steps by rote.

Ethan ran up toward his side of the aircraft. Beale closed the door in his face. "I'm not going to miss this."

Sam stuck his head into the cockpit.

Abby didn't even give him a chance to ask what was going on. "Everyone off. I need at least one crew chief. You're it. You have thirty seconds to clear them out."

She got the big twin rotors lumbering their way around. But

her *Charlene* was a beast of a bird and the ten thousand horsepower of her two engines overcame their inertia in seconds.

"Good to go?"

"Copilot good." Emily reported.

"Just a..." Sam was still hustling "...and we're clear. Good to go. You've got me doing the work of four."

Abby didn't care. The rear ramp clanged shut as she lifted.

Emily was handling the tower, which was good as Abby wasn't in the mood to talk to anyone. "Heading Two-Eight-Zero," Emily called out as soon as they were clear of the base's air space.

The SAS base lay only ninety kilometers northwest of Brize Norton, so eighteen minutes later they were landing at Stirling Lines. Her Chinook took up a third of their little helo runway. She shut it down right where it was, blocking everything.

"Sam, anyone tries to board, you have my permission to shoot them."

"Uh, yes ma'am."

"They're British, you might offer them tea first."

Abby didn't appreciate the colonel's humor. Which was a pity, it was a good line. The two of them climbed down at the same moment the security troops trotted up, a staff sergeant with a three-man fire team. An SAS staff sergeant, which meant he was more skilled than any soldier outside the SAS at any level. He saluted nicely, which was the only thing that slowed her down.

"You didn't give our base much of a head's up on your arrival or your purpose, ma'am. While Group Captain Cutcher cleared you—"

First Abby had heard of it. She'd thank Colonel Beale later.

"—she's RAF, not Army and not SAS. We need to know the purpose of—"

"Where is he?"

The sergeant blinked once, then showed that, like Delta, the SAS recruited for intelligence in addition to other skills. "American chap put his bum in a sling, did he, ma'am?"

"He did."

"Just a short walk." He did an about-face and, with a hand sign she didn't quite catch, had his squad form up around them—half escort, half guard. Then, correctly judging her mood, he set off at a fast walk. They were soon doing a light jog to keep up with the striding pace she set.

They crossed the grass and headed up a lane between long buildings. The SAS apparently didn't train out in the open where they could be observed by others. One building echoed with the hard snaps of an indoor shooting range, another with the grunts of hand-to-hand combat training. Straight ahead was an open field. Beside it parked a line of electric motorbikes, a pair of MRZRs, and a DAGOR.

Misty was the first one to spot her. She simply pointed. Abby shifted her course. Then Misty smacked Hot Rod and Compass atop their heads so they wouldn't miss the show.

69

Derek knew he was in for it the instant he heard the Chinook hammering down out of the sky. It was no gentle approach. One moment there was nothing. The next there was the great beast of a machine practically standing on its tail to shed speed. Chance had it silhouetted by the sun behind light clouds, a terrifying image that shot his heart into his throat. He'd expect the bird to crash on its tail any second. But it didn't. Instead, at the last impossible moment, the nose dropped and it settled as lightly as a feather behind the buildings.

He tried to prepare himself.

Abby was coming. And, based on that landing, she was some kind of pissed.

Looking around revealed nowhere private. They had been setting up for a demonstration of the extreme response their vehicles could achieve under crisis conditions. There was no rough driving course here at Stirling Lines, so this first part would be more show and tell and he wanted it to be good.

He didn't want—

Abby stormed out of the lane between the buildings, using

that impossibly quick stride of hers. An SAS security squad jogged alongside. Beale was...being Beale, wholly unreadable.

"Abby, I—"

At five paces, she yanked out her sidearm and shot him in the chest.

70

Derek flailed backward as if she'd shot him in the chest with an RPG.

She reholstered her weapon and crossed her arms while she waited for him to stop floundering about like a dead fish.

He finally tented the hands that he'd clamped over the strike point on his chest and peered in carefully before looking up at her.

"I know if I'm armed with a blue or not." She pulled the weapon out and held it sideways so that he could see the blue-painted handle of the training weapon. She'd kept it after the takedown of the MI6 team. Then she shoved it back in her holster. "Not that I wasn't tempted to drop a live round or ten in you."

"Abby, I—"

"If you didn't want to be with me—" And the full force of that statement slammed into her just as hard as that RPG, "—you could have at least told me to my face."

What was she doing here? Standing in front of all these people? Throwing her heart in the dirt for everyone to see? Why had she even come? She spun on her heel and sprinted back toward her *Charlene*. Only there did she know who she was.

Except...

She couldn't imagine what Colonel Beale was thinking. Throw her out of the 160th because she was now unreliable? At a minimum. She would certainly do it to herself if she was in command.

Heave her out the door at altitude! That was the old threat, wasn't it? She was not going to cry. Not throw herself to the dirt of the SAS training ground and whimper. No, she'd walk tall until they threw her out of the 160th Special Operations Aviation Regiment all on their own.

Though what could be worse than that?

She pictured Derek lying in the dirt and not wanting her.

Somehow, that *was* worse.

71

Derek rubbed at the spot where the round had hit him. At five paces, with just a t-shirt on, that would sting for a couple days. He looked down again at the small blue mark the Simunition had left there. It wasn't at the center of his chest as he'd first thought. Even in her rage, that would be too sloppy for Captain Abby Rose. No, she'd shot him directly over the heart.

He looked up as a shadow blocked the brightest portion of the overcast sky.

"Colonel Beale?"

She offered as many words of advice as Colonel Gibson might, as in none.

"Yeah, get up off my ass and go after the woman." Which was about the last thing on his list of smart moves. But he couldn't get over Abby's face. He knew it so damn well but couldn't pin down the emotion.

Not sadness.

Not fury, though that was there.

But something...

Betrayal!

Once he identified it he knew he was right. It went against his entire ethos. They were on the same team and he'd made her feel the commitment. And she was smart enough that *she* was probably right about what he'd done, even if he couldn't see it. He'd *never* turned his back on a teammate in pain before.

Pushing to his feet, he brushed himself off.

Hot Rod and Compass looked ready to sell tickets and open a popcorn franchise.

Misty's look said he should keep a weather eye on her sniper rifle—and it wasn't painted blue.

"Where—" But he knew. Back to her beloved helicopter, which she pulled on like an armored suit to hide in. The slim pilot in the Megatronic transformer-whatever giant killer robot machine. She never realized that what made her so impressive was that she could pull on that suit of armor and make it dance across the sky.

Derek started at a trot.

Then he heard it. The heavy wok-wok of the wokka-bird's rotors starting to spin. She was leaving. Without her commander. That desperate to be away from him. And he knew in that moment that he was equally desperate to be beside her.

He broke into a sprint. As the heavy rotors roared to full wokka-wokka and grabbed air, he reached the bird and jumped.

He had a grip on the lower edge of the rear gun window, then made the mistake of looking down. They were already fifty meters up and climbing fast. He'd never crawled through a window so fast in his life.

The cargo bay was empty. Up forward, he could see the shoulders of the two pilots. The tall one must be Sam. A lead crew chief could usually fly a bird well enough to test any repairs they'd made, making him fine as a copilot.

Derek would know the other one anywhere, even though all he could see was the rounding of her shoulder. Huh! He *would* know her anywhere. Abby had imprinted so deeply on his brain that he couldn't imagine being interested in anyone else.

Ever?

That question sat far more comfortably than he expected—ever.

She was headed west, which didn't make much sense. Perhaps her instincts were headed out over the Atlantic, heading home to her family's lobster boats. If so, she wasn't doing a very convincing job of it, cruising along at a few thousand feet going barely half of what this bird was capable of.

Then he spotted something and slipped toward it.

72

"Typical."

"Typical?" Abby asked in surprise before she recognized the voice over her headset.

"Yeah, you shoot a guy in the heart and run away."

"I should have used a howitzer."

"Now that would have *really* stung."

"Would have served you right."

"Probably..." Derek dragged it out. She could hear him think about it. "Yeah, it was a bad move. Definitely *not* typical for me. I'd say I'm sorry, but since you already shot me for it, I suppose we're about even."

"Not even close!" Abby shouted into the mike loudly enough that she saw Sam flinch. She still wanted to strangle Derek. "A bad move." She scoffed at him. "A bad move is forgetting where you dropped your lobster pot or if you drank too much and have no idea where you moored your boat the night before. This was—"

"—betrayal. I know. I finally figured that out while lying in the dirt with Beale standing over me."

"Did she kick you?"

"I'm shocked! You'd have her kick a good man when he's down?"

She scoffed into her mike again. "Just..." She closed her eyes and braced herself. It was the right decision. "...go away."

There was such a long silence that she was afraid he had. "Is that what you truly want?"

She almost said yes. But these last few days with him hadn't been like any other. Life had become fun and easy and... Like the one time she'd asked Dad why he'd never remarried. He'd only sighed and looked sad. That's how she would feel if she walked away. She didn't want a lifetime of that regret.

"Where..." She looked down at the cyclic and realized that she hadn't once touched the mike switch.

If he wasn't calling over the radio...

"Wait..."

The intercom? He was—*here!*

"This far enough forward?"

This time when she spun, he *was* close enough that she clipped his nose hard with her helmet. He sprawled backwards from where he'd been crouched, losing the intercom headset as he collapsed into the short passage leading to the cargo bay and clutched his nose.

"Yep," Sam said over the intercom. "I'd say that was close—some enough."

"Can you get us back to Stirling Lines' helipad? Our commander might appreciate not being marooned there."

She didn't bother to wait for Sam's answer as she shed her harness and helmet. She lunged out of her seat to show Derek how she really felt. A kiss on his battered nose should be a good start.

KEEP READING FOR AN EXCERPT OF THE NIGHT STALKERS #1, *THE NIGHT IS MINE*.

THE NIGHT IS MINE (EXCERPT)

IF YOU ENJOYED THAT, YOU'LL LOVE…

THE NIGHT IS MINE (EXCERPT)

THE CNN FILM CREW HAD MADE IT FUN. BUT NOW...

The laptop stood balanced on a couple of empty, dull green ammo cases for the Minigun. Sweaty pilots and crew stood gathered around the computer, waiting for the network to roll the clip.

Captain Emily Beale and her team rushed into the tent from the Black Hawk helicopter landing area, still in their hot, sticky flight gear, helmets clutched under their arms. Just past dawn here in Pakistan, late-evening news back home.

A dozen guys who hadn't been lucky enough to fly that night packed the already baking tent. They wore shorts and army green, sleeveless tees revealing a wide variety of arm tattoos. Some with girls' names, several snakes, and a small fleet-worth of helicopters—all with feathered wings. The men squatted on the packed sand that passed for a floor, perched on benches, or stood feet wide with arms crossed over muscled chests.

The observation jolted Emily a moment before she shrugged it back into her mind's dustiest footlocker. Simply another reminder that the entire female roster of this forward deployment included only one name—her own.

Brion Carlson came on and flashed his famous scowl, cuing his multimillion-person audience that the next clip would be fun, not war-torn hell, not drowned mother of twins, not car pileup at 11.

Emily's free hand rested on the M9 Beretta sidearm in her holster. Tempting. A couple of 9 mm rounds through the screen might cheer her up significantly. But then they'd all know how she felt. Be hard to laugh it off after that level of mayhem. She knew hundreds of ways to kill a person but how do you kill a newscast? Smashing a laptop failed to meet the ultimate criteria for complete suppression. She scanned the intent faces of her flight mates. Still, a bit of localized destruction held its temptations.

She'd only been in the company for two months. The first week or so, she'd been a total outsider. But as she'd proved herself on mission after mission, she'd gained acceptance—grudging at first, then not.

Now, on the precarious cusp of true welcome, this.

"Hot from the fighting front, at an undisclosed location in Southwest Asia, CNN caught up with Black Hawk pilot Captain Emily Beale as she cooks up a storm for her flight crew. She's the first, and so far the only, female pilot to qualify to fly helicopters for SOAR, the elite 160th Airwing."

"Aviation regiment," Big John called out. Someone shushed him.

"With the Night Stalkers, as the Special Operations Aviation Regiment call themselves—"

"Damn straight," John answered and then turned to scowl at whoever had been foolish enough to try and shush him before.

"—she flies, literally, where no woman has flown before."

The Night Is Mine (Excerpt)

The clip rolled a close-up of four steaks sizzling on a surface so black that it didn't reflect the scorching, midday sun.

Odd place to start, but what the hell.

The Black Hawk's nose cone covering the terrain-following radar assembly had been plenty hot to sear a steak. And the meat had tasted damn good. A humorous opening. So far she could live with this.

Then the camera pulled back.

First the nose of her helo, which was kind of cool. Made a nice surprise for the viewer who wouldn't recognize it from the curve of the Kevlar composite.

Then the camera swung toward the person wielding the cooking tongs.

She groaned...silently...but, damn! She'd given them loads of footage about why she flew, had answered a thousand probing questions about a female warrior in a man's world, and *this* is how they started?

Ray-Bans. Blonde hair running loose over her shoulders. A trick only Special Operations Forces and SEALs could actually get away with in all the US military. The elite fighting teams were *supposed* to wear non-military long hair, even mustaches and beards, to blend in wherever they were inserted.

SOAR pilots usually did the close-cropped military thing, but not her company. *She liked the sound of that, her company.*

She'd made it into the Black Adders, the nastiest and toughest company that SOAR had ever fielded. They belonged to the 5th Battalion, which was the nastiest and toughest battalion, no matter what the other four claimed. That's why the 160th Special Operations Aviation Regiment (Airborne) 5th Battalion D Company wore their hair long. It made them more like their SOF customers, the Special Operations Forces action specialists they transported to and from battle. Of course, none of them minded the added bonus of being able to thumb their noses at the establishment they'd give their lives to defend.

The laptop image scanned down her body as if she were a model for Playboy or Hustler. Army-green tank top. Running shorts and army boots. Standard desert camp gear. She was soaked in sweat, and the clothes clung to her like Saran Wrap. A point the cameraman had made the most of, both on his pan down and back up.

But this wasn't who she was. It wasn't the point of the interview. She flew the most lethal helicopter ever devised by man, and they were turning her into a porn star. Her grip on her still-holstered M9 sidearm grew painful, but she couldn't ease off.

At least it would be uphill from here.

"Em-i-ly!" "Whoo-hoo, Captain!" "Now that's what we're talking about!" The catcalls in the tent overrode the voiceover. Attracted attention from outside. More air jocks drifted in to see what was up. Is that how they thought of her every day?

To react would only admit her intimidation. And that door wouldn't be opened for anybody.

Even on the tiny laptop you could see good muscle definition. Emily had never been a bodybuilder but she lifted enough weights to hang right at her best fighting weight. And though the guys were still hooting over the narration, she wasn't particularly happy with how she looked. She'd never met a woman who didn't feel that way and ignored it as well as she could.

Did guys feel like that? This crowd seemed pretty pleased every time the camera caught one of them. A lot of macho shoulder punching, hard enough to bruise, each time one of them made national television.

The next clip showed her pulling out an emergency foil blanket, good for reflecting away the worst of the sun if you were smacked down in the middle of sand-dune nowhere. She'd demo-ed how to use one to hide from the sun, digging it into the sand before disappearing beneath.

But in the next instant, she knew this broadcast didn't go there. Instead they went with her quick origami moment to create a decent solar oven from the foil. It had taken her a while to figure that one out back when she flew for the 101st. They jumped to a finished loaf of sourdough bread, from a starter she'd smuggled in. Not bad. She could live with this, too.

Somehow.

And then the next image rolled.

Not a helicopter or flight suit in sight. How long was this stupid clip anyway? They'd dogged her heels for a full day and this was the best they could do?

Back to the solar oven. The soufflé. They wouldn't. They couldn't. They did.

A whole circle of broad-shouldered, bad-assed flyboys standing around her with their arms crossed over bare, serious-workout chests. A solid wall of shirtless, obviously posed male flesh she'd hadn't noticed the news crew setting up.

Then her tiny image on the screen lifted the chocolate soufflé from the makeshift oven. Perfect. And the desert was so frigging hot that the soufflé didn't start its inevitable collapse from cooling until after the camera moved on. The round of applause had tickled her at the time. But on the squidgy, piece-of-crap laptop, it made her look like a half-naked Suzy Homemaker in shades.

"Flying into battle, you know her well-fed crew will follow Captain Emily Beale anywhere because she's the hottest chef flying." In the parting shot, a helmeted pilot, visible only as a silvered visor and blue-black helmet, lifted off in a swirl of dust.

Her helmet was purple with a gold-winged flying horse on the side, the Pegasus with laser eyes of the Night Stalkers emblem, and everyone in the tent knew it. It remained clamped under her arm at this moment in case they wanted to double-check. She'd had no missions the day the film crew was in camp so they'd shot that dweeb Bronson, of all useless jerks.

That couldn't be the end of the clip. But the wrap shot was perfect, the camera following Bronson high into the achingly blue sky.

All those interviews about her pride as the first woman serving in The Night Stalkers.

Not one word made it in.

Descriptions of nasty but declassified missions that she had been authorized to discuss.

All cut.

Actually, they hadn't used a single word. She'd never spoken. Just cooked and been ogled.

And finally, to drive the hammer home, they'd used Bronson in his transport bird, not her heavy-duty, in-your-face, DAP Hawk gunship for the closer. When you wanted a joy ride, you called Bronson. When you wanted it done, you loaded up her MH-60L Direct Action Penetrator Black Hawk.

They had to include at least one—

"In New York's Bryant Park today…" The laughter in the tent drowned out the parade of anorexic women who probably couldn't shoot a lousy .22 without getting knocked on their narrow butts.

She pulled her pistol and let fly at the laptop. The first shot shattered the screen and flipped it off the empty ammo case. The second spun it in midair, and the third punched the computer into the sand.

The guys inspected the smoking laptop in the ear-ringing silence and then Emily's face as she reholstered her sidearm. More mayhem than she'd intended, but she was a pilot first, dammit.

Then, as if on cue, the crowd almost as one fist-pumped the air.

"Sexiest chef flying, Captain!" "They got that right!" "Whoo-hoo!"

"Well, your next thousand meals are gonna be damned MREs." She shouted to be heard over the rabble.

They hooted and applauded in reply.

"Cold egg burritos!" The worst of the Meals Ready-to-Eat menu.

"Ooo!" "We're so scared." "Show us how to make an oven." "Sexiest chef!"

She opened her mouth to offer a few uncouth words about how much they'd enjoyed watching their own lame selves—

"'Tenshun!" The deep voice sliced through the chatter like the rear rotor blade of her Black Hawk through a stick of softened butter. A voice that had sent a shiver down her spine ever since she'd first heard it two months before.

They all snapped to their feet as if they'd been electrocuted. Some part of the laptop still functioned; Carlson's voice sounded into the sudden silence, "At a recent concert, the Rolling Stones—"

A booted foot smashed down and delivered the coup de grâce to the wounded machine.

Major Mark "The Viper" Henderson stood two paces inside the rolled-back flap of the tent, one foot still buried in the machine. Six feet of clichéd soldier. Broad shoulders, raw muscle, and the most dangerous looking man Emily had ever met. His straight black hair fell to his squared-off jawline. His face clean shaven, eyes hidden by mirrored Ray-Bans. Rumor had it they were implanted and the Major no longer had eyes.

After two months, she couldn't say otherwise. He always wore the shades when he wasn't wearing a helmet for a night mission.

Even the first time they'd met, as purported civilians at Washington state's Sea-Tac Airport, he had worn them. Coming out of security, newly assigned to the 5th Battalion, she'd known instantly who waited for her. She doubted another person in the crowded airport would recognize him as a soldier; they'd both been trained to blend in. But she'd recognized Major Mark Henderson as if part of her body had known him for years.

In the tent, he swiveled his head once, the sunglasses surveying the crowd. Every man jack of them knew the Major had memorized exactly who was there, what they'd said, what they were about to say—and probably knew what they'd been *thinking*...at the precise moment they'd exited their mothers' wombs. If they weren't careful, he'd start telling them what they would be thinking about during their last moment on Earth, and none of them, not even Crazy Tim, wanted to run head-on into that level of mindblower.

"There will be no gender-based commentary in this unit. Understood?"

"Yes Sir!" Rang out so loudly it would've hurt Emily's ears if she hadn't been shouting herself.

Buy now at mlbuchman.com
and at fine retailers everywhere to continue reading

ABOUT THE AUTHOR

USA Today and Amazon #1 Bestseller M. L. "Matt" Buchman started writing on a flight south from Japan to ride his bicycle across the Australian Outback. Just part of a solo around-the-world trip that ultimately launched his writing career.

From the very beginning, his powerful female heroines insisted on putting character first, *then* a great adventure. He's since written over 75 action-adventure thrillers and military romantic suspense novels. And more than 200 short stories, and a fast-growing pile of read-by-author audiobooks.

PW declares of his Miranda Chase action-adventure thrillers: "Tom Clancy fans open to a strong female lead will clamor for more." About his military romantic thrillers: "Like Robert Ludlum and Nora Roberts had a book baby."

His fans say: "I want more now...of everything!" That his characters are even more insistent than his fans is a hoot.

As a 30-year project manager with a geophysics degree who has designed and built houses, flown and jumped out of planes, and solo-sailed a 50' ketch, he is awed by what is possible. He and his wife presently live on the North Shore of Massachusetts. More at: www.mlbuchman.com.

Other works by M. L. Buchman: *(* - also in audio)*

Action-Adventure Thrillers

Kate Stark
Final Taste
Ice Burn
Knife's Edge

Miranda Chase
Drone*
Thunderbolt*
Condor*
Ghostrider*
Raider*
Chinook*
Havoc*
White Top*
Start the Chase*
Lightning*
Skibird*
Nightwatch*
Osprey*
Gryphon*
Wedgetail*
Air Force One*

Science Fiction / Fantasy

Deities Anonymous
Cookbook from Hell: Reheated
Saviors 101

Contemporary Romance

Eagle Cove
Return to Eagle Cove
Recipe for Eagle Cove
Longing for Eagle Cove
Keepsake for Eagle Cove

Love Abroad
Heart of the Cotswolds: England
Path of Love: Cinque Terre, Italy

Where Dreams
Where Dreams are Born
Where Dreams Reside
Where Dreams Are of Christmas*
Where Dreams Unfold
Where Dreams Are Written
Where Dreams Continue

Non-Fiction

Strategies for Success
Managing Your Inner Artist/Writer
Estate Planning for Authors*
Character Voice
Narrate and Record Your Own Audiobook*
Beyond Prince Charming: One Guy's Guide to Writing Men in Romance

Short Story Series by M. L. Buchman:

Action-Adventure Thrillers

Kate Stark Stories
Miranda Chase Stories

Romantic Suspense

Antarctic Ice Fliers
US Coast Guard

Contemporary Romance

Eagle Cove

Other

Deities Anonymous (fantasy)
Single Titles

The Emily Beale Universe
(military romantic suspense)

THE NIGHT STALKERS
MAIN FLIGHT
*The Night Is Mine**
*I Own the Dawn**
*Wait Until Dark**
*Take Over at Midnight**
Light Up the Night
Bring On the Dusk
By Break of Day
Target of the Heart
Target Lock on Love
Target of Mine
Target of One's Own
NIGHT STALKERS HOLIDAYS
*Daniel's Christmas**
*Frank's Independence Day**
*Peter's Christmas**
Christmas at Steel Beach
*Zachary's Christmas**
*Roy's Independence Day**
*Damien's Christmas**
Christmas at Peleliu Cove
HENDERSON'S RANCH
*Nathan's Big Sky**
*Big Sky, Loyal Heart**
*Big Sky Dog Whisperer**
*Tales of Henderson's Ranch**

SHADOW FORCE: PSI
*At the Slightest Sound**
*At the Quietest Word**
*At the Merest Glance**
*At the Clearest Sensation**
WHITE HOUSE PROTECTION FORCE
*Off the Leash**
*On Your Mark**
*In the Weeds**
FIREHAWKS
Pure Heat
Full Blaze
*Hot Point**
*Flash of Fire**
Wild Fire
FIREHAWKS SMOKEJUMPERS
*Wildfire at Dawn**
*Wildfire at Larch Creek**
*Wildfire on the Skagit**
DELTA FORCE
Target Engaged
Heart Strike
*Wild Justice**
*Midnight Trust**
NIGHT STALKERS RELOAD
*Guard the East Flank**
*Hold the West Line**

Emily Beale Universe Short Story Series

THE NIGHT STALKERS
The Night Stalkers Stories
The Night Stalkers CSAR
The Night Stalkers Wedding Stories
The Future Night Stalkers Reloaded
DELTA FORCE
Th Delta Force Shooters
The Delta Force Warriors

FIREHAWKS
The Firehawks Lookouts
The Firehawks Hotshots
The Firebirds
WHITE HOUSE PROTECTION FORCE
Stories
FUTURE NIGHT STALKERS
The Lift (Science Fiction)

SIGN UP FOR M. L. BUCHMAN'S NEWSLETTER TODAY

and receive:
Release News
Free Short Stories
a Free Book

Get your free book today. Do it now.
free-book.mlbuchman.com

www.ingramcontent.com/pod-product-compliance
Lightning Source LLC
LaVergne TN
LVHW091533060526
838200LV00036B/587